BORN TO BE BROKEN

ALPHA'S CLAIM, BOOK TWO

ADDISON CAIN

Photography by Wander Aguiar
Artwork by Zakuga
Cover art by Raven Designs

For my loving husband.

1

By the time she'd found his home, Claire could little more than crawl. Scratching at the portal, fingers numb, she slumped to the floor. When the door cracked and squinting eyes showed in the dark, had she the capacity, Claire would have laughed. Never had a man looked more shocked.

She was filthy; stringy hair wet from snow and sweat, limbs badly scraped from her fall. About her throat, a bruise tellingly shaped in a handprint circled like a sad necklace. That was nothing compared to the state of her feet when he tried to help her stand. Torn and bleeding, more skin had been worn away than was sound. Corday hoisted her from the ground, her freezing body flush to his, and locked the door.

"Claire!" He vigorously rubbed his hands up and down the trembling woman's back. "I have you."

It's a good thing he did; once the door locked her eyes

rolled back in her skull, Claire unconscious. Corday rushed her to his shower, cranked on the heat, and stood with her under the spray. Her lips were blue, and no wonder considering that temperatures on this level of the Dome had grown near freezing. The Beta stripped off her ruined dress and washed every rivulet of blood from his friend, finding more bruises, more wounds, more reasons to hate Shepherd.

The gauze at her shoulder he'd left for last, grateful at least something had been tended to. But as it grew saturated, he grew worried by what was hinted at under the bandage. Peeling it back, Corday cursed to see what the beast had done to her. Shepherd's claiming marks, the tissue red and distorted—even after what looked like weeks of healing, her shoulder was a fucking mess.

The monster had mutilated her.

The water turned as cold as Corday's blood. He pulled her out, dried her the best he could, and tucked Claire into the warmth of his bed. There she lay, naked and badly damaged, a little color coming back to her hollowed cheeks. One at a time, he uncovered limbs, tending scraps, bandaging wounds, doing his best to preserve her modesty. That didn't mean he didn't see them, the telling bruises mottling her inner thighs.

She looked almost as bad as the Omegas the resistance had rescued…

It frightened him. Not one of those women was thriving. Even safe, they deteriorated—hardly spoke, hardly ate. More of them had died, and though the Enforcers could not pinpoint the cause, Brigadier Dane was certain with all that they'd suffered—the children and mates that had been taken from them—they had simply lost the will to live.

Claire had to be different.

Left arm, right arm, both elbows sluggishly bled. Salve and bandages were the best Corday could offer. But there was nothing he could do for her throat; the mottled yellow-brown bruises were not fresh. The Omega's injuries grew far more complicated with her legs—both kneecaps were grotesque; one gash deep enough to require stitches. He did his best with butterfly sutures, closing the gap of torn flesh, lining up the skin so that it might stand a chance of mending. Her joints would swell—that was unavoidable—and he hesitated to ice them as she was already shivering and still cold to the touch.

"You're gonna be okay, Claire," he promised. "You're safe with me."

Claire opened bloodshot eyes; she looked at the Beta whose face she could read like a book. He was scared for her. "It doesn't hurt."

"Shhh." He leaned down, smiling to see her awake. Stroking the wet, tangled hair from her face, he said, "Rest your throat."

She complied, and Corday worked quickly to finish, disinfecting every abrasion on her outer thighs, knees, and shins. Her feet were a different matter. There was little he could do, and she would hardly be able to walk in the days to come. He picked out the detritus, noting how she didn't move or twitch even when a fresh wave of blood followed a large chunk of glass once it was pulled free. He wrapped her feet tight, and said a prayer to all three Gods that the open wounds would not fester.

Once it looked like she was asleep, he rose.

Claire's hand shot out, her bruised fingers clawing into his sleeve. "Don't go!"

"You need medicine," Corday soothed, weaving his fingers with hers.

Claire held tighter, disjointed and afraid. "Don't leave me alone."

Brushing a pile of bandage wrappers to the floor, Corday did as she wished. He slipped under the covers beside her, offering body heat and a safe place to rest. Claire let him hold her, laying her head on his shoulder, still.

Ashamed to ask, beyond pathetic, she whispered, "Will you purr for me?"

Such a thing was an act of intimacy between lovers and family, but there was no hesitation in the Beta. Corday pulled in a deep breath and started the rumbling vibration at once. The sound was a little off—the act being something he was unaccustomed to—and though it lacked the richness of an Alpha purr, it was infinitely comforting in that moment.

"That's nice." Exhausted, Claire sighed. "Please don't stop."

Corday thumbed a spilling tear from her cheek. "I won't, Claire."

In the voice of a broken thing, Claire began to feel more than endless choking malaise; she felt disgust… for herself. "I hate that name."

Huddled close to her friend, like children whispering secrets, Claire woke. Though her body ached, she was warm, surrounded in a scent of safety, and grateful for the boyish smile Corday offered once she'd pried her sticky lashes apart.

Cautious and gentle, he smoothed her tangled hair. "You look much better."

They were so close she could see the night's stubble on his cheek, smell his breath.

He seemed so real.

Sucking her split lower lip into her mouth, Claire felt the sting. Tasting the scab left when that woman, Svana, had struck her for refusing to spread, made the nightmare real again. It was as if Svana were in the room with her, as if the Alpha's hands remained wrapped around her throat.

Claire struggled to breathe.

Corday broke through her growing terror. "You're okay, Claire. I'll keep you safe."

It wasn't a dream, it was real. Claire grew to understand that the more Corday spoke, the more he touched her, the more she felt the sun on her face.

How had she even come to be there?

She *was* separated from Shepherd, in a great deal of physical discomfort, naked, and Corday had taken her in, despite the fact that she had drugged him—lied to him.

She had to remind herself out loud; she had to make herself remember. "I jumped off the back terrace of the Citadel… crashed into snow."

"And you ran here," Corday finished for her.

She had, before air had even returned to her lungs she'd scampered up and fled. "I ran as fast as I could… right to your door." Voice breaking, trembling something fierce, Claire sobbed, "I'm sorry, Corday."

Seeing her panic, he tried to calm her. "There is nothing to be sorry for."

"I drugged you," she whispered. "I lied. And now he'll find you. He'll hurt you."

"He won't." Corday grew earnest and severe. "You can trust me. There is no need for you to lie to me again. I can't help you if you lie."

"If I had taken you to the Omegas, he would have killed you, just as he killed Lilian and the others." Claire looked to the pillowcase lightly crusted with her blood. "He punished me… I'm pregnant."

Corday already knew. He'd smelled it almost the instant Claire had been in his arms. There was only one way such a thing could have come to pass. Shepherd had forced another heat cycle.

There was very little he could say, little he could do, but one thing Corday could offer her. He looked her dead in the eye and asked, "Do you want to remain that way?"

What a question… Claire had to think, recognized she had been clinging to the Beta to the point where it must have made his shoulder ache. Easing her hold, she measured the little bit of human that she still was, and knew she had not wanted a baby yet. More so, she had foolishly allowed herself to develop an attachment to the monster who had filled her womb, a monster who was using her like a broodmare—a beast whose lover had tried to kill her.

Claire pressed her hand to the tiny life growing inside her. She could rid herself of the issue; abortion was a common practice, probably accessible even now. She could have Shepherd carved out of her.

After a shuddering breath she admitted her horrific truth, "I don't feel anything, you know. Inside… I feel nothing at all."

He gave her space, offering a lopsided smile. "I know it might seem like the world has ended for you, Claire, but you are free now. You're a survivor."

She could not help but sadly smile at a man who would never understand. "Survivor? What kind of future do you see for me? I was pair-bonded to a monster to be his toy, drugged into an unnatural heat cycle, impregnated against my will so I would grow devoted, and then forced to listen to the Alpha who was supposed to be my mate fuck his lover—a very scary Alpha female who wrapped her hands around my throat, who shoved her fingers inside me right in front of him."

He couldn't stop a grimace. "Shhh. This can be made right."

"It's okay for us both to admit there isn't going to be a happy ending for me." Claire sat up, holding the sheet to her chest, empty. "I have no future, but I can still fight for them."

Brushing back her hair, wanting to pull her nearer, Corday restrained the desire to embrace the sad-eyed woman.

"If you step outside that door and try to take on Shepherd, you won't win."

"I won't win… but I *am* going to act out." A goal, something to cling to, hardened her voice. Claire sneered. "I'm going to do everything I can to make noise. And if they catch me, I'll make sure they kill me."

"Please listen to me," Corday grew urgent, afraid to scare her off should he say the wrong thing. "Let's talk this through. The best thing you can do right now is grow stronger. "

"I intend to." She nodded, knowing he misunderstood. "Shepherd once told me there is no good in the people of Thólos. He was wrong. This occupation has stripped away our pretenses; it has made us naked to our nature. Don't you see? Integrity, kindness—it exists here…" Claire closed her eyes, nestled nearer once again. "You, Corday, are a good man."

He didn't hesitate to pull her flush. "And you're a good woman."

Resting her cheek on his shoulder, she sighed. She might have been a *good woman* once, but the truth was, she was not a person anymore. She was a shadow.

"I want you to know that while you were gone, we uncovered the distributors of the counterfeit heat-suppressants. Omegas were rescued. They are recovering and protected. The drugs were destroyed; every last man paid for his crimes."

There was a flutter in Claire's chest, a moment of feeling

she tore to pieces before it might infect her. "Thank you, Corday."

"You are a part of that, you know?" Boyish eagerness, a desire to see Claire pleased, infected his grin. "Your determination—you fought for them. They have you to thank for their freedom."

"I didn't do anything but get raped and cry about it."

"You're wrong." Corday took her cheek, made her meet his eye. "You stood up to the biggest monster of them all. You have escaped him twice now. *You* are strong, Claire."

But she wasn't. "No… you don't understand. The pair-bond, the pregnancy… I started to care for him, to need him." Saying it out loud made her mouth taste of vomit. "I was weak."

Corday knew none of that was her fault. "Given the circumstances, what happened was only natural."

"I don't know what it was… but *it* was. I stopped seeing a monster and wanted the attention of the man. And once he'd persuaded my affection, he made it the world's sickest joke. I should be grateful, I guess. Listening to him with her… it ripped the pair-bond out. He can't control me now."

The total lack of emotion in Claire's voice disturbed Corday. Whatever Shepherd had done had damaged the Omega, and a part of him wondered if every expression she was making was only because she was supposed to remember things like breathing and blinking.

Oblivious to the apprehension in her friend, Claire continued. "I get it now. This breach was not about gaining power. We're his puppets, falling rabid at the snap of his fingers. We dance on his stage. Shepherd, his Followers, they're punishing us all for…" she scoffed under her breath, "for blind ignorance. For allowing what was done to them."

"You are free of him, of his lies, and his evil, Claire. Remember that."

"The Dome is cracked. It's snowing outside. Not frost, *real snow*. We are not free of him, not when we let that happen. We let this all happen."

"We can take back Thólos."

Claire's breath hitched. "Not so long as he is alive."

"Your Omega escaped through a broken drainage gate. Blood on the scene shows the direction in which she fled and that her bearing was not affected by broken legs. The trail was lost when she slid below mid-level and moved out over accumulating sludge."

"How much blood?" Shepherd demanded, skimming the report in his hand for anything relevant.

"Considering the distance she fell, minimal. Internal bleeding may be an issue."

His unforgiving gunmetal glare caught the light. Impatient, Shepherd growled, "She has not eaten in almost a week. She will not have been able to manage a great distance malnourished, shoeless, and bleeding."

"Was she suffering from morning sickness?"

Shepherd turned toward his desk, his attention going back to the report. "Hunger strike."

Jules, unsurprised by such a statement, remained blank. “When she is returned, what are your expectations of Miss O’Donnell?”

Exceedingly irate, Shepherd hissed, “For her to resume her duty as my mate.”

Only psychological damage would lead a pregnant, pair-bonded Omega to hunger strike and jump off a building in madness. Jules grew blunt. “And if that’s not possible? Whom do you intend to serve as surrogate Alpha to see to her until she delivers your heir?”

Muscles straining, Shepherd warned, “You presume much, Jules. She will be returned and her behavior corrected.”

Jules was second-in-command for a good reason—he was shrewd and willing to act. Employing candor, he stated, “Without physical contact the Omega will willingly accept, she may miscarry.”

Shepherd was not to be gainsaid by man or woman. His final order was issued. “You are dismissed.”

Grasping that the situation was beyond his original assessment, Jules saluted and removed himself from the room.

Shepherd took to his desk, alone. Memorizing the reports flashing on his COMscreen, every so often he habitually glanced behind him, expecting to see Claire pacing. But she was not there. She was gone… He knew in his bones that his mate had sought out the *noble* man who had offered help. The Beta would take her in, tend her, comfort her, touch her. The very idea another might hold her… act as a surrogate…

infuriated him.

Gnashing his teeth, Shepherd swore. The Beta would die screaming.

Had Shepherd not purred, growled, stroked, followed every instinct to rouse her back from her stupor? He'd even tried to explain. *Him*! The Alpha, the strongest who was never questioned, had tried to reason with an Omega. But she had not even blinked.

She'd slipped so far out of his grasp.

It was her vocation to stay, to be devoted, to love him, to obey. Had he not seen to her needs? Had he not given her nice dresses and the best food? Had he not spent hours simply petting the girl until she was completely content? What was one unpleasant situation compared to that?

Had he not saved her life in more ways than one?

Impregnating her ensured her survival, justified her maintenance to his followers. No one could question the safekeeping of his baby. More importantly, it gave her purpose and distraction. Shepherd could not tell her in so many words—she was not one of them, remained far too determined in her ideal of *goodness* to comprehend the greatness of his calling. Furthermore, the reasoning behind his actions was unnecessary for her to know. Shepherd knew if Claire realized the true nature of what was coming, she would only fret more. She would cry for her pathetic citizens instead of giving all her attention to him. Direct treachery was best: it kept him in control of her fate. But she was willful, so damn obstinate with her foolish romantic notions.

Shepherd's fist crashed against the table. He roared,

upended the entire thing until papers flew and his COMscreen cracked against the cold floor.

Svana's unexpected arrival had been infuriatingly problematic. Not only was she displeased by what she had found, Svana would have ripped Claire's beautiful eyes out had Shepherd not pacified his beloved once she'd seen what he'd kept hidden away. You don't reason with provoked Alphas, you show action. Had he not fucked her loudly, broadcasting his favor to ensure the territorial female did not view the Omega as a threat, Claire would have been murdered the first moment he left her alone. He had done what was necessary, for both of the women.

It was the price to keep Claire.

Yet he had lost her anyway, even before she had run. Watching her mentally slip away, his rush of anger, his outright fury… it was the same rage that had burned him when he rose from the Undercroft to murder Premier Callas… only to find the leader of Thólos—the man who'd sentenced his mother to the Undercroft—was richly laced with the scent of Svana's sex.

Shepherd had drawn a deep breath, momentarily stunned as he processed what could not be—until he understood what Svana had done.

The speech he'd prepared for his greatest enemy, the one perfected night after night caged underground, was forgotten. What should have been a quick death, the body to be displayed, ended in blood dripping from the ceiling, Premier Callas' entrails flung all over the floor.

And then came pain far more horrific than any agony his

Da'rin markings might produce. His beloved had defiled herself, purposefully tainted her body by mating with the enemy.

Shepherd had confronted Svana, the woman he had loved from the first moment they'd met in the dark, the ethereal creature who was his whole life, who held his soul in her beautiful hands. The woman who had set him free, empowered him to gain control of the Undercroft—the very woman he'd killed for, suffered for, ached for.

Since their first sexual experience, Shepherd had only ever lain with the occasional estrous high Omega his beloved had procured for them—so they could fulfil the animal urge to rut together as they were meant to. For lesser beings, Alpha/Alpha pairings were difficult, as there was no pair-bond, and it was in their natures to challenge for dominance. But the two of them were beyond such sordid behavior. Or so he'd thought. He had never wavered… not once.

She had.

She had fucked the Premier, thrown what they had aside for some distorted ploy, as the final undiscussed crux in her plan. As Shepherd heard her speak on the matter, as she convincingly painted a grand scenario, he could not bring himself to question what she'd *never mentioned.* Svana had planned her seduction all along. Though she held Shepherd and spoke of her love, he was attuned to her; he could smell what was wrong in her scent. What had been done was even worse than he'd originally believed; Svana had chemically forced an unlikely ovulation. She wanted to bear the child of her enemy… to have a traitor's lineage continue the line—a man who wasn't infected with Da'rin, who was born with superior bloodlines—a man who might even be the carrier of the *alleged* antibody to the Red Consumption in his veins.

Not like Shepherd, who didn't know which of the countless prisoners who'd raped his mother had fathered him. His blood had not been fostered through generations with access to secret science and inoculations against disease. Instead, he was disfigured by Da'rin that burned in the sun and would always mark him as a castoff.

She had not voiced it, but Shepherd interpreted the truth. Svana found him wanting in the most primal of ways.

All those years, Shepherd's fidelity had been one sided. Svana did not hesitate to admit she'd taken other lovers. Hadn't he? After all, were they not Alphas? Was it not their right? She had stroked his chest and smiled so perfectly, reminding him that what they shared was beyond the physical. They shared a great destiny, an eternal spiritual bond of love.

Gutted, Shepherd had fulfilled his duty to his loyal Followers, to the dead mother he hardly remembered. Thólos fell, everyone playing their part to perfection; yet he was less for it. The world had shifted, he had achieved greatness, but what was he left with? Nothing. A big black hole where the light had gone out. He was incomplete.

But then he smelled something untainted hiding under the poignant stink of decay. Like a gift from the Gods, Claire was delivered; unlikely virtue born out of the filth of Thólos. A lotus. Claire, with her convictions and her timid bravery, walked up to a man like him—stubbornly waited for hours, a lamb amongst the wolves—to beg for help from the very villain inflicting suffering on the friends she would save.

One breath of her and he would have taken her, heat or no. The Gods had simplified his spiritual culmination by delivering her in estrous.

As he'd rutted the willful, strange thing, Shepherd found she wriggled so wonderfully, felt so perfectly snug encasing his cock, that he had to ensure she could never leave. As Svana had claimed their *devotion* was beyond the physical, their love divine, Shepherd felt perfectly justified in taking Claire, in creating a corporeal mate—an attachment that would only benefit the unruly Omega. He bonded to keep Claire for himself, his reward for service to the greater good of mankind reborn. The green-eyed little one's purity was now his own, her nearness succor. In Claire, Shepherd had regained that missing piece, the covetous need to possess something innocent, achieved.

Yet, now his bonded mate was gone with his child in her belly, wandering a city that was destined for plague.

The Omega would never come back to him willingly, not while the pair-bond was so damaged. Shepherd would have to return Claire by force.

He could almost hear the echo of her words in the air: *do not give me cause to hate you more.*

What had gone through the mind of the Omega he'd found unconscious on the bathroom floor? He'd anticipated anger, but found something impaired far beyond his reasoning. His coupling with Svana had left Claire unresponsive and empty—left the cord so fractured, all Shepherd could feel from her was an echo of desolation.

It was not a sensation he enjoyed.

No amount of attention or space had made a difference. Glassy eyes looked at him with judgment and hatred no matter how he tended her, touched her, or purred. All her favorite foods had been prepared, new dresses put in her drawer… she had not even noticed.

Claire O'Donnell belonged to him. Shepherd would find her, drag her back… and force feed her if he fucking had to. He would make her adore him like she was supposed to. Because she was his, only his, and he did not share his things. Ever.

He had even prevented the sharing of her body with his beloved. Was that not something?

CORDAY HAD RUSHED to carry out his mission for the resistance, eager to return to Claire. It wasn't because he didn't trust her to stay put, it was because he didn't trust her at all. The look in her eyes when Senator Kantor had arrived to guard her had been nothing but calculating. There was none of her former fear or skittishness, her reaction numbed as she sized up the Alpha.

The Senator could see the change in her as well, Kantor reacting with cautious courtesy. They exchanged pleasantries, Corday made them coffee, and then he left to meet Brigadier Dane. Corday's duties kept him out past dark, and the

Enforcer was utterly unprepared for the sight that met his eyes when he returned home.

Claire was asleep, curled up on the couch next to Senator Kantor, who was boldly purring in the dark.

A stab of something unwelcome drew Corday to frown. "Did she ask you to do that?"

"No. I knew what would lull her to sleep," Senator Kantor answered in a hushed tone. "Rebecca struggled to fall asleep too. I learned a lot tending my wife in the years the Gods blessed me with my Omega."

It was taboo to speak of deceased mates. Corday was surprised to hear the Alpha mention Rebecca—especially considering the sad circumstances of her long ago murder by Kantor's political adversary. It had been a sensation and had led to Senator Bergie, several of his staff, and even Bergie's son being incarcerated in the Undercroft.

Unsure what to say in response, Corday lit a few candles, and dragged a seat over from the kitchen, his face grim as he looked at the sleeping girl. "How was she today?"

"Better once she ate—less catatonic, more cognizant." Senator Kantor studied the wasted thing. "Miss O'Donnell's physical reaction after having parted from the father will be complicated. The pair-bond and the pregnancy will make her ill."

Corday had faith things might turn out better. "She told me the pair-bond was broken. As for the pregnancy, I will take care of her."

Senator Kantor shook his head "It doesn't work that way, son."

Shooting a look at the Alpha, Corday ground his teeth. "We'll see."

"Now that you are back, the three of us need to have a discussion." Senator Kantor sat straighter, smoothing his sleeve. "Get dinner in her first; afterward the two of us will explain."

It was unsettling to be ordered around in his own home, but Corday nodded and went to the kitchen. Simple fare was prepared. There was some fresh fruit for Claire, an apple he'd bartered for a handful of batteries.

When all was ready, Corday carefully took Claire's limp hand, stroking her fingers until her bleary green eyes popped open. It was obvious she was confused. For just a moment she jerked from his nearness, ready to run. Then it began. The rich rumble of an Alpha purr took Claire from startled to angry.

The glare she gave Senator Kantor would have been funny had her scent not turned so rancid with fear. "You can stop now."

The old man conceded.

Over dinner, the men chose silence. Claire did not. "Is there another bounty?"

Corday was not going to lie to her. "Yes."

She forced down another salty bite. "And?"

"When we observed the Citadel, there was a line of citizens dragging in women of your description."

Claire cringed. "That's disgusting…"

"From what I could see, the Followers were letting them go, but citizens are starving." This was Corday's chance to explain why Senator Kantor was really there. “The bounty on your head could keep a family fed for a year. We have to keep you hidden.”

The old Alpha broached the greater issue. “And not just from Thólos.”

Claire cocked her head. “What do you mean?”

“I need you to understand that what is said cannot leave this room.”

He’d insulted her. “I never told Shepherd a thing. Never,” she said.

“Dissention could be our greater enemy.” Ruffling his grey hair, elbows on his knees, Kantor sighed. “Many of our people believe that unification under the Follower’s governance would satisfy Shepherd. The fact is, these citizens are numerous and growing more loyal to the dictator’s regime than we could have imagined. Our own ranks, even some of our brothers and sisters in arms, have been tempted to the other side. Once ensconced, they cannot be reasoned with. Your appearance within the resistance might offer too great a temptation for any straddling the line. Corday and I both believe they will vie to give you back.”

“We would never let that happen, Claire,” Corday interjected, desperate to explain once he saw the look on her face. “Ever. Do you understand?”

Senator Kantor dared to squeeze her hand. “We need our troops focused. We must find the contagion. To do that, you must stay hidden. No one can know you’re here.”

Claire sat silent, processing such information. When she finally spoke, her words were not gentle. “You seem to be a wise man, Senator Kantor, but can't you see that time and further suffering will corrode those loyal to you no matter what? My pregnancy is the key to your success. So long as I am running wild in Thólos with his baby as my hostage, he won't infect the population—not at the risk of infecting me. Now is your chance to strike. Use me and rebel immediately."

"I disagree… Shepherd's treatment of you has been appalling, negligent in the gravest of ways." Solemn, Senator Kantor denied her. "If we move prematurely, he might release the contagion. I cannot risk millions of lives, your life, on a maybe. I'm sorry, Claire. Until the Red Consumption's location is uncovered, the resistance will make no move."

The line of Claire's mouth grew sharp. Sitting taller, she looked at both of them as if they were simpletons. "It's not the contagion that keeps us in his power. It's our own cowardice. Every day our people do nothing, the bastard is proving his view of our behavior is correct. The Dome is cracked. Don't you see the weather will kill us long before any virus might? *We* have to take back our city, or we die trying."

Senator Kantor put a hand on the Omega's shoulder. "Thólos' citizens are not soldiers. They're scared and have no comprehension of combat. You must understand; many are watching their families suffer, their children are dying."

Claire shook her head, swallowed her outburst. "No one in this city is a civilian anymore, there is no neutral. Either you are with Shepherd, or you are against him."

"It isn't that simple, Claire."

She looked to Senator Kantor, lost. “Isn’t it?”

A deep sigh preceded Senator Kantor’s explanation. “You are still young and will learn in time that things are not always as they seem.”

Claire cocked her head, her previously glowing image of so highly regarded a Senator distorted by the sad impotence of such a man. “Shepherd once told me the same thing… You just echoed the words of a madman.”

Senator Kantor offered a conciliatory smile, his look of pity disarming. “I’m asking you to trust me.”

Corday understood what riled her; bone deep, he felt the same away. “We make progress every day, Claire. I swear it to you.”

Claire looked to her friend and could see he had faith in the Alpha charged to lead the rebellion.

“I understand.” And she did. She understood that the longer they waited, the more people would die—that the world was a nightmare where the men and women who’d once sworn to uphold the law might hand her back to a despot for food that would only last so long.

She understood perfectly.

She hurt; everyone hurt. And it had to end.

Once Senator Kantor had left, Corday took her hand, and led her back to the couch to rest. When he had her to himself, Corday smiled and pulled a gift out of his pocket.

“I have something to cheer you up.” The Enforcer, his face dimpled, held up what was pinched between his fingers. “A few weeks ago I went to your residence. Everything was pretty smashed up, but I found this hidden under the lining of your jewelry box."

He slid a band of gold on her finger.

The gold was warm, but Claire's reaction to it utterly cold. "This was my mother's wedding ring."

As a child she'd hated the sight of it, still angry her mother had abandoned her, too young to accept what had happened. Claire had forgotten she'd even had it tucked away. Now it fit, just like her mother's disappointment in life fit. Holding up her hand to view the grim thing, she saw the correlation to her mother's impetus—a pretty, sparkling reminder that one could always choose.

"Thank you, Corday."

He took her hand again, stroked her fingers, and promised, "I want you to know that I understand the way you feel, but he's right. If the Senator's life was not gravely threatened, I don't know if I would trust even him with you."

Claire wasn't sure what to say. "Why haven't either of you asked me about Shepherd?"

Corday started to purr, scooting closer to put an arm around her shoulder. "Considering that you escaped once, anything he'd allowed you to hear may have been planted to mislead the resistance should you get free again. I hate to say it, but every move that monster makes is… brilliant. There is nothing you can give us."

No one was on her side, and though she tried to hide her look of hurt, it didn't matter. Corday saw.

She chose to tell him things anyway; she needed him to

hear her. "He was born in the Undercroft, his mother incarcerated by Premier Callas. His lover's name is Svana."

The Beta listened, Claire's words confirming what Brigadier Dane had conjectured. It would explain how Shepherd had been incarcerated off record, but the thought of a woman being thrown into that hell… that his own government had done such a thing, just could not be. Could it?

Claire continued, eyes far away as she blathered on. "Svana has an accent I've never heard before—like she's not from here."

"There are a thousand kilometers of snow in every direction outside this Dome, Claire. Outsiders cannot wander in."

"Just like women cannot be thrown in the Undercroft and entire cities cannot fall overnight?" To Claire it seemed there had to be more… dark truths about themselves that had to be recognized. Meeting her friend's eyes, she confessed, "I don't think Premier Callas was a good man. I'm afraid Shepherd's harsh opinion of us might not be wrong."

Corday's arm tightened around her. "Are you saying you agree with him?"

"No," she answered quickly. "No. Evil cannot change evil. Maybe his underlying motivation was once principled. I know he thinks it is, but it's not."

"That's right, Claire," Corday reaffirmed, worried to see her so lost. "Shepherd and his army are delusional."

Cheek to his shoulder, she agreed, "Aren't we all a little these days…"

2

Claire was not a violent woman. She did not know how to fight. She was not physically strong.

But she wasn't defenseless. Claire was fast and clever. She just needed to find a way to use those traits to further her agenda. Deceiving Corday *again* did not sit well with her, but his loyalty, his intentions, were tied up in Senator Kantor's leadership.

Maybe the Senator's plan would work… perhaps rebels could uncover the location of the contagion. Then what? Rally the people over a series of hard years while the Dome continued to crack and more snow fell? Claire was not going to wait to find out.

Feigning complacency, smiling when she was supposed to, Claire acted the part of a submissive Omega and fervently agreed when Corday asked for her promise to stay inside. Admitting she was terrified of being given back, that she trusted him to protect her, it only took two days of good behavior before he finally left to attend his duties.

Despite the pain each step cost, once alone, she began to pace and plot.

The monster himself had told her she'd failed because she believed in goodness in a city where there was none. He was wrong. Claire knew that she had failed because she hadn't tried hard enough, thought big enough because, in the end, she'd expected someone else to save her.

How very Omega.

How fucking ironic that the champion the women had chosen had been Shepherd! Laughing under her breath, sickened, Claire gripped her skull.

Nona, the other Omegas—not once had Corday mentioned them. It was the other Omegas, the one's he'd freed that slipped into conversation here and there. He was trying to shore her up, show that there was hope, but he never mentioned her friends.

Claire knew why. Corday was afraid the temptation to go to them would undermine her promise to stay put. He was right.

Just as he'd threatened, Shepherd had stashed those women in the one place no outsider could get to—the Undercroft. Claire was certain down to her bones.

Getting in would not be easy. Once inside, her quest would grow impossible unless… Claire could encourage the Omegas to stand as a pack and fight.

No one was going to save them—they would have to save themselves. All Claire could do was give them their chance.

In a way, Shepherd may have even done Claire a favor. He'd have seen to the Omega's basic needs, wanting them healthy enough for his men. After so many weeks with food, the women would be stronger, and Claire had a feeling that with starvation no longer clouding their judgment, they would also be very angry.

Anger was the only sentiment Claire seemed to understand most days. Anger was a great motivator.

Turning to pace in the other direction, her elbow winged Corday's bookcase, knocking a mess to the floor.

Bending over to clean up, Claire froze.

An Enforcer data cube…

Information on Shepherd might be there. Maybe even Svana's name was tucked into inside an Enforcer file.

Claire plugged it into Corday's COMscreen and typed out the name 'Shepherd.'

Nothing.

'Svana.'

Nothing.

This resource was too valuable to ignore. There had to be something on there she could use. Claire just needed to think. She needed to slow her mental chatter, to breathe. A cold sweat came as her finger tapped the screen, spelling the name of the only criminal Claire knew. The COM flashed, beautiful chocolate eyes staring back at her.

Claire knew the contemptuously smirking face on that woman's credentials, every angle of it. Even though it had been years, Claire still knew how she smelled, what her laugh sounded like. Leaning nearer the screen, the Omega almost smiled.

The next hour was spent absorbing every single detail the data cube contained on one repeat felon. Maryanne Cauley had amassed quite a record: assault, larceny, burglary, arson… her file was massive. From the looks of it, the stunning lawbreaker had gone from cocky repeat escapee of farm labor to… nothing. Her file just stopped—no record of further incarceration, no address, no date of death. She had just disappeared.

If Claire had not known what had been done with Shepherd's mother, it would not have felt like a very… *disturbing coincidence*.

She did not know what made her do it, but her fingers typed out one final name: 'Claire O'Donnell.'

It only took a moment to see the flaw on her citizenship registration. If Maryanne Cauley still lived, Claire knew where she'd gone to ground.

CORDAY HAD COME BACK to find his apartment cold and empty, lifeless where there should have been a small Omega resting on the couch. Corday had hated leaving her, but she had sworn so faithfully, admitting that she could hardly walk on her feet, that he had believed her.

Claire had fooled him. Claire didn't trust him. Claire had left him… again.

There was a note:

Dear Corday,

I can't live a lie and stay hidden. Not the way things are now. I want you to know that no matter what happens, I chose – fully aware of the consequences.

Love,

Claire

She had signed 'love' but there was no apology. He knew where he stood and the position was painful and deeply upsetting. Knowing her obsession with the Omega situation, Corday folded up the letter and shoved it in his pocket. Zipping up his jacket, he went right out onto the causeways and fought through the snow to where Brigadier Dane secretly sheltered the leader of the resistance.

Banging on the door, Corday refused to let up until the woman answered.

Dane glared. "You shouldn't be here."

Corday did not wait for an invitation, pushing his superior officer aside as he growled, "Like hell I shouldn't."

"Have you lost your mind?" The door was swiftly locked, the invading cold air shut out. "Showing up here in broad daylight endangers us all."

Looking back at the soldier, Corday deepened his scowl. "It's dumping snow outside, no one's on the street and my tracks are already being covered. Where is Senator Kantor?"

"I'm here," a voice sounded from the dwelling's back room.

Ignoring the snarling Brigadier Dane, Corday pulled the note out of his pocket and stomped over. "She left."

Senator Kantor set down his COMscreen and took the

note. One brief read over and the old Alpha shook his head. "I'm sorry, Corday. It's not like we could have locked her up."

"Claire is going to do something crazy!" Practically tearing out his hair, Corday snarled, "We've gotta stop her."

Senator Kantor shook his head, his tired eyes bloodshot and sad. "We cannot risk exposing ourselves on a manhunt. We both know she recognized we couldn't help her. Do you understand that, kid?"

"She's going to get herself killed!"

Speaking in a low voice, the Alpha tried to convey sense and a much needed measure of calm. "The Omega is pregnant, she's pair-bonded and mentally detached. She doesn't have much time left, and she knows it."

Rubbing his forehead as if he could wipe away his frustration, Corday demanded, "What are you saying?"

"I am saying that Claire is fighting what must be a nightmare inside her. Her timeline is short and she is making her choice."

"I told you. The pair-bond was damaged."

Senator Kantor dropped the fatherly tone in place for one far more authoritative. "*She's* damaged. Her determination is the only thing keeping her together. You try to cage her, or stop her, she'll fall apart. And that would only open her up to his influence again. It might be best to let her do what she needs to do while she can still do it."

"We both know she's going to try to get those Omegas out of the Undercroft," Corday hissed. "It would take an army and she's just one girl."

Senator Kantor fully understood what was at stake. “She has an advantage, a hostage, and you don’t know where she is. Nothing can be done. Believe it or not, my bet’s on her.”

“He’ll KILL her.”

“Read the letter again.” Senator Kantor handed the crumpled page back. “No one can comprehend the consequences like she can. She’s a grown woman who’s made her choice, just like we ask our brothers and sisters in arms to make every day.”

“This is fucking insanity!” Corday stormed out of the room, the note crushed in his grip. “I’m going to find her. I’m going to bring her home.”

Brushing past a frowning Brigadier Dane, Corday found himself caught.

His arm in her grip, Dane’s face was red and her hiss nasty. “You will do no such thing. Return to your home. Cool off before you jeopardize the entire resistance with your impulsive stupidity. Think, for once. Whatever this Claire has planned, distracting her or getting yourself killed won’t help anyone.”

Corday was strongly tempted to violence. “You don’t know Claire.”

“I don’t, but I know you. And I know when you’re wrong.”

THE WEATHER WAS ABSOLUTE SHIT. A blessing and a curse, as it seemed Thólos was hiding from the unfamiliar storm. No soul walked the streets to pester her, and though falling snow made the path difficult, the trek left her soaked to the bone and shivering violently.

In all the years since Claire had last walked the midlevel promenade, she'd forgotten much. The tight dwellings were still celery green, but it took her some time to remember which window had once housed a flower box full of red poppies.

There were no splashes of color now… no flowers. Soon even the withering trees would be nothing but sticks. All there was, was that too cheerful green peeking out from clinging frost, broken windows, and refuse.

Three flights up, third domicile on the right.

Standing face to face with a once familiar door, Claire jiggled the handle and found it locked. Running her fingernail around the frame, she felt a bump in the crack—a spare key hidden just as it had been when she was a girl.

The inside was dark. No one was home.

In place of the woman she sought lay junk: wires, filters, air scrubbers, pipes, and whirring machines piled all over the room. The selfish magpie had stolen them right out of the Dome's infrastructure, and by doing so had weakened everyone else.

It was unspeakable, infuriating and, worst of all, after reading her file, Claire was not remotely surprised.

Mouth sour, Claire stripped off her wet clothes, hung them to drip in the galley kitchen, and helped herself to something dry. It was night before she finally heard the scratch of a key in the lock.

A tall beauty slipped into the chilly room, rubbing her mittened hands together. It only took the woman a second to spot Claire lounging on her couch. "You should not be here."

"You always were such a cunt. You know that, right?" Claire snarled back.

"That is a big word coming from you, little girl." Cocking her head to the side, blonde hair moving like a waterfall behind her, the Alpha changed her snarl to a provocative purr. "Do you have any idea how much you're worth?"

"Don't get too excited. He won't pay you… Shepherd hanged the last batch who brought me in, Maryanne." Claire looked at what had once been the smartest girl she knew and saw a stranger. "Fact is, he takes offense that anyone would expect payment for returning what's his."

Shoulders tight, Maryanne eased closer, eyeballing every corner of the room. "Did anyone see you come in?"

"No."

"That means at least three people did."

Claire let out a breath. "My face was covered and I'm sure you can smell for yourself that I am nothing special right now."

Full lips smirking, Maryanne lifted a handful of Claire's hair for a sniff. "True…"

Claire took Maryanne's hand, the hand of who had been her closest childhood friend, and held it. Large eyes pleading, she whispered, "I need your help."

"No."

"Why?"

Maryanne pulled her fingers free and sauntered off. "You

have no idea what these guys can do to you, Claire. Whatever you did, just find a place to hide and wait it out… but don't drag me into it."

"Actually, I do know what they're capable of," Claire spat at Maryanne's back. "I'm pregnant with Shepherd's child."

"Fuck me!" Maryanne spun in horror, staring down at the diminutive Omega's belly.

"I wouldn't, remember," Claire teased, trying to mimic the mischief of their youths. "You were all over me during school. That's why we aren't friends anymore."

"Shut up, bitch." Maryanne laughed, unable to suppress a wolfish grin, "You wish. It was Patrick Keck whom I wanted to fuck… and I did. Often."

"Then you disappeared. You were my best friend and you never even said goodbye." And that had hurt a great deal. More so because Claire knew Maryanne had been capable of so much more than the mayhem she'd accomplished. "I read your file. Is it true you broke into the Archives?"

"Several times… only got caught once. Shoveling pig shit for a year was worth it. You have no idea how much some folks will pay for something as mundane as forbidden, tattered books."

"How did you get in?"

Maryanne licked her teeth and motioned to herself in a sweeping gesture. "This girl's got skills."

Claire grew serious. "And I need them."

The woman edged closer, trailing her fingers down

Claire's tangled black hair, cooing, "You can't afford me, sweet pea."

"I know. Which is why I hate to do this." Claire looked for a moment like she might lose her nerve, but she drew a deep breath and began. "The Omegas are locked in the Undercroft. I need to set them free, and you're going to help me, or I am going to tell Shepherd you laid a hand on me. He will rip you to pieces, because I'm not only carrying his child… we're pair-bonded."

Maryanne turned full Alpha. "I WON'T FUCKING DO IT!"

"You will."

The blonde paced towards the window, checking for the twentieth time for a sign of trouble. "Goddamn you, Claire. Goddamn you and your pointless humanitarian bullshit. You always were a goody two-shoes when we were kids. It was disgusting then, and it's even more pathetic now."

"But I was never a pushover." Claire took Maryanne's arm, her expression one of desperation. "I am sorry, but I need you. I need the *skills* you have that I lack. If you do this for me, I will never bother you again."

A deadly look came with the question. "Why not just ask your mate?"

"He's the one who locked them up." Claire pushed her hair behind her ear and stood her ground. "Like you, he's blind to what is right and wrong."

Maryanne cursed. She raged for hours, trying to talk Claire out of such madness, but the outcome was inevitable. Maryanne Cauley had no choice, and she knew it.

They fought over the plan vehemently. There was no time for reconnaissance, the pair blind to what may or may not be waiting. Diversion was one thing, but what Claire intended was insanity. But it could be done, Claire knew it in her bones. She could make it work. She had to, because if she did not give her all, risk everything, then nothing would change.

In the end, it was a shot in the dark at best… suicide at worst. But Claire, it seemed, had come to the right woman.

Maryanne Cauley knew the Undercroft—she knew entrances, she knew secrets—and though she refused to speak of why, it was obvious that once upon a time, Maryanne Cauley had been disposed of down in that dark place.

Shepherd's mother was not the only woman thrown into hell.

At dawn, Claire was exhausted but determined. Maryanne swore up and down and yanked Claire to bed when the Omega would not stop yawning. Once under the covers, it was so simple to fall into old patterns, Maryanne braiding Claire's hair just like she had when they were little.

Hoping the answer would not be as disappointing as she anticipated, Claire sighed, "The way you talk about the Undercroft, the look in your eye every time I say the name Shepherd… You know him."

"Everyone knows him."

No, it was much deeper than that. Claire rolled over to look her friend in the eye. "Don't lie to me, Maryanne. He scares you. He scares you because you *know him.* Somehow you were once involved with that monster. Are you still?"

Maryanne tried to be flippant. “Involved? I should be asking you that same question. After all, your romance is probably going to get me killed.”

“I am not mated to Shepherd by choice.” Claire would not let herself blink or stutter. “I went into estrous unexpectedly in front of him. He forced the pair-bond.”

Maryanne had the decency to look stricken. “Don’t take this the wrong way, Claire, but this is Shepherd. He’s a powerful man. It seems a little strange that he would bond to a woman he didn’t know… I mean, he’s a warlord. People probably give him Omegas for Christmas.”

Svana’s words echoed in Claire’s head. ‘*We have not shared a heated Omega in some time.*’

“They do… I don’t know why he bonded to me, and the one time I asked, he gave only pointless, empty words.” Her green eyes grew harder, as did Claire’s demand for answers. “My question, Maryanne. How do you know him?”

Pursing her lips, Maryanne confessed, “I, um, needed friends once.”

“I was your friend. I would have been, had you not run off… and”—Claire sighed, knowing Maryanne well enough to see she was not exactly an innocent—“done the things you did until you got thrown into the Undercroft.”

Maryanne snorted. “Before I found a way out.”

“From Shepherd.”

“My services in exchange for my life.” The girl who had never felt guilty about a single trespass she had committed in her life looked at her old friend with uncustomary regret. “I was the one who recovered the access codes to the Judicial Sector and the Citadel."

Brows drawn tight, Claire hissed, "How could you?"

"I didn't know their plans for Thólos. I swear."

Claire didn't want to hear it. "What did you think he would do once freed?"

"He was already free…" Maryanne whispered. "How do you think I got out?"

Claire's brows shot up. "What?"

Maryanne snorted at the small woman's naiveté. "Sorry, bitch, but we've been screwed for a long time."

"Do you know where he keeps the virus?"

Smirking, Maryanne shared a hard truth. "If I did, do you really think I'd be here, stockpiling and preparing for the end of the world? Listen to me, Claire, they don't know about this place. I wiped it from the records almost a decade before I was tossed downstairs. I have enough food, enough air scrubbers to get through almost a year. You don't need to follow through with your crap plan. You can stay here with me. Should the worst happen, all we'd have to do is wait until the virus did its work."

Claire shook her head. "The Dome is cracked, Maryanne. You'd freeze to death as the ecosystem fails. It's like he planned for people like you. We're all going to die. We're all going to die if nothing is done."

THEY WERE BOTH ANXIOUS, tired… just like everyone else in Thólos. There was no point in further argument. Instead both Claire and Maryanne fell into hurried preparations. Things needed to be built for Claire's scheme, and technology learned. Maryanne's explanations, the way she could make something dangerous from nothing, reminded Claire just how out of her element she was.

Rudimentary bombs, how to override basic access panels —Maryanne was teaching her instead of just making them herself, wordlessly reminding Claire that their association would soon end and that the fumbling Omega would be on her own.

When all the tools were ready, Claire showered, scrubbing off any lingering trace of Corday's scent. Maryanne was in that bathroom applying lipstick as if they were planning an outing, not an attack against the tyrants holding the city. Blinking at the mirror, Maryanne froze, jaw agape at the sight of the Omega's naked body.

The Alpha touched without asking. "What is all of this?"

Claire didn't need to look down to know what Maryanne found so disturbing. "The price of my freedom."

Careful fingers traced the yellowing handprint over Claire's throat. "And your neck?"

An incoherent noise, a mockery of speech got stuck in Claire's mouth. "It's nothing."

Maryanne took her chin and turned Claire's face to meet her own big brown eyes. She smiled, teasing. "Your feet are disgusting. You're bleeding all over my floor."

And the pain was a blessing, the perfect distraction.

"Shepherd didn't allow me access to shoes. I had to run in the streets barefoot."

"Does it hurt?"

"Yes. But it doesn't bother me and it won't slow me down."

Maryanne crouched to see why fresh blood was running down her old friend's shin. "Your knee needs stitches."

"Nothing I can do about that right now."

"Sit down, I'll do it."

It was so backwards to have Maryanne Cauley be the one to tend to her; as kids it was always the other way around. Watching the fully grown woman pull a needle and some metallic thread through her skin, feeling the pinch and burn, the world seemed so very strange. "Whatever happened to your mom?" Claire asked.

"Who fucking knows," Maryanne muttered as she made another tight stitch. "Probably OD'd years ago."

Claire just hummed, distracted. "My dad died four years back. Roadway accident."

"Your pop was always pretty cool."

Claire had to agree. "Yeah… I'm glad he's not here to see this."

Maryanne rubbed her lips together as if she wanted to say something but thought better of it. Instead, she stood and gathered clothing appropriate for the mission and shoved the horrid black garb of Shepherd's Followers towards Claire.

The Omega didn't balk, just dressed silently while Maryanne squeezed her limber body into a matching uniform.

"You know, Claire," Maryanne was dead serious, knotting her hair to tuck under a cap. "Underground there's a whole 'nother world. Those who follow Shepherd are beyond dangerous."

"Whatever they are doesn't matter."

Maryanne's voice fell flat. "What I am trying to tell you is, pair-bond or no, they have an agenda. Shepherd might just kill you."

Claire had no illusions on that score. "I'm counting on it."

"I could save us all this trouble and kill you right now," the Alpha offered.

"That's awfully sweet of you," Claire teased, standing on tiptoe to press a peck to her friend's ruby lips. "But I will already be dead to you after tonight. Give me what I need and you have my word."

Maryanne tucked a loaded gun into Claire's pocket. "Promises, promises…"

"And, Maryanne," Claire added, forcing a playful smile. "You look like a slut in that outfit."

3

"This is the entrance to Purgatory." Maryanne pointed to the map alight on the screen between them. Tracing the snaking tunnels that lay right below the concrete footpaths of the Lower Reaches, she said, "This floor is for administration and separated from the true Undercroft. If your Omegas are being kept in this shithole, Shepherd would not stash them any lower than here. Not if he wanted to keep them alive."

Claire stared down at the COMscreen. Seeing her people locked away like livestock brought a wave of unbearable sadness. The Omegas slept ten to a cell, segregated by age, and there were less than the fifty-six that had been taken. Three Shepherd had hanged, the remainder Claire assumed had either died or been pair-bonded and dragged away. There were hardly even forty, and one was in estrous, isolated and being rutted by a stranger… the girl only sixteen.

In her heart, Claire had been terrified Shepherd may have allowed his men to inject the Omegas with the same drugs he'd used on her… to set up a brothel of mindless estrous sex for the taking, and she had to admit she was marginally relieved to find he had yet to stoop so low.

"Looking at them like that isn't going to change anything, sugar pie," Maryanne cooed, crouched at her side.

"Even you must see how sick this is." Frowning, Claire looked away from the COMscreen so her friend might meet her eye. "Don't let me down."

"I'll get you in. Then I'm gone."

Claire nodded. "For your own sake, I suggest you run fast."

As per their agreement, Maryanne tapped into the system and hacked the prison's upper level controls. Handing over the technology, she gave Claire patchy dominion of Purgatory's security systems.

"You need to know, small fry, not every castoff was released when Shepherd staged his coup. There are paths in there you don't want to stumble down. If you get lost… you let Shepherd find you." With those final, frightening words, Maryanne gave Claire a quick kiss and disappeared.

Claire had to make the next move alone. Holding a device constructed from duct tape and a few stolen circuits, praying to her Goddess that their plan worked, she flipped the switch.

Scattered explosions went off, all four of the handcrafted bombs Maryanne had distributed functioning flawlessly. Right on cue, Claire began phase two. As her friend had promised, the Followers on screen rushed towards the disturbance with alarming precision. When the soldiers were separated and in halls or elevators, she trapped the men with updated overrides to the systems they would have to countermand at each terminal.

Lips a hair's breadth from the screen, Claire took control of the prison's internal communications system. "Omegas, the doors to your cells are unlocked. Anyone who would prefer freedom to Shepherd's slavery, claim it. The guards are scattered, trapped, but I can't hold them for long. Band together, I'll lead you out. Do not forget your sister being held in the room at the end of the corridor." Venom dripped from Claire's voice. "I don't imagine Shanice dreamed her first heat would be spent mounted by a soldier three times her age."

On her small monitor, seven women, Nona included, stood and rushed out of their cells. More stood to watch, afraid but rallying. Over lingering seconds, the numbers began to grow, women throwing back the bars and racing out to join their sisters. But Claire's attention was elsewhere; a band of Followers had already overridden control and broken free.

Lacking the skill to manipulate the system with the same finesse as Maryanne, Claire cried, "Four Followers have made it through. You have to stand up for yourselves! If you want out, you must fight back!"

At first sight of the unwelcome Alphas, the Omegas fell upon them like locusts. More Followers tried to grab at the women, only to discover supposedly weak Omegas attacked in packs. Even the strongest male could not stand against forty enraged females. Gunshots were fired, two of Claire's sisters fell—but all four of Shepherd's soldiers were destroyed as the group forced their way forward. By the time they descended on the room where the estrous high Omega was being rutted, the pack had fallen into a frenzy.

The rutting male was ripped away, torn apart by teeth and claws.

They scooped up their sister, and followed every last direction Claire shouted over the speakers. In less than five minutes, women began to flood the very passages the Castoffs had employed the day they broke free.

Once they had pushed past the final doors, Claire stepped out of the darkness and called out to them. Nona reached her first. Over the sound of shouting, Claire yelled hurried instructions into the woman's ear. One nod of understanding, and Nona took Claire's COMscreen.

Claire pushed her crude trigger's final button.

Blinding flashes preceded cloying green-grey smoke—it filled the prison's access road to the point where Claire could no longer see Nona, she could not smell her, and she would not have the chance to wave goodbye.

The screech of tires and trucks packed with Shepherd's Followers skid to a halt outside the causeway. In moments, armed soldiers had created a perimeter; the only plausible exit blocked.

There was no turning back. This was the end.

Claire recognized the blue-eyed Beta leading the men, watched him squinting when the billowing smoke parted just enough to show who'd dared strike a blow at Thólos' new regime. With a gun held to her temple, Claire walked forward until she was exposed to Shepherd's men.

Eyes sharp, Jules commanded, "Put the gun down, Miss O'Donnell."

Seeing them so close, so organized, the Followers were exactly as Maryanne described—killers, remorseless, walking nightmares—and she was just one woman standing up against far more powerful men.

Raising her chin, defiant, Claire shouted over the fray, "Every Omega here gets to walk away, or I pull the trigger and kill Shepherd's child."

Ignoring the accumulating smoke, Jules marched to the edge of the barricade. "And how far do you think they will they get?"

The Beta was expecting an answer; Claire did not give one. All she did was stare right back into those unsettling baby-blues.

When long minutes of silence continued, when no further move was made by the female, Jules finally seemed to understand.

Claire smiled.

"Now that I think about it," the gun still pointed at her skull, Claire took a deep breath. "Putting the women in the Undercroft was actually an excellent idea. I think we'll stay… without the debauched visitors and scheduled rape, of course."

"Do you really think a handful of women will be able to hold the prison from us?"

"Yes."

A strange look passed through the man's eyes. He looked about to speak but was silenced by the sound of heavy footfalls approaching from the shadows.

The nightmare was coming.

She felt him before she saw him. Her eyes never left Jules, but it took every ounce of Claire's self-control not to step back into the blanket of smoke and ruin her plan when Shepherd emerged in her periphery.

"Little one," Shepherd's voice was soft and enticing, flowing just like the vapor at her back. "Point the gun at me."

He was so very big. Even with a good fifteen paces between them, Claire had the impression that all he needed to do was reach out to drag her back to hell.

Though she was afraid to look his way, though she kept her attention anchored in the vibrant blue of Jules' stare, Claire's words were for Shepherd. "If I thought I possessed the skill to aim and be certain a bullet blew right through your skull, I would not hesitate to shoot you. But I've told you before, I'm not stupid. Pointed where it is, I don't have to worry about missing."

Shepherd took a step closer; Claire stiffened.

Showing her teeth, she forced herself to look at him. "Your approach is making it very tempting to pull the trigger. If I die, your child dies with me. Stop. Moving."

With her attention on him, Shepherd paused, guiding the conversation as if they were having an afternoon chat. "It is good to see that you are mostly uninjured from the fall, and that you have been eating."

"I didn't fall, I jumped." Claire lifted her chin higher,

exposing the bruises blotched across her pale throat for every last Follower to see.

Only with some great effort was Shepherd able to speak levelly. “You have made your point. I will even admit I am impressed with your little coup. But it’s over now.”

“I don’t give a fuck what you think!”

A stifled bark came from the Alpha, his mouth curved into a snarl. “I know you are angry—”

Her voice dropped low, coarse as she hissed through clenched teeth, “Angry does not even begin to describe what I am. I have been defiled, manipulated, betrayed, and broken. *I am way past angry*.”

“Everything that was done was necessary,” Shepherd countered, taking another intimidating step closer.

“You may have had me for a moment there, but your woman opened my eyes to what you really are.” Fierce, Claire’s lip curled in threat. “I should be thanking you, Shepherd. Your horrible lesson of insurrection was an inspiration. You taught me that even the weakest can rise up against tyranny with the right encouragement. Well, I’m rising up against you and the perversion of your ideals.”

She had stood there long enough.

Trembling so hard she was certain every last man there could see her fear, ready to do what she did best, Claire took a backwards step into the smoke.

Shepherd countered, struggling to rein in his rage. “Do not make me come and collect you, little one. You may get injured, and I would prefer that not be the case.”

“What are a few broken bones and a potential gunshot or

two?" She pressed her free hand to her heart, Claire's face the image of anguish. "They wouldn't matter. I feel nothing. Nothing at all."

Even Shepherd could not deny the echoing truth in the fractured bond; it was like she wasn't even there—the greater fragment of her spirit simply gone. But she was more at that moment than she had been when her every hour was spent in a stupor underground.

She would recover.

Looking deep into such pain-filled eyes, Shepherd spoke in a voice of certainty, of authority. "Your place is with me. You will return to your mate."

"You are no mate to me." Claire spat on the ground between them. "I will stand with my people on my terms! If Thólos is to suffer, your child and I will suffer with it."

Shepherd was going to reach for her, she knew it. Claire spun, black hair flaring as she darted into the smoke. Shepherd was so very fast for a man of his size, and Claire could feel him and his Followers bearing down on her. But out of the dark, thin arms reached for her.

The embrace of an old friend was followed by a sudden loss of gravity.

Maryanne Cauley had come back, a cable propelling them high above the Lower Reaches before the raging giant or his men had even seen where Claire had gone.

THE AMOUNT of security protocols that had been overwritten during the Omegas' escape was extraordinary. All the surveillance footage had been wiped, many of the mechanized doors manipulated to trap his soldiers still malfunctioning. Purgatory's grounds had been turned into a maze that took Shepherd's most skilled Followers over an hour to penetrate, only to find there was not even one Omega inside.

The females had vanished as if teleported by the smoke.

Seven Followers dead, twenty-four trapped, and one man barely breathing. Claire's plan had been either extremely well-coordinated, or she was gifted with sheer dumb luck.

Deceitfully complacent, Shepherd turned to his second-in-command. "Explain to me, Jules, how an Omega female who paints pictures for children's stories accomplished this feat with only four days to plan?"

"I can't. Not yet, sir." The Beta stood at attention, unsmiling and severe. "We tracked the Omegas to the sewer access and know they went north, but the scent…"

"Was lost in the waste they rubbed all over themselves," Shepherd finished, knowing exactly what they would do. His lip curled. "And they are armed with weapons taken off our fallen men."

"Weapons they do not know how to use," Jules offered.

"Those women went on a rampage and killed five Alphas with their bare hands. I am fairly certain they will learn how to fire assault rifles in no time." A strange feeling came to the pit of Shepherd's gut, the sensation quickly ignored in favor of the satisfaction of clenching his fists until joints popped.

"We have profiles and photographs of all known

surviving Omegas. The odds that one will be seen are exponentially higher with so many. They will be found."

"The situation with Claire takes precedence over retrieving the Omegas. Her escape route was divergent. She must be moving through Thólos as we speak. Assign our best trackers, and when she is found, no one approaches but me."

Jules knew the female had been serious about ending her life; it had been the only reason he'd not disarmed the quaking woman at first glance. "Cornering her would not end well. Her mental state is unbalanced. Miss O'Donnell is a danger to herself until her desperation recedes."

Shepherd cut a dangerous glare at his lieutenant. "What is your point?"

Intense blue eyes sat static in a face devoid of emotion. "Your appearance turned her fear to rage; her finger tightened on the trigger. I had a measure of rapport with her; you did not."

The slight flare of Shepherd's nostrils, the intake of breath, was nothing compared to the growl that stained his reply. "Her entire plan hinged on distracting us with the ploy. She did not pull the trigger, she ran."

Jules did not baulk. "Her success will give her confidence, and may lead her to expose herself to needless danger in order to fulfill her agenda. Shall I create a situation she'd want to resolve? We could draw her out on our terms. Miss O'Donnell could potentially be captured before any more trauma accumulated."

Shepherd momentarily considered the suggestion before he shook his head in the negative. "She is too clever for that."

"Where do you think she'll strike next?"

"I do not think she will strike at all. Not one of her bombs killed a Follower. She could have executed all our comrades trapped inside. Casualties were kept to a minimum. As far as we know, she never fired the pistol or pointed it at anyone but herself. No matter the show she put on, Claire O'Donnell is a pacifist. Her ideal would be to inspire, just like she threatened."

"If she exposes herself to the public, they will bring her in," the Beta assured.

"Her faith in the scum of this city is far more dangerous to her than any gun. If they knew of our bond, the people of Thólos would not deliver her home. They would rip her to shreds."

CURLED TOGETHER like kittens in Maryanne's bed, Claire slept with one hand over her belly and a troubled frown on her brow. Maryanne watched her fitful sleep, certain again that she'd lost her mind for going back to drag the obstinate fool away.

After witnessing the showdown with Shepherd, watching as the hulking killer spoke as softly as he could even though he was clearly furious, Maryanne couldn't wrap her head around it. When she'd been forced to work for him, she had seen him at his most ferocious, and it was nothing compared to the cautious demeanor he displayed to his mate.

The man was fucking terrifying. But just for a moment there, Maryanne had seen it. He'd been desperate.

Pair-bonds were strange things, a condition Maryanne had purposely chosen to avoid until the day she died. Who would want to give up their freedom and be tied to another person forever? The very idea was repulsive. Sex was sex—and Maryanne loved sex—but the urge to forge a tie, to bind oneself… no thank you!

As an Alpha female, options of whom you could fuck ranged far and wide, and fear of getting knocked up was basically non-existent. The only way to ovulate required the use of hormone injections or a male Omega in heat to inspire such an event. Maryanne didn't have a thing for scrawny guys, which was good, since the likelihood of finding a male Omega was pretty dismal. It was Beta boys she preferred, though a girl now and then had been fun, too.

Being born an Alpha had been a boon. She was stronger, aggressive, quick, and able to move through society in a position people like Claire coveted. The small thing in her arms had always resented her dynamic, even when they were little. Maryanne couldn't blame her. Once Claire's scent began to fill the room with sweetness instead of just little kid stink, the world started treating her like she was made out of glass. That was half the reason Maryanne had dragged her into more… interesting pursuits.

Childhood shenanigans had been good for Claire.

Or were, until Claire began to hide what she was under the practiced mask of a Beta—the pills, special soap. It was sad to see someone try so hard to be something else.

Considering the alternative of being bonded in a heated stupor with no real protection if the Alpha went against the Omega's wishes, it was understandable.

After all, look what had happened to Claire's mom—the paragon of the downside. It was no surprise Claire had never embraced her true nature. Looking at her now, Maryanne wondered if the dark-haired woman even knew the absolute finality of her bond with Shepherd, and the lengths to which he would go to recapture his mate.

Or he would just kill her… he probably would kill her after tonight, at least.

Grinning stupidly, Maryanne thought back on Claire's taunts and the burning vehemence practically rising like flames from the giant. Maryanne would have paid good money to watch that show. If she wasn't so anxious that Shepherd was going to rip the wall off the side of her den and come to fetch back his very unbalanced mate, she would have probably laughed at how perfectly Claire had owned him. She'd got her prisoners out, she'd stood alone against the Followers, she'd even threatened to kill herself and probably would have… simply to give the Omegas more time to follow through with the second half of the plan.

But Claire had always been a stubborn, sentimental fool.

A little fool who was clinging to her in sleep with a face so full of misery, Maryanne almost didn't recognize her. Claire was ten kinds of messed up. It was more than the scrapes and bruises, or the gross state of her feet; it was something in her makeup. The Omega female stood like a marionette missing a few strings—not at all the spirited girl she had been when they were kids. A small part of Maryanne wanted to ask what had happened. The larger, more reasonable part, was determined to wash her hands of this trouble as soon as possible. Whatever was going on between Claire and Shepherd, whatever had caused Claire to provoke a man of his size and deadliness, Maryanne did not want to get dragged into it.

Defiled, manipulated, betrayed, and broken...

Well, that happened to everyone. Apparently it was just Claire's turn. Threading her fingers into the tousled, sooty hair, Maryanne began to comb out the knots.

Claire pressed nearer, a whimper catching in her throat. "*Shepherd...*"

And that was the final reason Maryanne would not be able to keep her. Everything went back to that pair-bond. Claire might be fighting it, might be fueled by rage and pain, but eventually she would waver and crack. It was inevitable, a tie of souls or some such nonsense. So long as she was running wild, Shepherd would hunt her, be fixated on a rampage, and Maryanne was not going to get trampled when nothing would change the outcome. She didn't owe Claire a damn thing; in fact, the way it looked now, *Claire owed her*.

Maryanne closed her eyes and cursed Shepherd to hell.

When she woke, there was no need to make a complicated decision regarding her lodger; Claire had made it for her. The little black-haired Omega was gone.

It was strange to walk through Thólos.

Claire may as well have been walking through the apocalypse. Everything she saw was far worse than the nightmare where the rabid pack was chasing her through the streets. Nothing seemed alive. No stores were open, no restaurants offered food. Buildings stood in shambles, broken glass and debris scattered about. Even bodies were left in the streets to freeze.

As her stroll continued, the warmth of Maryanne's bed leached away as if Claire had never known the comfort. She wandered, confused… wishing she could unsee all of it. In less than a year, the city had become a wasteland, another world that poisoned all it touched with frost, ice, and loss.

Shepherd's plan had been a success. Thólos was destroying itself, and all the man had to do was sit back and watch.

A whoosh of breath left her lungs and Claire stopped walking. Hunched against the wall was a dead child—blue, frozen—a little boy no older than nine.

Kneeling over the stiff corpse, Claire reached out and brushed back his matted hair, wondering how Shepherd could think this child's death would satisfy his plan. What great lesson would society learn by a lost life no soul would remember?

Slumping to the kid's side, mimicking the body's posture, Claire tried to find a reason for any of it. Tragedy in Thólos was nothing new. Since the occupation, orphan children died all the time.

More children were orphaned every day.

This was the new norm.

And who took them in? Where were they to go?

The people failed. Claire was not even sure if she could justify it anymore, not after seeing this. Leaning her head to the side she rested her cheek on the dead boy's hair and stared forward. There was no pleasure in her freedom or her view of the sky… there had not even been a sense of victory at her success freeing the Omegas.

Even in Maryanne's company she had only played the part, falsified emotion on instinct.

Closing her eyes, she let out a breath, ruffling the stiff brown hair under her lips. There was no point in being Claire anymore. Instead, she would be nothing, as hollow as Thólos had allowed itself to become.

It was the sound of a sob that woke her, and for a moment she thought it was from the boy she slept against. Waking abruptly, her bleary eyes darted around and found nothing—just the same empty alley and the same piles of icy garbage. The only difference from before was the darkness, a thing her eyes adjusted to quickly after so long underground.

Oblivious to the freezing cold, Claire stood, ignoring the crack of stiff knees. Her pillow, the forgotten corpse, sat as rigid as before, the child staring forward into the same future as hers… into nothing.

Claire claimed him, and with more strength than she felt, she hoisted the boy up on her back, the corpse's limbs not easy to manage.

Not a soul disturbed her as she walked with her macabre prize through the streets of hell.

4

Corday looked over the newly freed Omegas, silently observing as they assembled a living space from piles of garbage. The mid-level Incineration Plant no longer created compost for the farm levels—not since citizens had taken to dumping their garbage in the streets. Now rotting mounds of muck protected an enclave of frightened women. Every breath stank of putrid food, mold, and things better left undescribed.

One thing it did not smell like was the young Omega still writhing through estrous, the girl moaning and begging for relief.

Corday was admittedly not an expert on Omega heat cycles, but whatever had been done to her, her sobbing response could not have been normal.

He kept his distance. The other Omegas also gave her a

respectful berth, the group huddled together for warmth, gnawing on the rations he had provided.

An old woman, Nona, had come knocking on his door. It was Claire, she said, who'd directed her to find him. It was Claire who'd promised the resistance would feed and supply the freed Omegas.

It was the name Claire that made him come running.

He'd taken supplies without the permission of his commander. Brigadier Dane was going to kill him, and he was going to tell her straight to her face to go fuck herself. He was not going to let Claire down.

When he'd arrived the previous night, the Omegas had been… hostile. They were filthy, reeking just as badly as the garbage heap they'd chosen to shelter in.

Nona had warned him the women were dangerous, that they were armed and might shoot any male on sight. She had even warned him not to follow her back once she'd procured supplies.

Corday was having none of it. He needed to see Claire.

But Claire was not there. Even hours after the women had settled in, their liberator failed to show her face. The night dragged on, morning came, afternoon, Corday stiff from leaning against a slimy wall.

Had Claire been captured? Had the tyrant killed her?

Nona gently told him that Claire's plan required her to arrive from a different path; that the woman most likely was waiting for dark before she moved; that she had always been overly cautious when away from the safety of the group.

Corday scoffed. The Claire he knew was reckless. She was also badly hurt.

Over and over, Nona reminded him that if Claire had been taken, Shepherd's men would have already come for them.

Claire O'Donnell was out there.

And so he waited past the point of exhaustion, exasperation, and flat out fear. Evening fell. At first Corday thought his eyes were playing tricks on him. A two-headed hunchbacked beast staggered down the plant's dark garbage chute. Milky eyes stared right through him; they never blinked—just as the mouth beneath those dead eyes gaped in a fixed expression of hopelessness.

It was the face of a corpse.

Hidden beneath it sat a much dearer countenance, the struggling woman's eyes half-covered by a curtain of black tangles.

"Claire!"

Corday rushed towards the Omega and her burden, unraveling the frozen limbs of a cadaver unwilling to release its host.

Claire did not seem happy to see him. In fact, she didn't seem herself at all. "I found that boy alone in an alley, Corday… forgotten."

Once the dead child lay safely upon the ground, Corday pulled her against his chest. Warmth of his cheek against hers, stubble scratching, he breathed, "Nona came for me. I know what you did."

After the atrocities Claire had seen in the city, the attack on the Undercroft… facing Shepherd, seemed to have happened in another life. "The city's become a horrible place. I saw things… What's happening to us?"

Existential talk on the human condition could happen later. Tugging her towards the Omegas' fire, Corday urged, "You're freezing, Claire. Sit."

Nona ran over at first sight of her friend, the older woman throwing herself around her. "Your mother would be proud. You know that, my girl?"

Claire didn't want accolades, she just wanted to collapse.

There was no shyness. Corday ignored the watching women and tugged Claire down to rest between his thighs. Arms and legs wrapped around the girl's shivering frame, he put his chest to her back and purred.

The Omegas were openly confused by the state of their hero. Where was the confident deliverer who'd faced down an army? Why was she letting a Beta male hold her in an intimate embrace?

Why wasn't she speaking?

Nona smoothed the hair off Claire's forehead, watched her young friend close her eyes, and waited until Claire's breath became steady in sleep. Only then did she sniff.

Cautious not to wake her friend, Nona mouthed the words, "She smells pregnant."

Corday nodded and whispered, "She is."

It should not have been possible—not when Claire's last cycle had come the day she'd entered the Citadel.

Pressing her thin-lipped mouth in a frown, Nona's heart broke. "Shepherd has done this to Claire. This is…."

Corday cut her off. "I know," he tightened his hold, "but she won't be alone."

Nona's severity lessened, she even smiled at the boy. "You care for her."

Corday did. "Swear to me you won't let her leave when I'm gone. Swear you will keep her safe."

The inevitable was unstoppable. "She is pregnant and pair-bonded, Corday. Even if you tend her constantly, she won't be able to stay for long."

Looking Nona dead in the eye, Corday chewed out each word. "Shepherd damaged the pair-bond. It has no bearing now."

Older and wiser, Nona spoke as gently as she could. "That is not possible… what he damaged was Claire."

"So you'll just let her wander back to Shepherd?" Corday would be damned first.

"You are not an Omega. You can't possibly understand the finality of a pair-bond." Nona began to smooth Claire's hair, looking at her friend with pity. "The only way for Claire to be free, is with Shepherd's death or hers. I guarantee she knows that, no matter what she may say."

"But…" Corday chose denial. "Claire told me…"

Her friend had always had misplaced altruism. "She would want you to have faith." In a hushed voice, Nona confessed, "I know better than to give you false hope. But know this, so long as she is pregnant, she is precious to Shepherd. That makes her safe."

Corday pulled down the scarf around Claire's neck. Nasty bruises sat on display. "Would you call this something treated as precious?"

Nona took in the marks, tears gathering in her eyes. Words were difficult. "It's more than just the pair-bond. Everyone here knows she is mated to Shepherd. They will not trust her. They will drive her off."

Corday glared at the collection of women stealing glances in their direction. "Claire saved their lives."

"Listen to me, boy," Nona urged, fervently whispering. "That does not mean every Omega in this room deserved it. It would only take one to bring us all down again."

Had the Omegas not learned? "The women who turned her in last time were hanged by Shepherd. I watched their executions myself."

"You and I both know that fear makes people do very stupid things."

"Then she comes home with me."

Nona, her face full of compassion, agreed, "That might be best."

Looking down at the sleeping woman in his arms, Corday felt shaken… because he knew what was wrong with his scheme. "But she won't stay unless I lock her in."

Nona nodded. "I think you're beginning to understand. Keep purring. It will calm you both."

Puzzle pieces were his specialty. Jules understood the finite operation that motivated people, he was second only to Shepherd in that particular skill. He was also the only other person who'd had any access to Claire over the last few months. He knew what she smelled like, even pregnant. He knew her voice and had pegged her at once for a brooder.

She was almost sweet in her misguided agenda, and Jules grasped exactly what had drawn Shepherd so strongly. Claire was an enigma, all wrapped up in a little moral bow.

Claire was everything Shepherd falsely believed Svana to be.

His commander had never *lived* amongst Dome civilization, not like Jules had before he'd been imprisoned. Shepherd's rearing underground—surviving the extreme of Undercroft society—had wired the man to thrive in acute circumstances. No matter how preternaturally brilliant Shepherd was, his lack of empathy in dealing with conventional people was obvious. Yet he was an amazing leader, drew men to his standard, could see the world in a way others could not.

He'd freed the outcasts… even before the breach.

One man had driven back the nightmare underground. Shepherd had organized a feral population, given slaves purpose, hope. Yet, like all prisoners, if Shepherd wanted something, he took it, and God help you if you disappointed him.

Shepherd remained incapable of understanding Claire's *hesitations*.

Even for all the Alpha's aggression, there was no one in the world Jules admired more. His respect even withstood the flaw in his superior—Shepherd's universe began and ended with Svana.

The fact the two Alphas were lovers was no secret. Even Jules had witnessed Svana's enthusiasm for Shepherd for years. He knew the story of how she had drawn him underground, approached Shepherd as if she were an angel with her passcodes and rare food. At the time they'd both been young. Perhaps they had seduced one another—two miscreant wild things enslaved by the system. But where Shepherd had been born in hell, Svana had come from heaven.

He practically worshiped at her feet. He had made himself the mission for her, built her an army.

She claimed to be special, chosen…

Worst of all, it was true. All of it.

She owned something no amount of money could buy: a valuable bloodline.

Svana was the key to freedom, to a new world, to a land where no one would look down on them for Da'rin—where no one would hiss the word 'outcast.' With her help, all of them would be heroes, redeemers, saviors.

They would all be reborn.

Svana had not been born in Thólos Dome. Instead, she'd been *gifted* to the people of Thólos…

None of this was public knowledge, of course. Very few knew Svana had arrived on a transport two decades ago as part of an Interdome trade of viable females. Even less knew who that child in rags really was. Her adopted parents didn't know, and from Jules' investigation, even Premier Callas was not privy to such information. The secret belonged to Shepherd and to the chosen Followers of the man sworn to lead them to freedom.

Svana was cunning on her own; she used her position to develop access to everything… secrets, money, favors—even lovesick teenaged Shepherd.

It was a fancy she'd grown out of. Shepherd, on the other hand, had been entirely unaware of the fact that his beloved had moved on. She knew what she was doing, feeding his regard for her, nurturing his devotion. It seemed pathetic, had you not seen what the two of them could accomplish together.

That Jules hated. She was necessary for the plan. Shepherd, all the Followers, *needed* her.

But she also needed them. Without Shepherd's army, there was no way the woman could reclaim her birthright. Svana was the only surviving offspring of Greth Dome's ruling family; a monarchy that had been deposed and disposed of. Insurgents had killed her parents, and had foolishly thought to extend mercy to a little girl considered too young to remember.

Svana may have been small when her life under Thólos began, but she had been coached to corrupt from birth. But, just like her parents, she believed herself beyond reproach.

The affair with Premier Callas… Whether the Alpha admitted it or not, Shepherd had been forced to face a glimpse of what she truly was.

In response, Shepherd had acted against his beloved; he took an Omega mate. A fact Jules had known Svana would not be pleased about once discovered. Was this not the very reason Shepherd had kept the Omega obsessively hidden? Not a soul was allowed near her, and even Jules had been cast out for only looking once… until recently.

The Beta did not know what had spurred Shepherd to take quarters away from his room for days; he didn't ask. He had instead been stuck dealing with an irate ruler who possessed far less patience, and a pregnant Omega who looked heartbroken each time he brought her another of the blasted trays.

For reasons unknown, Shepherd had reduced Claire to a position of breeder, not mate. Jules accepted it and did his duty. It was less than a week before the lieutenant opened the door to find Miss O'Donnell on the floor, altered, and trapped in a room with an odor Jules had smelled in his leader's quarters before—the spiced scent of Svana's Alpha slick. The Omega who should have been nesting was as far away from the bed as she could get, so still she seemed corpselike. It was the only reason he'd spoken when she asked his name.

On closer inspection, it had been impossible for Jules to miss the split lip and the discoloration on Miss O'Donnell's neck. Even more, he had recognized the look in her eye when Shepherd approached outside Undercroft; every nuance of her expression Jules had read with precision. The Omega was devastated—not just afraid—emotionally crippled, and clearly suicidal no matter Shepherd's denial on the subject.

And that was where the issue lingered. Jules presumed the obvious assumption was correct. Shepherd had mated with his long time consort… and he was aware of their habit of sharing heated Omegas.

Claire had reacted badly to whatever the Alpha female's visit had inspired.

The situation was irreparable in the allotted time. Shepherd's denial and Svana's vindictive nature had done the damage. If what Jules suspected was true, Miss O'Donnell now had good reason to hate the man beyond just the initial fear of her situation and misunderstanding of his true agenda. Even more, Shepherd's current demands that Miss O'Donnell be returned to resume her position as his mate made the situation far more complicated.

It would almost be more convenient if the little Omega just died, the entire situation being nothing but troublesome. But she was carrying what would be Shepherd's heir.

Claire was important now.

THE GROUND WAS hard beneath her, the unyielding floor setting her hip to aching. But there was the smell of safety… a well-known Beta. They were wrapped together, covered in his coat like an overripe bug cocoon.

She cracked open an eye, finding Corday already watching her, his expression too controlled to read.

Claire admitted guilt. "I knew you'd help Nona if she used my name."

Corday put his lips to her forehead; he held her tighter.

"She told me what you did. You held a gun to your head, Claire."

She had done that… and she had been very scared. "I did."

He could play the belligerent game just as well as she could. Still holding her, he moved his face until their noses were touching. "Claire, please."

Claire glanced to the side and absently worried her lip. "I'm not sorry for setting these women free."

"I don't want you to be!" Urgent, Corday whispered so the spying women might not hear. "What I want is for you to trust me. You don't need to fight alone."

But she did… both Corday and Senator Kantor had explained their position. "I am not going to attack Shepherd or his pig army. The Omegas are free, it's done."

"I don't believe you."

Still bone tired, Claire sighed. "I give you my word that I will not attack Shepherd. Such a thing would be pointless."

"Look at me," Corday urged, face grim and determined. "Swear it."

She held his gaze. "I swear I will not attack them."

The Beta seemed satisfied. "How long has it been since you've eaten?"

"I ate at your house."

Frustrated, he squeezed her. "That was three days ago, and you threw up afterwards."

"I had more important things to worry about than food."

"Claire, you are not superhuman."

No. She did not even feel regular human. She felt quasi-formed and misshapen. “I will eat.”

A twitch curled Corday’s lips. “Good.” He sat her up, rubbing at her neck when her bones cracked. “And while you are eating, I am going to ask you what other crazy schemes you have planned. You don’t need to keep secrets from me, Claire. Let me help you.”

They had an audience, several sets of eyes watching their low, murmured exchange. Corday went to pillage through the crates he’d brought. A piece of fresh fruit and a packet of protein rich supplement in hand, he returned to her.

Others approached Claire.

A few even sniffed the black-haired Omega, backing away quickly as if she might taint them once the rumor had been confirmed.

If Claire noticed, she did not react.

Corday could see that Nona was right. No matter what she had done for them, Claire would not be tolerated by the pack for long. “Come home with me, Claire.”

Claire looked to the man offering her an apple as if he’d gone mad. “I can’t put you in that position. No.”

“Then I’ll come here every day until you change your mind.” The Beta took her cold fingers and urged, “I want to take care of you. When you come to your senses, I will take you home.”

Claire mumbled, looking to the fire, “Should the time come, I look forward to going home.”

It was Nona who’d sat quietly through the exchange, who’d touched Claire’s arm in understanding.

It was time for Corday to go. Claire stood, pulled him into a hug, dismissing the man as she teased, "Next time you visit, bring decent coffee."

He chuckled.

Suddenly serious, she gripped the fabric of his coat. "And if you are foolish enough to get caught, I will charge the Citadel to get you out."

Corday's laughter faded. "That's not funny."

"I wasn't joking."

Frustrated, running a hand through his hair, Corday argued, "You set the Omegas free. You moved mountains. It's time for you to rest."

Claire agreed. "Nona would not allow anything else. Now, get out of here, Beta. No boys allowed."

Corday did not want to go, but he gave her space, swearing he would return.

With the Beta gone, Nona placed an arm around her young friend, the old woman muttering, "He doesn't understand."

The broken Omega whispered, "He doesn't need to know."

THERE WERE ONLY four in the room: Corday, Brigadier Dane, Senator Kantor, and a stranger.

"There is a new member come to join the resistance." The typical exhaustion that had aged Senator Kantor since the Dome's fall, lifted. The pleased Alpha gestured to the beautiful woman at his side. “We made contact with my niece… This is Leslie Kantor.”

Smiling softly at her uncle’s heartfelt relief, the brunette Alpha female reached out her hand in formal introduction. “It is a pleasure to meet you, Corday.”

There was a glint in the older man’s eyes, a long lost spark returning when Corday grinned and took her hand. “It’s rare we get good news. Welcome.”

Dwarfed in her layers, bundled up warm, Leslie offered, “And I hope I have more to buoy you. Before Shepherd’s invasion, Premier Callas had been my betrothed. Our circumstances had yet to be announced.” She waved a flippant hand. “These things have to go through the proper channels, be approved by the Senate, and so on. In the interim, Callas arranged for me to have deputy access to everything. As it was done in secret, Shepherd’s men are unaware that I can infiltrate their communications network.”

Corday’s mouth gaped. “Holy fuck…”

“Yeah, son.” Senator Kantor chuckled. “Holy fuck.”

This changed everything, gave the resistance an actual chance. “Do you know where he’s hidden the contagion?”

Leslie shook her head. “No. The language they communicate in, it’s difficult to understand. But that does not mean we can’t crack it. I just need time.”

But this was still great progress. The secrecy of the meeting began to make sense, no one could know Leslie Kantor’s secret. She would have to be hidden, the information restricted. Corday said as much. “No one can know about her. If Shepherd got wind, it would be an easy thing to revoke her access."

"Agreed." Senator Kantor had Corday's next orders. "If we kept her here, too many people would see her. We can't have questions raised. I'm entrusting my niece to you, Corday."

The honor bestowed on the low ranked Enforcer came at a very bad time; however, there was no way to refuse such an important mission. Claire needed him, but the entire population needed the intel Leslie might uncover. Corday shared his news. "You should know sir, the Omegas were freed. Today we've struck two victories against Shepherd."

The Senator genuinely smiled. "I told you my bet was on Claire."

"You did."

And that was it.

JULES FROWNED, a rare thing, and listened to the audio surveillance of Thólos' pathetic resistance headquarters. The hunt for Claire had been waylaid when report arrived that a certain Alpha female had presented herself on the resistance's doorstep.

Svana—Leslie Kantor—had a different part to play in the fall of Thólos. She had a specific mission that had nothing to do with playing rebel. And if she'd known where they were all along, why not pass that information to Shepherd.

Jules knew exactly what the bitch was up to.

Svana was hunting Claire. Of course she'd know the Omega had escaped. It was the reason he'd had the Alpha female followed since Shepherd's mate had gone missing.

And now she'd lead them right to the resistance.

The woman was truly foolish to think this act would go unnoticed. Shepherd might have lauded his beloved, but Jules did not find her cunning clever. Oh, she was useful and she was powerful, and for that reason alone, Jules had not engineered an accident for her years ago.

But she was trouble.

No matter the plan or the promises, the female was self-serving.

Jules didn't trust her, and was eager to prove that she needed to be curbed. It was the reason he chose to follow them, to make a preemptive visit to the listed domicile of one Enforcer Corday.

It wasn't difficult to breach the building. All it took was the acquisition of one terrified rebel and a few minutes of torture to learn the location of Enforcer Corday's home, and a few well-placed distractions for the dubious couple working their way across the city. While the Enforcer and Svana were still meandering through the dangerous city streets, Jules opened the door to the sad little apartment.

That first breath of air… and the Beta froze. The room was saturated in Miss O'Donnell's scent—the couch, the bed, he even found her bloody dress tucked in the bathroom hamper.

Svana could not have intended it, but she had delivered Jules right to the Beta who'd taken in Shepherd's mate.

Even if the Omega was not in the domicile, Enforcer Corday had access to her. Miss O'Donnell's retrieval was imminent.

Bugs were placed, the surveillance team handpicked by Shepherd's second-in-command, situated nearby. The job was done quickly. All that remained was to report personally to Shepherd and explain the *complicated* situation.

5

Entering Shepherd's den, Jules could scent his commander's extreme agitation. "I have picked up the trail of your mate."

Shepherd's demand for an answer was immediate. "Where?"

The Beta detailed his report, handing Shepherd a dossier on a young male. "Since Miss O'Donnell's disappearance, as a precaution, I have had Svana shadowed. Today, *Leslie Kantor* chose to contact the resistance—inadvertently she led us right to their doorstep. While she was there, a Beta by the name of Enforcer Samuel Corday was charged with her protection. I personally went to the Beta's residence to bug the location before he could return with Svana as his ward.

"Miss O'Donnell was not on the premises. Her scent, however, permeates the dwelling. I also found the shredded dress she was wearing when she leapt off the roof. Enforcer

Corday is the Beta with whom she found refuge before her assault on Undercroft. I believe he knows where she is. By tracking him through the grid, he will lead us straight to your Omega."

Looking up from the photograph of the handsome male, Shepherd let the weight of his glare run over his second-in-command. "You can confirm that Svana approached rebel leaders of her own accord?"

"Yes." And that was the greater issue, in Jules' opinion. "The niece of Senator Kantor has offered her passcodes to help the resistance."

The stiff set of Shepherd's shoulders, the pulse of danger in the air, warned him the Alpha was not pleased with the news. "Did she?"

"Svana is acting autonomously for purposes of her own." Jules, his chin held high, ignored his leader's silent dismissal of Svana's unsubstantiated misdeeds and outlined the remainder of the report. "She will have recognized Claire's scent the moment she entered Enforcer Corday's domicile."

"That will not matter. Claire will be recovered immediately." Shepherd could always tell when Jules had something more he wanted to say, it was in the shiftiness of his hardened glare, and the uncomfortable lines around his mouth. Standing, his huge arms crossed over his chest, Shepherd's own posture made it clear his subordinate had better get to the point. "Speak."

Jules explained in the same steady monotone that displayed acute sincerity. "Aside from the threat of Svana, Claire O'Donnell is willing to kill herself, brother. By starvation… a bullet to the head… she will find a way if she wants to."

The single step closer put Shepherd within the distance to behead Jules with little more than a flick of the wrist. Eyes flared, Shepherd threatened, "You presume to tell me what she will and will not do? You presume much lately. I am quite certain I made myself clear before."

The Beta was loyal; it was his duty to speak. "You are responsible for Claire O'Donnell's current state. Your open infidelity has altered what you created when you chose to pair-bond. That kind of hatred will not disappear simply because you drag her back."

The beast emerged. An arm bulging with muscle struck, slamming the smaller man against the wall. Dangling Jules by a grip on his throat, Shepherd roared, "You do not know of what you speak!"

Gasping, his boots high above the floor, Jules grunted despite the grip of the giant, "You allowed Svana to manipulate you into dishonoring your pregnant mate. You are responsible for what broke her, and must recognize the consequences of what you sanctioned. I cannot return her as she was."

Jules was thrown clear across the room. Before he might break the man's bones, the bellowing giant's fists attacked the wall instead. Huge chunks of concrete broke off, his knuckles tore, and blood flowed, but Shepherd's outburst did not exorcise such rage.

When the provoked, panting monster spun to face the Beta, eyes full of murder, he found Jules standing, loyal and unmoving as always. Shepherd poked Jules roughly in the chest. "I should kill you."

Before answering, Jules wiped a trickle of blood from his mouth. "For speaking the truth, brother?"

Shepherd rolled his shoulders, snarling a defense, "I did what had to be done and sent my mate from the room so she would not have to watch as I pacified Svana."

The Beta outlined the facts. "In choosing to *pacify* your former lover, you destroyed any potential for Miss O'Donnell to be your mate the way you seem to wish her to be."

"And you think given the fact that you once had an Omega wife, your opinion has value?" Shepherd's face was red, his pulse thundering at the bulge of his neck.

Jules offered an alternative. "The only way you will gain influence over the Omega is to give her what she wants."

A minute passed, a minute where Shepherd had to fight every instinct that told him to crush the Beta for questioning him. "Explain."

"Her profile is one of a martyr. If you offer to leave the Omegas and her *allies* in peace, you have a bargaining chip—influence over Miss O'Donnell you can wield to gain compliance and the behavior you prefer. If approached correctly, I expect that she will agree to return of her own free will in exchange for the lives of the others. Suicide will no longer be an issue, giving you time to progress the pregnancy that may soften her hatred towards you."

Shepherd detested what he was hearing, but there was wisdom in his second's words. "Is there more?"

For once, intonation, bitterness, inflected Jules speech. "I didn't only have a wife. I also had two sons."

There was a hint of remorse in Shepherd's retreat. Ignoring his bleeding knuckles, the Alpha pulled on his coat and left the room. "I shall lead the surveillance of the Beta personally."

Jules radioed an underling to clean up the mess and repair the wall, as usual, three steps ahead.

As ordered, Corday had escorted Leslie Kantor to his apartment. The journey had not been simple. In fact, it seemed that every causeway they'd tried to walk contained some obstruction or Follower presence that required the pair to choose another path.

It took hours of doubling back just to make it a few steps forward. It didn't help that Leslie Kantor did not have a clue how to fend for herself. The female, though charming, had no business on the streets.

Corday could hardly believe she'd survived as long as she had.

He did not voice his opinion, but she could sense it. When they were finally sequestered and safe in his apartment, she admitted, "I have been sheltered since the city fell. My family's housing holds a secret panic room that was stocked with enough food and water that I had little need to leave."

If only everyone had owned such a luxury. Sizing up the

woman, Corday asked, “You were alone in your bunker?”

Eyes downcast, Leslie nodded.

“That must have been hard.”

“I didn’t know my father had been hanged outside the Citadel. I didn’t know my mother had been strung up beside him.” Tears fell free down her high cheeks. “I’ll never forgive myself for not trying to find them… I should have sought my uncle sooner.”

Leading her to his worn sofa so the weeping woman might collect herself, Corday said, “Your parents would have wanted you to stay safe.”

Rubbing her eyes, Leslie sighed. “I will do anything I can to help the resistance. Shepherd must be stopped.”

A smile was offered in agreement. “And we will stop him, but we cannot make a move until we uncover the location of the contagion. That must be your priority.”

“I’ll do my best.”

“We can start tonight.”

“Of course. Just let me clean up first.” Leslie glanced down at the fine coat that had grown grimy with their crossing, at the scarf, the mittens, and began to strip the layers away. “The scent of your mate leads me to believe you’ll have some fresh clothes I can borrow.”

Corday stood and moved to the kitchenette. “I don’t have a mate.”

Leslie smirked, coquettish and feminine. “I just assumed… Omega scent is on your coat… and in this room. But I can see it’s a sore topic. Forget I said anything.”

“No, it’s okay.” Gathering food so they might eat and get

straight to work, Corday said, “Claire just sleeps here sometimes.”

Leslie bit her lip, eyes sparkling. “And she sleeps in your coat?”

The charm worked, Corday was amused. “And sometimes in my coat, yes.”

“I pegged you as a cuddler.” Leslie stretched her arm across the back of the couch, looking over her shoulder and bantering as if they were friends. “She’s a lucky female to have the attention of a man who fights for what he loves.”

With a half-hearted smirk, Corday shook his head. “It’s not like that. She couldn’t even if she wanted to… or even if I wanted to. My friend was pair-bonded to a stranger, someone who mistreated her. Any kind of physical relationship is off the table for now.”

“Pair-bonded?” The woman went deadpan, cold calculation slipping into her expression. “That is unthinkable.”

Corday gave a sorry shrug. “So you see; it’s not what you imagine.”

Leslie shook her head, contemplating something monumental. “It cannot be the case that this *stranger* pair-bonded to her.”

Corday brought over their rations, plopping down beside his guest. “I wish it wasn’t. She’s a wonderful girl whom I like very much… even though she’s as infuriating as she is sweet.”

Leslie’s smile returned, her bearing once again playful. “What is she like, your Omega?”

Corday gave a small, caustic laugh. “Stubborn. Determined to be a one woman resistance.”

Patting his thigh, Leslie warned, “One woman can’t stand alone against Shepherd’s power.”

“I hate to admit it, but she’s done pretty well so far. She’s accomplished more than we have.”

Leslie inched closer, fascinated. “How did she stand up to Shepherd?”

There was little Corday could say. “By simply being Claire.”

The beauty at his side was unsatisfied. “Be cautious of her, Corday. Don’t allow yourself to foster feelings. If she is pair-bonded, as you say, then she could never commit to you.”

“Yeah, well… she ain’t exactly committed to her mate, either. He made that easy enough by allowing some psycho female to unhinge the pair-bond.” Corday scoffed at the irony. “Well, now it seems he woke the beast. The Alpha monster and his lover unleashed a storm.”

Leslie’s voice grew lower. “What are you talking about?”

“Claire broke Shepherd’s Omega prisoners out of Undercroft two nights ago.” Corday grinned, proud to the bone. “I’m starting to think the bastard doesn’t stand a chance.”

“What of the woman? Shepherd’s lover?”

Corday cut a glance at his guest, frowning deeply. “I didn’t say it was Shepherd.”

Leslie blinked, the picture of naiveté. “Not in so many words…”

“All I know is that the woman behaved like your run-of-the-mill sex offender." Reaching for his COMscreen, Corday grit his teeth and growled. "Sounds to me like Shepherd and the Alpha bitch are a match made in heaven—or maybe hell is more appropriate."

EVEN WITH THE popped collar of the leather jacket Claire had stolen from Maryanne, it felt as if the cold constantly cut right through her.

Cold was the only thing she could feel.

The Omegas were beginning to stir, the shuffling sound of movements soothing. Claire was glad to observe the group adjusting to freedom, even if it was in a reeking dump, even if she was not a welcome part of it. The women had maintained a respectful verbal distance, had asked very few questions, and had been as comforting as they were able.

That did not stop the troubled glances, though. To them, she was contaminated.

They could not have been more correct.

It was unsurprising that wariness should come from the knowledge that she had been claimed by the biggest monster of them all.

There was only one there who kept to Claire's side.

"Did they discover who you really are, Nona?"

The old woman wrinkled her brow. "I don't think so. Even if they did, they had little interest in me. Interrogations were only about you."

"That seems rather pointless." From the sound of it,

Followers had compiled a file packed with random inaccurate information. Most of these women hardly knew her, and would have probably said anything they thought Shepherd wanted to hear. Staring dull-eyed at the fire, Claire murmured, "You need to make sure Corday doesn't find out."

"It's not exactly like he can put me in prison, dearest," the woman whispered, pulling Claire to rest her head in her lap.

"But when the city is free…"

"We have other things to worry about now."

Claire sighed. "I wonder what happened to the others, the Omegas who were bonded?" Were they locked underground as she had been? Were they frightened? "I never saw anyone else. I don't know where they are. I can't help them."

"Shepherd told me that all had settled into their new place. You were the only one having difficulties." It was a subject that disturbed Nona as much as it troubled Claire. "Did you know he came to speak with me a little over a week ago? Your mate claimed you were withdrawn and demanded I tell him how to end your depression."

Hearing such a thing, Claire turned green, doubling over to vomit. That was the end of any mention of Shepherd.

Nona was a modicum of comfort, but Claire felt adrift—isolated even in the companionship of her kind. It led her to stand, to wipe her mouth, and to leave the Omegas' sanctuary without another word.

Though it was obvious she wanted to, the old woman did nothing to stop her.

Just like the last two days, from dawn to dusk Claire wandered Thólos like a wraith.

Her absences were hardly commented upon, but Nona was always there with a portion of rations she pressed Claire to eat. Once she had her dark-haired friend warming by the fire, she would talk nonsense; she would make Claire communicate, until the exhausted Omega forgot to keep answering.

For two nights straight, Corday failed to return.

If Claire noticed, if she was relieved or saddened, she said nothing.

Nona was not even sure her friend had any concept of time passing.

Claire was too beyond herself, too detached. But when she walked, the city seemed to open up to her—every path leading to some new awful landscape. The buildings were hollow because the dead were piled in the street. Marks of violence were everywhere, roving bands of looters still pillaging as if there were treasure to be found in the decay.

That was reality—exposed reality.

Half cognizant, Claire almost found her wandering had taken her right to the Citadel.

The black specks of Followers in the distance startled her out of her stupor. She drew back with such speed, she slipped on an unseen patch of ice. Heart in her throat, Claire fell into the gutter, scampering blindly until she zigzagged through the first open door in her path.

It took almost an hour to snap out of her panic, to look around at the wreck of a stranger's home and recognize why every frigid draught filled the room with whispers.

It was paper bowing in the wind. Overturned shelves, fallen books scattered over the floor.

Under her hand lay the words:

He who does not know the evils of war cannot appreciate its benefits.

Disgusted, Claire snapped the worn book closed to find Sun Tzu's *The Art of War*.

She wanted to throw it, to rip every last page from the spine, but instead found her eyes drawn back to the dog-eared pages. Sprawled on a pile of some dead soul's ransacked things, she read until it was too dark to continue. Then she slept, passing another night free of Shepherd, utterly lost, and broken inside.

When morning came and she woke stiff, Claire rose from her makeshift burrow and walked out the door as if she'd never been there. It was not until she was back at the Omegas' haven that she realized her bloodless fingers were still gripping Sun Tzu's masterpiece to the point they'd gone white.

She was staring at it like it owed her an explanation for being there.

Nona crept nearer to see. "What is that?"

Eyes on the book, the green-eyed waif muttered, "Sun Tzu said to appear weak when you are strong, and strong when you are weak." Claire began stripping off her clothes. "Go get the COMscreen. I need you to make me look strong."

In a building opposite the generic apartment Enforcer Corday dwelled in sat a seething Alpha—one on the verge of snapping. Shepherd prided himself on his steadiness, his focus and dedication to purpose, but at that moment, after bombardment, accusations and indignity, he was not at his best. Where the pair-bond connected, Shepherd felt some strange pulse. The force that burned and stole his focus condemned his rage. The sensation had denounced his actions often over the past months, brought with it severe discomfort. It was discomfort he bore, knowing that the final result made what were sometimes reprehensible deeds necessary for his mate.

He could tolerate the pain of the bond just as he tolerated the pain of such extensive Da'rin infection. Tolerating being challenged by a subordinate, even if it was a man he respected, was not quite so easy.

No one questioned him. He ruled the Undercroft, had toppled the Dome's disgusting government, and controlled an entire puppet population. His Followers recognized and bowed to such greatness, and no puny Beta had the right to dictate what was best… as if to share wisdom… as if to say that what he demanded was impossible!

Jules' insinuations looped on repeat in Shepherd's thoughts, the Alpha dissecting each word, finding the flaws in the other man's argument… determined to prove he was right and Jules was mistaken.

Shepherd would have his Claire on his terms. Everything would be as nature intended, Jules' idea of *consequences* be damned.

But there was a deeper message between the words, a sly list of allegations Jules would have to be corrected for.

'*Infidelity...*'

'You allowed Svana to *manipulate* you into *dishonoring* your pregnant mate…'

All this implied a breach in code: castigation. Jules had inferred Shepherd was corruptible and that Svana pulled his strings. His second-in-command's gall was unspeakable.

Even aware of his simmering wrath, the blue-eyed Beta stood vigilant at his side.

Stuffing down bitter rage, unwilling to be seen as less than perfectly calm, Shepherd continued his surveillance and kept his growling to a minimum. Jules would be dealt with for his failure once Claire was returned. As Alpha—the creator of the bond—Shepherd would prove to the lesser Beta that his Omega would come to heel without pointless negotiation or bribery. That was the natural order of things.

Claire would be found, and she would submit. In time, she would love him.

But the bond whispered that she wanted to die, that she would find a way soon. And that possibility was the tiny mustard seed of doubt cracking his obstinacy.

In hindsight, Shepherd recognized that he should have coddled her after Claire's tantrum all those weeks ago. But he wanted his mate to see why she'd suffered the meltdown. She had to admit she desired him, responded to his presence, that things had improved. Shepherd had given her the space to consider such weighty insight—left her to feel the loss of the mate she needed—so that she would know without question what her true, natural feelings were.

So she would behave and adore him.

Even Shepherd had to admit that his attempt to condition, his rejection of her presence, must have made his mating with Svana seem deliberate—another punishment.

The feelings inside Claire once it began, the degradation, it could not have been worse.

Improvement did not come with time. Her terrible desolation had not abated with freedom or success; Shepherd could feel it flowing from her like an endless bubbling poison. Claire was past the point of despair. It was a thing he had witnessed countless times in the Undercroft—a cessation of spirit. But the Omega had spoken; her eyes had been full of fire when she faced him on the streets, a marked improvement from the vacant figure who had subsisted on air in his den.

And it was the Beta smiling at Svana that had roused her. Corday was the one Claire had run to, his food she'd accepted. He was the man Claire preferred to him.

Shepherd deliberated on such an outrage, frustrated further to see Svana playing the fine lady—touching Corday, wooing him gently, all the while digging less than subtly for information.

What game was Svana playing?

Svana had a great many strengths, but the Alpha female had a tendency to miss the minutiae. It was for that reason Shepherd was sure she had no idea he was watching, that the Enforcer's apartment had already been bugged… that Followers were listening to their would-be queen.

As the conversation between Corday and Svana continued, the stiffness of his second-in-command was impossible to miss. Jules found the whole thing distasteful.

Svana had no cause to get involved, to distract. Her only duty was to keep the contagion hidden and unleash it once their exodus began. If she were to be captured or killed in this ploy, the finale of their great insurrection, of their great revenge, would fail.

Worse, every minute Corday was stuck tending *Leslie Kantor*, he was not giving them the location of Claire.

Her interference was a disappointment.

Svana's initial displeasure with his keeping of a mate had been addressed, handled, and resolved. Shepherd had paid the price for Claire—a far steeper price than he had expected—ruining the Omega's growing affection. He had even fucked Svana in the same bed he shared with Claire, watching the Alpha female grow excited by the scent of his mate, a thing Shepherd hated allowing.

Breathless, Svana had claimed their mating to be the most glorious yet, satisfied when Shepherd's orgasm was finally achieved. As always, he'd ensured his knot remained on the outside of her cunt; Svana unwilling to let them be linked in a position that left either vulnerable—a long standing sexual rule between them.

Grunting as he gushed, he had offered the answer the female sought, *"Glorious indeed, beloved."*

Shepherd pulled out, lay at her side while she petted his

broad chest. In a silken voice, Svana had purred out her absolution, *"I forgive you."*

The words had seemed unfair. Had Svana not herself fornicated and tried to lure her Alpha body into highly unlikely pregnancy with their enemy? Were not her very words the idealization that their love was beyond the flesh… a thing of spirit and destiny?

Shepherd had fucked her twice more, once almost immediately, simply to keep Svana from speaking on the subject, and again to ensure he'd exhausted her. There had been no more pillow talk. In the end, there had been no demands about Claire at all. As if the hiding Omega was of no consequence, Svana had simply dressed and left. All that was left behind was Alpha female scent saturating the air of his den, blending oddly with the sweeter smell of Omega.

No, that was not all that was left. The Omega who had only a few days prior begun to respond, who for once had been eager at last to be near him, had lain crumpled on the bathroom floor—everything between them left in wreckage—all his effort dismantled and ruined.

He had not seen Svana since, and now he was forced to listen to her subtle manipulations as she sat beside the hated Beta.

"I just assumed... Omega scent is on your coat."

Shepherd growled so violently at the presumption that Jules ordered the other Followers from the room.

"It's not like that. She couldn't even if she wanted to... or even if I wanted to."

Shepherd gripped the table, the wood beginning to buckle.

Did Claire want to have sexual congress with that male?

"My friend was pair-bonded to a stranger, someone who mistreated her. Any kind of physical relationship is off the table for now."

And if it couldn't get worse, like magic, it did. Svana's reaction to Corday's words was authentic. Shepherd saw her face through the feed, the beauty of her exotic bone structure lost the mask of Leslie Kantor. Svana showed herself. *"Pair-bonded? That is unthinkable."*

That disgust was genuine.

Outraged, Shepherd was forced to conclude Svana had believed he'd kept a female under lock and key in his quarters that was not his rightful possession. Rape was beneath him, as Svana well knew considering his mother's sad history, and Shepherd did not break his code, ever!

Vibrating with utter indignation, Shepherd felt energy build up, crest, years of anger threatening to seep out as a low endless howl of rage. Only one thing stopped the outburst, one phrase that carried him beyond explosion and straight into stagnant shock.

"The little I know is that the woman behaved like your run-of-the-mill sex offender."

Blood throbbed in his skull. Was that Claire's interpretation of Svana? Of him? She had called him a rapist once, and he had taken her when she was reluctant… but she was his bonded mate. Claire grew willing once she learned he took the time to pleasure her; the Omega relished their mating once she let herself enjoy it. Even the first time, he had not touched her without her consent. The one time he'd punished her physically, he had not hurt her. When she'd cried so pathetically afterward, he could not bring himself to do it again, even though it was his right as Alpha to correct her bad behavior and establish dominance. Never had it been rape. Her hesitation was due only to misunderstanding her position as an Omega, and her fear of her unfamiliar Alpha. After their time together, she had been coming around… he had painstakingly melted that ice.

He would not dishonor Claire, nor would Svana. His beloved had never touched Claire, he'd ensured it himself!

But he'd found Svana choking the life out of his mate… the Omega pushed back on the bed, her lip split and bleeding.

A new feeling, a sort of churning sickness stole his breath. Perspective shifted. Svana *had* come into his room and attacked a pregnant Omega clearly under his protection… but she would not have sexually assaulted her. It was against everything they stood for.

But Claire had been very frightened; it's what drew you from the Citadel to rush to your mate.

No! Such a thing was impossible. His beloved would never degrade herself in such a way. Perhaps this was based off Svana's suggestion that Claire join them in intimacy—the very statement which had sharply commenced the decay of the bond. Shepherd had not missed a nuance of Claire's reaction to those words, had felt her repugnance, her disgust pulse through their link.

She'd looked on him like he was a monster.

Consumed with separating the opposing factors, far too determined to maintain the status quo, Shepherd had not regarded the exchange's baser intent. How had he not seen? Svana had preyed upon the Omega so flawlessly… spoken every word to shame and debase. Thinking of it now, Svana's verbiage seemed so very beneath her, so calculatingly terrible.

The more Shepherd considered, the more he hated: hated Jules for daring to do less than he was ordered. He hated the handsome Enforcer Corday who had the audacity to feel fondly for his Omega—a man who spoke as if he knew Claire intimately. Corday couldn't *know* her. A base Beta could never have the bond that exposed Claire's very soul and perfection to her Alpha mate.

Shepherd *knew* her. Every breath she took, the music of her hum, her purity, her light. That was his alone.

The hate expanded, and even for the briefest of seconds, he hated Svana for effectively taking Claire away. The fleeting feeling of something other than reverence for his beloved confused him. Mechanically, Shepherd looked to the only other person in the room, as if the man might have the answer.

All was written in the smaller man's flat expression. Not one word spoken had surprised Jules.

Placid despite the tempest inside, Shepherd rose. "Once the Enforcer is asleep, pull Svana. I desire a private meeting."

"Yes, sir."

Shepherd's eyes narrowed. "What? No unwarranted opinions?"

There was no hesitation or fear of imminent recourse. Jules spoke openly. “I only stated facts. I have not shared with you my opinion.”

“By all means, Jules, SPEAK!”

The sharp edge of the man’s dead stare displayed more than enough. “Choose an Alpha surrogate for Miss O’Donnell.”

Rising from the chair, all the waves of provocation, the violence Shepherd had been restraining, flowed out in the simple phrase. “I would kill anyone who dared to touch her.”

Jules rebutted, unflinching, “Not anyone.”

6

The other Omegas probably thought she was insane, and maybe she was. At this point it didn't matter anymore. Claire knew her time was almost up, that the group was starting to chafe at her presence, that her behavior was a threat to them.

Claire understood exactly what was happening; that was the very reason why it was so important she hurry.

With the city's shops stripped clean of *valuables*, it wasn't hard to find the 'nonessentials' useful for her ploy. With Shepherd in power, COMscreens and networks were beyond Claire's reach but, like the book in her back pocket, paper had power.

A printed leaflet embossed with her image stared up at her; reproduced over and over again until no more paper could be found.

Nona had been brave enough to join her. To find the

machines and make the copies… Through the madness, the old woman had not left her side, not once. Her friend had even helped as Claire created what would ruin her in the eyes of the world.

Senator Kantor had warned Claire of the consequences should anyone learn who she was to Shepherd—of the potential outcome should the resistance get their hands on her. The conversation had been burned into her memory, had carried her away again and again over the silent hours she walked the city.

There was no great hero to stand for what had once been Claire O'Donnell; even her own people found her useful only as a commodity.

So be it. If that was what she was to be, she would make them all eat it. She would sell herself, choose how to manipulate the product, before she was out of steam.

Claire was not a leader of men or a great orator. She was an Omega who enjoyed painting pictures for children, who once believed she had a future full of promise. Now she knew there would never be a loving mate or smiling children. Distorted and ruined, she was just a faceless statistic in a city full of nightmares and indifference. Well, not anymore. She had nothing left and nothing to hide. So Claire created the voice she'd lost, the last piece of resistance she could manage—something horrific from her weakness that could give others strength.

Nona had captured the brutality of the image perfectly.

Though the flyer was black and white, something about

those large, enthralling eyes pierced brilliantly as the girl on the flyer stared forward. It was the profound expression of pain, the tracks of tears, the defiance, all balanced with the set of her mouth and the obvious cut in her lower lip. Claire stared out at the viewer over her shoulder, displaying the violence of her scabbed claiming mark—the grotesque thing still bruised like a rotting flower. Her chin was cocked high, her black hair pulled back so the damage to her throat was exposed. She was absolutely naked, the fullness of one breast round above thin ribs, the nipple just covered by the arm clasping her hair. The world would see her as she was: captivating and beautifully tragic.

It was her handwriting, the feminine script her final statement to Thólos:

I am Claire O'Donnell.

I am your mother, I am your sister, I am your daughter.

Look at me.

I am what you have done to yourselves.

I was pair-bonded to Shepherd against my will. I carry his child.

I fought back.

I fought back for you.

Each Thólosen who does nothing stands with evil. There are no excuses. Confront the abuse perpetrated on the streets, stand up to rape and violence.

Do not turn a blind eye again.

Do not make me stand alone.

Claire fled the warehouse as soon as the dark gave her cover, racing her own shadow like a wild thing. For a body that was strangely listless, she flew through the streets, sheaves of paper clasped to her breast.

It took all the dark hours of the night, multiple trips back and forth to gather more stacks of paper Nona handed off to her. The flyers were placed on the tops of buildings to blow in the icy wind like garbage through the streets, to continuously rain down on common areas where in only a few hours citizens would congregate.

Her portrait was like a virus, almost unnoticeable as it infected Shepherd's system, her image blowing about like leaves.

When her body gave out and her vision began to blur, Claire dropped the last armful of flyers from the highest causeway she could reach. Once it was done, she crawled like a wounded animal into the nearest building. In a dark corner she collapsed, oblivious of where she was, and uncaring.

It was simple enough for a man of Jules' skill to enter the apartment of the sleeping Enforcer. Svana was collected, and from the monitor in Shepherd's hand, it was clear that Jules' appearance had been somewhat surprising to her. When he crooked his finger, she swept from the room with her customary air of superiority, head held high like the royalty she was.

Shepherd kept her waiting, entering Corday's domicile, finding it typical, small, and full of the trappings of city life.

The Beta was asleep on his bed, snoring just loud enough to make the continued assurance of his slumber simple, the Enforcer completely unaware that the very terror of Thólos slipped through the darkness like a demon to stand over him.

Claire's scent was rich in the room. Even, to Shepherd's extreme antagonism, rising from the bedsheets. Watching the handsome Beta, his lips parted in sleep, the predator awakened. The beast licked his chops, ready to tear out the throat of his prey. But the giant needed the naïve young Enforcer alive long enough that the fool might lead him to Claire. Once that mission was accomplished, he would personally tear Corday limb from limb, relishing each scream. Staring down at the Beta, Shepherd could already imagine the tactile pleasure… feel the warmth of blood running through his fingers.

Moving away before he could give in to the temptation to carry out such a punishment before its due time, Shepherd forced himself to ignore the other traces of Claire lingering on the bed: the long dark hairs on the pillow and smears of her blood on the sheets.

In the bathroom, Shepherd found the dress she'd worn when Claire refused to eat, ripped and ruined, stained from wounds accumulated from a highly dangerous fall—a fall that could have easily killed her.

Shepherd did not know how long he stood in that dark cluttered space clutching that dress, wanting to rip at the fabric just as badly as he wanted to take it with him. But no sign of his visit could be left behind. Stuffing it back into the laundry container, he noticed the waste basket brimming with wrappings and white paper of used bandages, blood soaked cotton balls, all the signs that the Beta had tended her wounds.

It made him want to squeeze the man's neck until he felt his vertebrae pop apart.

The very air in the apartment was offensive.

Corday's smell had scented his female once before. It was clearly his sweaty clothing she had been wearing when the Omegas had turned her in. Worse was the odor of Svana's musk, picking apart Claire's sweetness in a gross reminder of what had been created in his den when all his weeks of dedicated exertion to draw out his Omega were spoiled by an action as rudimentary as sex.

Through his inspection, his ire only grew, and Shepherd knew he had to leave before the stink of his outrage escaped his carefully buttoned coat and high collar. Vanishing like a phantom, he moved at last to confront his beloved, finding her unaware of his entrance into the dark apartment chosen for their private meeting.

Closing the door to face down the subject of his anger, Shepherd addressed her with a blank expression. "Greetings, Svana."

Svana purred over her shoulder, her voice full of the richness of their shared history. "Must I remind you, Shepherd, that you do not summon me and leave me waiting."

Ignoring the lack of subtlety in the reprimand, Shepherd stepped closer. "How very beautiful you are this evening."

She smiled, her lips curving up like a cat lapping milk. "Am I not beautiful every evening?"

The warmth of his hand came to her shoulder. "Enforcer Corday is a fortunate acquisition. Exactly when did you infiltrate the resistance?"

"My love?" Svana's hands were already slipping up to cup his neck, to press to the small amount of warm exposed flesh so that nothing might be between them. "Are you not pleased at how easily they trust me? I can control them… mislead them."

The feel of her body under Shepherd's palms was familiar. "Nothing but ourselves could stand in the way of our success."

At once the soft, luring quality of Svana's blue eyes went sharp and narrow. "It is unlike you to make such a reference, especially towards myself."

Shepherd hissed. "Your undiscussed appearance amidst the resistance was unsanctioned."

At once, Svana moved out of the comfort of his touch. "I am not a child to be corrected, Shepherd. Remember to whom you are speaking."

Watching Svana in the dark, the shine of moonlight over the perfection of her face, did not bring him peace. Instead he found himself growing aggravated that there had still been no outright mention of Claire. Did she think he didn't know? That she would keep knowledge from him, purposefully, again… that she would presume not to admit her doings… it did not sit well in his gut. "Equivocation does not suit you. Let us speak plainly on the subject and be done with it."

The way she stood, with the city backlighting her silhouette, the silken tone of her voice, all of it was to allure. "Can it be that you are displeased with me?"

His large hands came to the lapels of his heavy coat, gripping tightly as he spoke. "The Followers overheard every word of your conversation with Corday, and nothing relevant towards our mission was even pursued. What is it you seek to accomplish in this game? You risk exposing your identity and purpose to chase the scent of my mate."

"Mate," she spat the word, revolted. "When I had originally heard of your toy, I figured it was some passing fancy to fill the hours you could not spend with me. Finding her pregnant was staggering enough, but I can hardly believe what that fool downstairs described. You *pair-bonded* with something so beneath you!"

"You have had many lovers to satisfy your body. I chose to have only one. I could not rightfully keep Claire without bonding. Accepting her as my mate keeps her in my power and in line with the Gods' plan." Sucking in an angry breath, Shepherd took a step nearer. "Furthermore, you should take care where you would point that finger. *You* attempted to produce an heir with Premier Callas!"

It was a rare thing for Svana to display surprise, but it crept into the corners of her expression.

Shepherd did not wait for her to speak. "Did you really believe I was unaware of your attempted conception? I smelled the effect of the drugs on your body. It did not go unnoticed by my Followers, either."

"It was necessary, Shepherd," she argued at once, fisting her hands in his shirt. "His genes house a treasure that cannot be lost—immunities, resistance to disease. Why should it have been wasted? What better revenge than to have Premier Callas' child one day leading our people?"

Shepherd reached out to run his fingers through Svana's hair, watching the brown slip right through his touch. "You would have preferred to carry the offspring of the man responsible for the corruption of Thólos. He threw my mother into the Undercroft. I would never raise a child of that monster as my own. What crawled out of you would never rule."

Svana's expression twisted into one of disgust. "So you seeded a weakling out of spite? I feel both honored and disappointed that you would act out so from petty jealousy, my love."

His own great anger fell back behind an alarmingly placid expression. "Was it not your explanation that our love transcended the physical? My desire for a corporeal mate should mean nothing to you."

The woman circled Shepherd in the dark, calculating her next move. Something seemed to register and Svana's eyes grew warmly seductive; she licked her lower lip. "It is not too late should you wish to breed me. Think of the greatness of our combined power. The necessary drugs could be found and we could begin at once."

"Even as glorious as you are, the chances of an Alpha female conceiving with Alpha male sperm are very slim—carrying to term even more so." Placing his great hands on her shoulders, Shepherd outlined what was unchangeable. "Claire will bear my offspring and serve as my mate, and you will rule at my side once Thólos is in ruins and my army has delivered Greth Dome from those who usurped your family's claim to the throne."

"The Omega is unsuitable. A foul creature of this city is unworthy of such an honor!"

Shepherd hissed, agitated that she would further question him on the matter. "Claire was untouched, her body pure and receptive. I was her first. That is only one example of how Thólos has not tainted her."

Svana laughed, scoffing. "An Omega of her age… No, dearest, such a thing is not possible. You have been fooled."

"Through the bond she can hide nothing from me." Where the flawless cadence of the words came from, he did not know. Nor did he miss the tiny shift in Svana's expression when he said, "I have absolute faith in Claire's former celibacy and her current fidelity."

"*Fidelity*. I see… you question my behavior." Svana understood his deeper meaning. Composing her face into an expression of pain she asked, "Are you trying to hurt me?"

"No, beloved." Shepherd bowed his forehead to hers, working to calm the torrent of anger before it swept him away.

Her body softened against his, conformed to his strength, seeking to mollify. "If you wish to keep a pet then I expect that you will share her with me."

The concept turned his stomach, felt incredibly wrong. "I am certain, given your introduction, that she would be unwilling to mate with you if asked. It is impossible."

Svana's derisive snort preceded, "It would not take long

for the Omega to learn her place… one which is below me. She may have fought my initial touch, but you are her Alpha; her opinion matters little. She is nothing but a physical vessel for your needs."

"Initial touch?" It was like the spark of a forest fire, Corday's accusation, *sex offender*, wrecking Shepherd's last vestige of calm. It cost him a part of his soul to accuse, "You tried to touch her sexually and she resisted. That is why you struck her…"

Svana seemed unperturbed, shrugging. "She refused to spread so that I could taste… I merely wanted to confirm the scent of her pregnancy—which I did."

A surge of violence almost overwhelmed his control. He shook, felt the dagger of the link twist hideously in his chest. The female Alpha had dared to touch his mate inappropriately! Svana had hurt Claire simply for being defensive and sexually obedient to only him. Shepherd blinked, fighting not to reach out and break bone. "That is unacceptable, Svana! Beyond your needless attack of a weak and pregnant woman, such behavior is so very against your nature that I question if you have lost yourself. How would you even consider what you have done as appropriate?"

Her eyes narrowed; she showed her teeth. "You keep her to fuck her. What is yours has always been mine."

"I claimed her as a mate!" It was almost a roar but so soft it seemed strange that the windows shook with unseen force.

"And then unquestioningly fucked me right in front of her, proving she is nothing but a sorry replacement. Because I am the one you adore. The scrawny Omega is only a diversion you believe to be more important than she is because you foolishly pair-bonded in a moment of weakness." A purr came from Svana's chest. "I understand now that I have neglected you. The situation will be rectified, and from now on I will see to your physical needs. There need be no animosity between us."

Shepherd blinked, jaw clenched as he looked down. His beloved had reached out to lower his zipper, her elegant fingers pulling out the flaccid length of Shepherd's cock. Svana began to stroke. It was the anger that sent his blood pumping and made him stiffen in her grasp, the fury that pulled forth the low animal growl as he latched onto sensation to escape the unbearable realization of what his beloved had done.

Rubbing her thumb in smooth circles over the tip of his cock, she cooed and leveled him with a hungry stare. Caught up in the grip, in the way Svana knew exactly how to earn a response, Shepherd tore at the fastenings of her pants, already rutting her hand in desperation to redirect so much wrongness into something right.

The apartment they were in was in shambles, the stained mattress he pressed her to as disgusting as the rotting chain in his chest. Gripping his staff in his fist, he met her eyes, lined up with the opening slit of Alpha pussy, and shoved in remorselessly hard.

The immediate sense of victory he saw in her shining eyes was appalling. Gripping her legs and turning his attention to look out the dark window over the city he'd conquered, he rammed hard and fast, just as he'd done on Claire's nest to save the Omega's life.

Just as before, Shepherd found less satisfaction in rutting a female who did not possess the smaller frame and the tighter cunt that would milk him when she came, that would draw out his essence until every last drop had been savored. There was no musical voice sighing his name as if it were the most beautiful sound in the world. Alpha females did not respond that way; they were built to mate with Omegas, to be dominant… they hardly even self-lubricated.

Shepherd felt no humming connection, no mental depth, just aggressive, angry sex… and it was eating at him. Svana was performing well, making her calls and trills, spreading wide to show the beauty of her body. It was not enough. His abject fury did not abate, it only distorted, it left him in ruins, and Shepherd began to feel the unsettling wrongness grow with every thrust.

He did the unthinkable and flipped Svana over, to mount his beloved from behind so he would no longer have to look at her. She gasped, tilted her hips at his strength, and seemed to relish the rough handling. To keep her head forward, Shepherd fisted her hair, immediately noticing the tactile wrongness of it. It was not silky black, but a coarser brown, and his growl led to no surge of wetness that bathed his cock and beautifully scented the air.

The woman he rode was not his mate.

Even with his eyes closed, even thinking of another, all he could see was Svana… altered, seemingly tainted by what she had done, by what he knew and could not forget. Once she came, tugging at her clitoris in little flicks of her fingers, Shepherd could not continue for another moment. Pulling out, he tucked away his already softening dick.

Spinning about, she gaped at him. "Dearest… everything will be as it was. Come, let me soothe you. I know what you need."

Already she was reaching for his zipper again, leaning forward from the bed to take him into her mouth.

Brushing her hand aside, he continued to right his clothing. "No, Svana." Shepherd felt an impure film on his skin, everywhere Svana's hands had crept over him unclean. "It was wrong for me to take you now. Your assessment was correct, we have surpassed physicality, and I will not defile our bodies by attempting to mate with you again. Things have changed, we must both accept that."

Her voice cracked. "You cannot possibly prefer another to *me*." Svana stood before him, demanding he see reason. "Especially a woman who defies you, who prefers the pretty Beta downstairs."

Shepherd lowered his chin to his chest, the deep furrow between his brows sinister. "Claire is unenlightened and misunderstands my purpose. The very fact that she abhors what I've done to her people demonstrates her worth."

"I am the one who loves you," the beauty pleaded. "Do you not see that she *hates* you? Has run from you… The Omega could *never* love a marked man from the Undercroft. You disgust her."

The sharp sting of Shepherd's tattered bond concurred. "But she is still mine, carries my heir, and is under my protection." He grew, cracking bones as he postured. "You will not touch her again, Svana. Do you understand me?"

"You will come crying to me when everything you imprudently created falls apart." Svana nodded, staring forward as if she could see into the future. "And I love you so greatly that I will give you the comfort you do not deserve."

Shepherd could not tolerate another moment of such spite. After what he had heard earlier, the lie spilling from her lips, it was painfully obvious Svana had never intended to let him keep his due. She'd expected that he would cast off the Omega. Nothing he had done had satisfied her—and like the monster Claire believed him to be, he'd stood by and let Svana debase his mate… even willingly participated.

Squeezing his eyes shut, he heard Jules' words echo for what felt like the hundredth time: *You allowed Svana to manipulate you into dishonoring your pregnant mate.*

Shepherd had accepted his beloved's liaisons, even though the revelation had dumbfounded him. He had even adored Svana despite her foulness with Premier Callas. The same respect was not wielded in his direction, her expectations contradictory, immature.

Every word Svana had spoken when they'd faced off over Premier Callas had been carefully chosen to extradite herself of blame, to justify her own actions. Now he understood—she'd never expected him to seek sexual fulfillment with another.

His beloved had taken him for granted, made his devotion common.

There was something so very cutting in the revelation.

After all, her actions had led to his response… his needs apparently considered less important than hers.

Svana had never truly been concerned about Shepherd's feelings on the matter, and now she stood before him and openly lied.

Faith shaken, Shepherd nodded sadly. What had once been the adolescent who'd climbed atop him at her first urge and mated, swearing to be his forever, was not the woman he found he could not look at.

Shepherd left in disgusted silence.

Back in his room, he showered in water so hot his skin burned, found the discomfort cleansing, but still felt the taint of what he'd done—found the recoil of the bond, the violent sting, a welcome penitence for mating in a way that degraded them all. No stranger to suffering, he relished it as his due, just as he had each time he had purposefully harmed Claire for her own good.

A knock came to the door. One of his lieutenants entered to hand him something far more disturbing than anything else he had faced in the last grueling twenty-four hours.

Shepherd held a wretched piece of paper in his hand, unable to look away.

Even with the consuming sadness of Claire's expression, even with the arrogant tilt of her chin and judgment in her eyes, she was beautiful. But it was the marks on her neck, the split lip… wounds created when Svana had forced Claire to spread, that held Shepherd's attention.

Look at me. I am what you have done to yourselves.

"Sir," the Follower began, "these are blowing all over

Thólos. Reports say they were discovered scattered at six locations so far. They have already been seen by the citizens lining up for rations."

Shepherd's unresolved anger, the long hours of poisonous rage, vanished at the realization of what her actions could mean. His silver eyes darted all over the page, absorbed every curve of a body that was only for his eyes… read her words… and could not look away from the complicated pain.

He wanted nothing more in the world than to hold her, to touch that naked skin, to do anything necessary to remove that expression from her face.

I was pair-bonded to Shepherd against my will. I carry his child.

Her message to the world, the exposed expression of her spirit—it was the final rebellion. Death was coming for her, and she was going to feed herself to the city in an attempt to show them all the truth of what they had become. The foolish, brave little Omega.

Do not make me stand alone.

There would be no sanctuary for Claire after this. She would not live long enough to know the pain of Red Consumption. Thólos would slaughter her, rip her apart like dogs fighting over a bone if he did not get to her first.

Knowing the Beta Corday had been with Svana and under surveillance all evening meant the man could not have known the Omega had done this. If the Enforcer did care for her, even a little, he too would know exactly what that flyer meant. Banking that once Corday saw the image he would impulsively run straight to Claire, Shepherd grabbed his coat and organized a team to make sure the Beta stumbled on that very flyer the second he stepped out his door.

The hulk addressed his soldiers, resolute and indomitable, with a mind as still as a frozen river. “A team must keep visual contact on Svana. Should she attempt to interfere or leave the Enforcer’s domicile, I authorize interception and detainment.”

“Yes, sir.”

Not one man questioned him.

How could one female cause such havoc? Corday was furious, looking down with a scowl at the suggestive image. At first he saw only rubbish on the ground; most of it wet from the sludge, and then he saw familiar eyes.

Naked, she looked out at him from the page, marred and damaged, but so fucking proud. Then there was her message… her goddamn message! What the hell was she thinking?

As he made his way to her, Corday passed people on the street who had their own copy, whispering the name ‘Claire’ amongst themselves.

Corday moved as cautiously as he could through the city until the mid-level byways spread out before him. The flyer crushed in his hand, past pissed off, he found the Processing Plant shut up, desolate and lifeless, just as the Omegas intended it to look. But a careful eye could see the sentry with one of the Omegas’ acquired automatic rifles guarding from the chute hatch. The way was opened for him and he went inside, barreling through the space to find Claire and shake some sense into her.

"Corday has made contact with the Omegas. No visual on O'Donnell."

Shepherd and a team of twenty had already surrounded the clever home Claire had found for her pack. There was little view within. Even so, from Shepherd's invisible perch on the building opposite, he and Jules could see the females mulling about in the dim space… but just like the Beta Enforcer scanning the room, they saw no sign of Claire's raven hair amongst the herd.

7

Nona had been expecting the young Enforcer, and walked forward to greet him. "When you did not return, I was worried you'd been killed. Claire assured me you were not—said she could feel you still lived."

There had been no chance to sneak off with Leslie demanding so much of his time. Three days he'd worked on translating the Followers' written language. Every hour they learned more, but at the cost of time he needed to be with Claire. Had he been here, he could have stopped Claire's lunacy. "Do you know what she did?"

Nodding, Nona gave a tired smile. "I do."

Corday held up the crumpled flyer. "How could you allow it, Nona?"

"There is no stopping that girl now." Nona gripped his

arm, trying to get the boy to see what was right before him. “There is no stopping what’s coming.”

Corday cocked his head and had to agree. “You’re right. Claire unleashed a storm of trouble with this shit.”

“Corday—”

He didn’t want to argue with an old woman. Corday wanted to argue with Claire. “At least tell me she is here.”

“She is with the boy.”

Corday narrowed his eyes, teeth clenched. “What boy?”

“Her dead boy.”

“Oh…”

“She buried him in the compost pile out back.” When Corday shifted away, Nona gripped his arm again, stopping the Beta so she might speak her piece. “Claire only just returned. She is tired, don’t expect much.”

Not interested in wasting more time, Corday held his tongue, marching right through Omegas who were less than happy he’d called again. A reinforced door swung in, sunlight invaded, and there she was, head bowed over a freshly turned pile of dirt.

THE ANGLE of the building hid her from view, forcing Shepherd to shift from his perch and move like a shadow over the roof. And then there she was, still as a statue, less than thirty feet away, staring down at a small mound of snow-dusted earth. Captivated, Shepherd let out a breath, watching the Beta approach her.

It was as if she didn't register Corday—not until the Enforcer shoved the flyer under her nose. "What is this?"

The Omega brushed the hair off her face, rubbing her skull as if it ached. "A picture of me naked."

"Do you think this is funny?" Corday snapped, working hard to keep from raising his voice. "Do you realize what you've done, Claire? Everyone will know. There will be no safety in anonymity, EVER!"

She would not need anonymity, but she did need Corday to move. "You are standing on my boy."

After a quick exhale, Corday stepped off the mound, pulling her to him. He hugged too hard, his voice breaking. "Your message… it is going to cost you any type of life. You will be hounded until the day you die."

The Omega pushed away, sniffed, and wiped her tears with the heel of her hand. "I know what I did. I know you cannot understand, that our agendas don't line up, but I cannot wait for the resistance to stop dragging its feet. There is no hero, Corday. There is no savior. Thólos has become hell, and I cannot even heap the blame for it at Shepherd's feet. What has happened here, we did to ourselves. Either the citizens see what complacency in the face of evil has cost them, or they are all going to die."

Corday pressed his hands to his face to keep his frustration in check. "Are you trying to inspire a revolution? You promised me you would not attack Shepherd's men."

Claire took his hands, pulling them down so he could look at her. She looked like death, exhausted, dark marks under her eyes. "It is not an attack on Shepherd. It's an attack on conscience. It's an attack on the people of Thólos."

Why couldn't she understand? "They will hate you…"

"I don't care." Claire took a step back, her temper flaring. "I told you there was nothing left for me. Don't you get it yet? This is all I can give, so let me give it and stop being so goddamn selfish!"

He tucked a stray piece of hair behind her ear, saying, "Survival is not selfish. Citizens who hate the bastard will simply kill you for sport. This was suicide."

Claire's voice was flat, steady as she affirmed the obvious. "I know."

"Have you lost your mind?"

She licked her chapped lips. "Look at me, Corday. I'm running out of steam, I throw up everything I eat; sleep gives me no peace… I am already dying."

"You are not dying, you are killing yourself!" the Beta shouted, clutching her shoulders as if he might shake sense into her "If you would just rest… If you would come home with me, I could take care of you."

"No."

"Aside from Nona, the Omegas hardly tolerate your presence here. It's only a matter of time before you're cast out." Why wouldn't she see that he could cherish her? "Why won't you listen to reason?"

"I CHOOSE HOW TO SPEND MY LIFE! NOT YOU, NOT SHEPHERD, NOT SENATOR KANTOR, NOT THE FUCKING PEOPLE OF THÓLOS. DO YOU HEAR ME, BETA?"

He had never once seen her with such fire in her eyes. “You’re upset.”

Throwing her hands up in the air, Claire agreed, “Of course I’m fucking upset! All I want to do is scream. Knowing that all I can offer Thólos is a naked picture on a flyer makes me loathe myself. How DARE YOU reprimand the fact that at least I am trying to do something while I still can? Your precious resistance does nothing!”

“Claire.” He reached out to hold her, soothing what made her tremble and cry. “Please…”

“I can’t be what you want me to be,” she sobbed against his chest. “I can hardly be myself anymore.”

“I am sorry,” Corday whispered, his heart breaking to see her so sad. “Don’t cry. I will purr for you, and you can rest. Okay? I should not have shouted.”

His offered low vibration began, Claire weeping like a child in his arms. Her arms went around him, her broken apologies lost in the wretchedness.

Muttering nonsense, Corday stroked her hair. “We’ll go inside, we’ll eat and you won’t get sick… I will stay so that you can sleep.”

He had to carry her and she let him, clinging to his neck as if he would disappear otherwise.

From a distance, Shepherd fought every instinct that told him to rush in and take her from the man comforting what was his. He hardly registered Jules’ hand gripping his forearm, the silent reminder to be still and measure the consequences. Because it was clear now his second-in-command was correct. Even if he dragged her back, she would not survive in this state.

Claire had lost the will to live.

THROUGHOUT THE DAY, Shepherd observed her actions inside the reeking plant. Corday was correct in his assessment. The Omegas avoided her and Claire seemed utterly unconcerned as she kept to her corner, purposefully distancing herself. All but the old woman had turned on the very catalyst of their freedom.

Envisioning a long row of women swinging, their hanged corpses on display to any who would deny his mate, Shepherd measured each wary look they turned towards Claire, even hating the women who gently ignored the suffering, dark-haired girl.

They were all unworthy of her, every single one, just like this city of lies and evil.

The Beta did tend to her, made her eat and held back her hair twenty minutes later when it all came up. He fed her again, pressured the small thing to drink water, all the while holding her in his lap, chest to chest, her legs wrapped around his torso, as if she were a child or his lover. The second serving seemed to stay down and in minutes Claire was dead to the world, snoring on his shoulder.

It was impossible to hear the exchange between Nona French and the Enforcer, especially with the man's lips pressed against Claire's hair. Eventually the Beta lay down, and the old woman pulled the man's long coat over the pair.

The dark arrived, Claire cried out in her sleep. When Corday's horrified eyes looked up to find Nona's sympathetic expression, Shepherd focused on the movement of the Enforcer's mouth and watched his lips form the words.

"She just called for Shepherd."

The absolutely crestfallen expression on the hated Enforcer's face brought a curl to Shepherd's own lips. The Beta might be the one holding her, but even damaged as the bond was, his Omega's mind was full of thoughts of her rightful mate. A sign from the Gods, a reminder to them all, that Claire was his.

Claire woke less haggard. "I am feeling better. Thank you."

In a voice so low that no member of the spying Followers could hear, Corday pressed his lips to her ear and whispered, "Claire, it's going to be over soon, we have access to their communications now. So hold on. Hold on until I can kill him. I swear to you I will."

Doing her best to pretend she wasn't ill, Claire nodded and kissed his cheek. "I have a great deal of faith in you, Corday. You are a wonder."

"And you will be free."

"I will," she acknowledged, eyes soft.

Slender fingers carefully pulled off her mother's wedding

band. Under their makeshift blanket, she took Corday's hand and slipped the band on his pinky.

"What are you doing?"

"I want you to keep this for me." Claire smiled as she gave her token. "A reminder, so that you don't forget I'm rooting for you."

She was making him uneasy. "I can't keep this."

"I am only lending it," she corrected, squeezing his hand. "You are to give it back to me when Thólos is free."

He hugged her, felt his heart soar. "Claire. I have faith in you, too."

"You are my hero, you know."

Corday wanted to kiss her, was so very tempted to thread his fingers in her hair and pull her lips to his. But that was not what they were; that was not what she could be…

At least not yet.

"Now," Claire broke the moment, shy. "You need to get out of here before the sun comes up. If I don't feel you're safe, I'll worry."

Already untangling herself, she eased out of his embrace. Corday was not allowed to linger, Claire urging him to leave before light might make his journey dangerous. It was obvious he did not want to go, but she seemed so much better, her eyes more alive and a smile on her lips when she spoke.

The Beta retreated. The second he was gone far enough down the causeway not to hear her, Claire doubled over, and quietly lost her stomach all over the frost by the chute.

Corday did not hear her vomiting, nor did he see even a

hint of the Followers that had surrounded him so flawlessly when he stepped out of her sight. He popped his collar to warm his neck, and shuffled off with his hands buried deep in his pockets—smiling.

Shepherd left Corday in the hands of Jules' team, his attention on his ill Omega and the change that came over Claire the instant the boy was gone. The false smile fell, and she moved far from the group and their fires to sit in solitude, as if invisibly drawn nearer to the place where Shepherd hid in the dark.

He could almost reach out and touch her.

Once comfortable, the female pulled a worn book out of her pocket and lay back to read. Shepherd cocked a brow. His little mate was reading a book he knew by heart, *The Art of War*. It was oddly endearing, the man imagining future conversations about the text.

What was her favorite passage?

Claire read while most of the women still slept; she read the same book she had read every day since she had found it, and let her eyes linger on memorized quotes. Sometimes she fancied that it was like reading a segment of Shepherd's soul. She could see his mentality in the book, his tactics, and sought vainly to understand—fixated to the point where she did not notice that Nona stirred.

The old woman prepared instant coffee, readying a serving for Claire.

"What wisdom do you have for me today?" Nona asked, pressing a steaming cup of swill into the young woman's hands.

Claire tossed the book on the ground as she always did when done with it, treating it badly. "According to Sun Tzu, great results can be achieved with small forces… But I choose to interpret that as: pissing off a bunch of women is a really bad idea."

The old Omega chuckled softly, eyes dancing as she watched Claire sip the coffee and grimace.

Nona stroked back Claire's dark hair and teased, "You always did love your cappuccinos, but I'm afraid that's the best I can do."

Looking down at the shitty watered down beverage, Claire tried to banter. "I have many reasons to hate Shepherd, but reason number one is that I have not had a decent cup of joe since I was run out of my home… the jerk."

Her friend offered a soft chuckle.

Claire took another sip of the steaming brown water. With Nona at her side, she sat in miserable stillness, her bloodshot eyes growing resolute. She did not know what was causing it, but her ennui was beginning to fade. What was replacing it was acutely painful.

She had altered… crushing indifference warring with an unbearable sense of loss.

She should have felt victorious—she didn't. She should have felt pride; she'd forgotten even knowing such a sensation.

Nona was speaking some nonsense about the coming sunrise, Claire robotically drinking the tasteless beverage. When the brew was finished, the cup was set aside.

It was time.

Claire stood up and just walked away, leaving her friend without a goodbye.

She would see the sky for herself, observe the sunrise alone. But it would not move her. The sky had lost its magic.

The old woman watched her go, watched as dark hair disappeared… and knew Claire had made her choice.

Outside it was cold, colder every day. Claire wrapped her arms around her body and stumbled away from the Omega's haven. There had been no direction in her death march, but somehow she found herself standing at the edge of the Thólos water reserve. The top had crusted with ice, covered in white as blank and colorless as she had become inside. But if she squinted, she could see through it to a world of water, where everything was washed clean.

Tucking a loose piece of hair behind her ear, she shivered and waited for the cloud heavy sky outside the Dome to glow. Just as it turned an off-shade of pink, Claire felt that if she allowed any pleasure from such a moment, pain would seep through instead. The only way to continue was to feel nothing forever. So she took a step forward, then another one, and alone out in the earliest gloomy light of the morning, Claire walked the ice.

There was no question of hesitation; her work was done. She had completed her mission, given everything she could. She had earned her release from prison. Air crisp on her face, the unmistakable smell of cold, it began to soothe where salty tears burned her cheeks.

Those first steps and the ice already began to whisper complaint. The next ten paces were met with misleading silence. Claire chose to fill the quiet with the customary Omega prayer whispered into the wind:

"Beloved Goddess of Omegas, great Mother who nurtures and protects, I thank you for the life you granted me."

It was not until she was standing near the center of the reservoir before the sound she anticipated arrived—the crushing threat of cracks and imminent death.

"I am your image. I am your delight. For you hold me in your care. Watch over the world—"

"*Do not move, little one*."

The first thought at hearing the sound of that commanding voice was that she should have known he would be there. The devil would have to witness her final moments. There could have been no other way.

Her focus left the horizon and moved down towards her feet, to the fractured pattern that bloomed under her stolen boots. Claire sucked in a slow breath, felt it stretch her chest, and glanced over her shoulder. "The city is a horror show and I don't have anything left. You win, Shepherd."

"You willfully misunderstand." The urgent coarseness of his voice was insistent… nervous. "Svana would have killed you had I not—"

Claire felt her mouth form a small smile at the man behind her. "At least I know what made you the way you are. It wasn't only your life in the Undercroft. It was her."

Shepherd held out his hand, his eyes wide and unblinking. "It was the only way I could appease her and keep you."

A look of pity—and it was pity she felt—saddened

Claire's face. "You tell that lie almost as if you actually believe it. The choice you made was not the only way; it was the way *you* chose. You chose to do that horrible thing… to do many horrible things… for her."

Shepherd's lips wavered, he looked confused. When he spoke next, it seemed as if the words were foreign to him, "If I was to offer an apology, would it make any difference?"

"No."

"Then I will offer this instead." He stretched his hand out farther. "If you return to me, I will give you what you want. I will leave the Omegas in peace and see that they are left alone. You have my word."

Claire hummed, her attention returning to the cracking ice under her feet.

He tried again, determined. "Svana will not be allowed near you; nor will I ever touch her in that manner again."

Claire ignored him.

Exasperated, he gritted out, "I will even allow you to see your sky."

She mouthed the words, spoke them as if the very idea meant nothing anymore, "My sky…"

"I will care for you."

Water fell from her eyes, ran down her cheeks. Her voice was so sad. "It almost sounds like you mean it… how funny."

It took a great deal of effort for Shepherd to manage the last inducement. "I will spare the Beta, Enforcer Corday, whose death will otherwise be very slow and painful."

That was the tipping point. The hazy quality of her green

eyes sharpened and her soft lips pressed into a firm line. She listened closely.

"I am offering you the lives of forty-two people, little one." Shepherd employed a voice of reason, his purr rumbling to show sincerity.

Claire looked at his upturned palm, at the largeness of it, the lines and the calluses. She thought of Corday, of his vow to free the city… of everything that had been whispered between them in the dark. She thought of the child she felt utter indifference for, and put a hand to her stomach.

"That is right, little one, think of our baby."

She would never allow Shepherd's evil or that horrible woman to have the child, but she could buy Corday time. If he failed, she would kill herself and the life growing inside her before it might be born; she could do that, and she would. The smooth turn of her step, the little movement necessary to face the giant made the ice crack further, yet still she stood above what should have been her watery grave.

Shepherd knew she would say yes, that she would subject herself to him to save every life he'd mentioned. Claire could already feel it through a link that should not have been there; a burning barb knocking about where her lungs fought to expand. Her breath hitched painfully, and she fisted the leather of her jacket over her heart. "There is one more life I want."

"Who?"

Despite the invasion of the clawing worm, Claire sneered at the Alpha. "I will only tell you if you give me your unequivocal word that this person will *never* come to harm."

"And if I do this, you will return to me and live fully as my mate?" It was what he wanted, she could see it, feel her just a little bit more through the link, and he did not stop the malicious greedy evil that fostered his grin.

She felt his pleasure, glanced into rapacious eyes, and saw every ounce of his desperate elation. "Yes."

Shepherd nodded and crooked his fingers. "You have my word."

"Maryanne Cauley."

There was a flash of insight, a minute narrowing of the eyes. The Alpha nodded in understanding—the slippery traitor… Maryanne Cauley, a prisoner who'd once sworn her allegiance to him in exchange for safe haven in the Undercroft, was the one who had helped Claire free her Omegas.

Claire took a step towards total abasement, cursing the Gods when the march to Shepherd did not shatter the ice and suck her down. The weight of her cold fingers she set in his, not returning the smile when the devil's hand engulfed hers. Shepherd touched her face, and she instinctively jerked away when the heat of his palm cupped her cheek.

His large thumb brushed away the line of tears. He knew she was in pain by the burden of the intensifying bond clawing its way past her resistance.

Intense, overexcited, he reached for her, unwilling to wait another moment to cart her home. Claire continued to fight the claim, clutching at her heart, battling to maintain the sense of endless nothing that had carried her to the ice. She did not want to be Claire anymore, oblivion had become her armor. If there was no Claire, there was no pain. Nothingness was her pride… then she remembered she had no pride. She had lost it all the day she started to care for the man cradling her in his arms.

As if he knew her thoughts, he gripped her a bit tighter to his chest and gloated. “Forty-three lives, Claire.”

Her eyes screwed shut at his use of her name, the unwelcome anguish at the memory of the only other time he had spoken it ruining her. She lost the war—Claire felt something: the hurt and grief she had been unable to feel that day, and everything shattered.

Her pick-up had been organized with military precision. Shepherd held his reclaimed prize, purring loudly in arrogant triumph as he carried her through the subterranean halls towards his den.

It seemed a waste of noise. The purr was not soothing Claire. She was past comfort as the worm inside her swelled, each breath hurt, corrupted and hated.

The sound of the deadbolt, the finality of the moment, all this went past her as she fought so very hard not to show what she was feeling—not to give him the pleasure of acknowledging he had the power to hurt her again. But he wouldn’t stop touching. He even pried her fingers from where she clutched at her chest so he might rub the heat of his palm where she was so very clearly pained.

Shepherd encouraged the meltdown because he knew what was tearing at her insides. “We will start afresh,” he crooned, his huge hands pulling at the layers she was dressed in, stripping her clothing just as he stripped away her freedom. "My little mate."

Green eyes flew open, full of outrage, full of all the seething vehemence she should have screamed at him two weeks prior. "Mate? MATE? You are less than nothing to me! A deceiving monster I abhor. You are depraved; you disgust me! What you did was unforgivable. I HATE YOU!"

Even as she screamed, even as she beat against him, he stroked, he hushed.

Claire ranted, the stream of vileness bouncing off grey walls, until screams turned to great soul-wrenching sobs. She cried so very hard she could hardly draw breath. She begged him to kill her, cursed him to hell for tempting her from the ice, and only found the softness of the mattress under her back his answer to her pleas. Those great hands were everywhere, tracing the scrapes, the stitches in her knee, exploring every bruise, until Shepherd commenced his inspection with a long possessive stroke of his fingertips along the outline of his still healing claiming marks.

There seemed to be no end to the agony of the cancerous tether inside her. It twisted like an outraged alligator, tearing out her organs. She had her eyes shut tight, trying to will it all away, until naked lips came to her chest, to the very spot that had been so corrupted. Claire began to fight back, shrieking like a banshee. There was no stopping his penetration, or the throaty groan that escaped him at feeling her tight heat gripping his cock. Shepherd suckled her breasts, ran his teeth lightly over her neck, tried to kiss her mouth between licking away the tears and restraining her flailing.

The sounds from the beast, the soft noise that issued forth over the rending of her brokenhearted wails were those of a thirsty man who had finally been given water. Every stroke of her tight velvet channel as he thrust his cock lifted him closer to that unattainable heaven: to freedom. She was his again, trapped and tied, and he would take her any way he could—even if she hated him, even if she was only a slave to the bond. Because he needed her.

He growled so low and deep it made her flutter and ooze, made her shriek in horrified hatred, and he moaned into her mouth at the slick and scent. Taking what he needed, he rode her gently, spread her legs wide to see the thickness jutting from his groin enter her over and over. Rolling his hips and toying with her nub, he stole what he demanded and the wave blasted through her resistance until Claire reached a shattering, uncomfortable climax that made her arch and choke.

He drove her back powerfully against the bed, knotted as deep as he could, and shared her completion, filling her with heat, with his very essence, breathing hard at her ear as he groaned the words, "I love you, little one."

It did not lessen her pain. It only cut her deeper.

Claire keened as Shepherd held her through it all, still gushing, still knotted, swearing he would never let her go.

8

Shepherd had hurt her in his fervor, in his need to see her mated while the bond reformed… to ensure that she could not escape it. There was a little blood between her legs, as she had been dry and aggressively resistant when he first thrust. Even her mouth was swollen from his unwelcome kisses. New bruises were forming around her wrists and between her thighs.

Shepherd relished each one of the stinging scratches marring his own flesh, his reminder that she was his again—each wound a trophy, and testament to what was between them.

His little one had put up a good fight, but Claire had quieted over the hours, though not calmed completely. The thread in her chest was frazzled. It pained her, so Shepherd held her tight and kept the heat of his palm where her nails tried to scratch through her skin. The tears had ended and instead, she was in a trance, fighting sleep, yet clearly exhausted.

The purr never ceased, and though she gave him her back, Shepherd stroked and soothed, allowing her little defiance. She needed nutrition and hydration, yet he withheld his immense dissatisfaction at the state of her body to allow her some respite after her struggle—to let her think she might rest on her terms for a moment.

Unwilling to leave her, he sent out an order for medical supplies, and covered Claire from sight. Holding her in a grip of iron, he allowed Jules to set what was required on the small table beside the bed. When the door was locked, he found her still refusing to look at him. It didn't matter.

Shepherd had seen her reaction to food, was certain that she would hold nothing down as upset as she was, and took her arm. When the needle pierced a vein, she remained unresisting. Intravenous fluids were administered. While the IV emptied, he bathed her with soft towels, each wound treated and bandaged, the stitches grunted at, and her feet, a thing that made the beast openly angry, were wrapped in soft strips of cloth.

When the process was finished he gathered her again in his arms.

"I will build you a new world, little one—a kingdom worthy of you and our son." He whispered his distorted ideals, raking his fingers through her tangles. On and on Shepherd elocuted, articulating all he would accomplish, how he would be a legend, how he would do this for her.

In Claire's hazy understanding, Shepherd had never spoken so much and said so little.

On her belly, with her back to him, she found herself listening to the pipedreams of a madman until she could not stand it another instant. Rolling over, interrupting his game with her hair, she argued with that same passionate defiance, that same misplaced goodness that had yet to vanish no matter what had happened to the rest of her. "Do not use me as an excuse for the horrible things you do. I will have no part of it!"

He grinned, smiling darkly at her hoarse complaints. Hand molded to the shape of her belly, Shepherd patted where their child grew. "The very fact that I have you back proves the Gods side with me."

Claire had cried herself dry, her chest was rotten mush. "You have me because I would rather save the lives of forty-three people than kill myself."

"Shhh." His hush was brushed over her chest. He kissed where their bond thrived. "Everything is mending and your sadness will fade in time."

It was not mending, it was scarring.

There was a gleam in his eyes, confidence. "We *will* begin again."

Lip curling, Claire laid out his sins. "You forced a pair-bond, drugged and impregnated me, fucked your crazy Alpha *beloved* in my nest…" She did not finish. Instead her pain surged again and Claire found her eyes could indeed leak more tears. "I recognize, Shepherd, that I am only here to be your toy. I'm a slave, a kept thing. I sold myself for them."

It was predictable, the storm of fury in his eyes. What was surprising was the small dash of regret. Where he had been rubbing her chest, his hand moved to a breast and began to roll and pinch the nipple until the soft pink darkened and the bud elongated under his fingers.

Of course he would fuck her again no matter how unappealing Claire found the idea. That was always his recourse for her mouth. That was his answer every time she was resistant or unhappy.

Lying still, too tired after hours of struggling to put up a fuss, she remained limp… ready to get it over with.

The other nipple received the same treatment; all the while Shepherd watched her with that calculating gaze. A thumb traced over her lips and dipped just a bit between them to play against the flat of her tongue. The growl was made, the aroma of her slick scented the air, and his free hand began to play with her pussy.

Shepherd pressed his chest to hers, growled low and deep once more, watching so very carefully.

She closed her eyes and chose to ignore him.

With his fingers coated in her slippery fluid, he began to speak. "In the Undercroft, I had my mother for so short a time, I hardly can remember her face. She died from the harsh use of many men." A slippery finger slid to her puckered anus and Claire started. Shepherd slowly added pressure against her rectum, her breath catching at the uncomfortable cramp of that place being stretched. Wide eyes showed her distress. Claire reached down to grip the wrist of the offending limb, her complaint lost around the thumb still teasing her tongue.

When she had stilled, realizing he was not moving, not penetrating further, Claire watched him with absolute attention.

"As women never lasted long, prisoners took their pleasure from men in this way." The probing finger slipped past Claire's clenched ring. "Or by using the mouth of another. The beasts in that hole would howl in the dark as they gratified their bodies on the small and weak. The sounds of screams, of tortured begging—even the moans of those who took pleasure in such things—that's the lullaby that lulled me to sleep every single night."

The sensation he was creating was unpleasant, the tip of his finger wriggling. Claire tried to squirm but his weight was on her, and Shepherd growled again until more slick dripped down to coat what penetrated her rectum.

She whimpered.

"I was smaller than you are now the first time I was cornered. My back was to the wall, a man with sores on his face pulled out his member and reached for my throat. What he didn't know, what nobody knew, was that my mother had whored herself for a knife. I shanked my attacker. During the struggle, I earned the scar across my lips that you in your estrous called beautiful."

Had she?

There was a purr, a short offer of soothing as he pressed his digit further up her ass, knowing the stretch was unwelcome, but using it to make sure she listened to every damn word he said.

"I left his corpse strung outside my cell, his cock hanging from his mouth as warning to others. He was only the first, and I was surrounded by dark-hearted monsters. As I grew bigger, grew stronger, the small and feeble would come to me, offering their mouths or their bodies for protection from those same men who hounded them. I found them repugnant, weak, and beneath me. I killed several just to make my feelings on the topic clear."

The thumb in Claire's mouth stroked her tongue in little circles as he spoke. "One day, something from the light found me in the dark, a young woman with a knife of her own. It was already bloody."

Svana.

"She'd heard of me, had crawled into hell to seek me out. She gave me the means to rule and asked for nothing. Her visits were often, her affection splendid. Like me, her mother had been killed before her. Like me, her future had been stripped away.

"Her mind, the things she knew, were beyond anything I had been taught. She offered to share such wisdom, brought me books, found worth in the monster whom inmates feared. The angel even brought me the file with my mother's name on top." Shepherd nuzzled her cheek. "In that missing person's dossier was a photograph. My Beta mother, before the Undercroft rotted her teeth, had been very beautiful, like you. I hated hearing her screams."

Claire put her hand to his flank, she felt his pain break against her.

The Alpha continued. "I could not save her, and to this day could not tell you which one of the demons underground was my father."

Claire did not want to let his history touch her, but it was so pathetic she could not help but feel pity.

"I was not the only man trapped in that dark by corruption above. Like my mother, more than half of the men forced below were innocent enough, but inconvenient to the powers that be. I learned secrets from them, things you cannot imagine… if you only knew the infection creeping through the hearts of this city, little one, if you could read the stories scraped into the rocks below us."

Why was he telling her this? She began to struggle, and flinched when his finger inside her surged deeper, stretching her until she stilled.

"Open your eyes, little one." The growl was menacing, guttural. "You will look at me when I say this."

She did not want to look at him, felt invaded by that single, oversized finger, and the way he still teased at her tongue with his thumb. Jerking from the penetration, she met his gaze.

"These men, this rotten society—in your goodness, you fail to see the flaws. I could tell you things that would keep you awake at night. Everyone, man and woman, hanged outside the Citadel participated in, or knowingly ignored, atrocities. Like the imprisonment of my mother.

"And yes, years ago Svana became my lover, and I

thought she was also, equivalently, my mate. I learned I was wrong. She is a driven woman, powerful, but you are the mate the Gods designed for me. Had you been dropped into the Undercroft, had I smelled you once, I would have killed every man who tried to touch you. I would have claimed you and dragged you to my cell, bent you over my cot, and fucked you where every convict might see through the bars… so that they all knew you belonged *to me*. Do you understand?"

There was no answer for such a barbaric statement.

Shepherd sniffed her, growled. With his finger still submerged in her ass, he worked his cock deep inside where she was wet and ready. She gave a little scream, muffled by his thumb as he began to rut. There was nothing tender, it was pure aggression, but it satisfied in a strange way. The overfull feeling, the way he left no place untouched as that uninvited digit squirmed around. She climaxed so quickly it was startling, felt his knot press against her quivering passage as he removed his finger from her rectum.

Claire screamed when her orgasm twisted into a tuneless vibration that wracked her bones.

When he shot his load against her womb, each spurt was matched with a roar. Head buried at her shoulder, lips at her neck, Shepherd pressed his chest to hers, to the place where they were tied. The cord sang, burned, ached, pleased, and consumed.

His thumb left her mouth, Shepherd pleased when he ground his knot inside her and his little one came again.

Crushed under him, his Omega moaned, lowered her

lashes, and found sleep in the clinging arms of what may, had circumstances been different, been a good man.

"WHAT DO you mean she's not here?" Corday demanded.

"I mean, Enforcer Corday"—Nona offered a tired sigh—"that she isn't here. Claire slipped away days ago and has not returned."

Behind narrowed eyes, Corday's mind raced a mile a minute. The worry was making his stomach churn, and by the look in Nona's eyes, it was clear she was just as upset, only concealing it better.

As if trying to offer the young man an explanation, Nona said, "I think she simply decided to go home."

"To Shepherd?" he snapped, anger written all over his face. "Claire would never do that."

"She had been low on spirits, Enforcer. What I am trying to tell you is that she most likely went *home*."

"You are wrong," Corday spat the words. He had spoken to Claire only three days prior. The Omega had given him her ring… she'd made a vow. "Did those women run her off?"

"No, but they would have in a matter of days. She knew that."

The agitated Beta looked at the old woman as if she was stupid. "So she went somewhere else for shelter."

"Perhaps," Nona admitted, debating if it would be best for the young man to have something to hold on to.

"When did she leave, precisely?"

"The morning of your last visit."

Corday threw up his hands, growling at the ceiling. "God-damn it, Claire!"

Nona took his shoulder again, squeezed his coat, and pulled him away from the gathering Omega crowd. "Sit!" The Beta male obeyed out of decorum, Nona glaring. "Claire did not want me to tell you who I really am. But I am going to anyway, because you are a Beta and I know you care for her, but you do not understand."

Nona made him be still, composing herself beside him. "When I was sixteen, I was abducted from my home, kept under lock and key for days until I was sold like cattle—bought by a man named David Aller, and forced into a pair-bond at my next estrous by a stranger twice my age.

"Once bonded, he revealed me to the public again, and my family accepted what could not be changed, even though I begged them to help me. I had no advocate; I was just a bonded Omega with no rights. When I ran the first time, I made it less than two weeks before I began to lose touch with reality. I was found wandering, confused, through the streets. The Enforcer that picked me up took me back to David as if I were a stray pet.

He beat me, a common practice for correcting renegade Omegas. The beatings grew worse, and I ran again a few months later. It was always the same, that unwavering pair-bond to a man I hated persisted and controlled me. I tried everything, every hinted course, but it was the same nightmare. It was ten years before I poisoned him and acquired a new identity. I still dream of him, sometimes I think I hear him… and David has been dead almost forty years."

Jaw loose, Corday looked at the gentle, old woman and knew she spoke the truth.

"There is no way out of a pair-bond, no recourse for Claire. One of them has to die for her to be even marginally free. Killing Shepherd might have saved her, but her time was running out and she knew it. She just did not want to worry you… because she knew you had affection for her."

"Claire is stronger than you."

Nona agreed. "That is absolutely true."

"She told me herself that the bond was damaged. Why do none of you listen when she speaks? Why do you all assume?"

"Corday." Nona took the boy's hand and spun the ring on his finger. "Claire is gone. She gave you her ring so you would not forget her, because she had affection for you, too."

The man argued vehemently. "She swore to me that she would survive. I choose to believe she had a plan. We have all seen just what she is capable of. I have faith in Claire."

"I love Claire as if she were my daughter. I knew what she was suffering, what she had sacrificed for us, and I hope you are right. But if you are, the only way that would have happened is if she purposefully went back to Shepherd."

Gritting his teeth and glaring at her, Corday growled, "She would not have gone back to Shepherd."

"I agree."

Beyond frustration, Corday turned and left, furious with the old woman.

THE WARMTH of a large hand softly stroked back loose hair from her face, waking Claire from a dead sleep. The purr was light, enticing her to stir, and from the way the mattress dipped, she could tell Shepherd was sitting on the edge of the bed.

It was the smell that made her comply, the aroma of roasted coffee beans and something sweet. Blinking salt crusted lashes, she looked straight at the bedside table. Sitting in a white cup atop a saucer was a steaming cappuccino made by someone who possessed the skill to create the little pictures in the foam.

It did not take a genius to figure out he had been watching her in the processing plant. Shepherd had heard her conversation with Nona, and he had done this in response.

"Please don't tell me you kidnapped a barista," Claire groaned, sleepy, stretching forward to sniff.

"The chef I kidnapped months ago to prepare your meals needed company."

Claire could not tell if Shepherd was trying to make a joke. Scowling, she glanced up at the man still petting her elongated back and pursed her lips. From the look in his eyes it was clear the brute was absolutely serious.

He picked up the saucer to hand to her, using his other hand to lift and turn her to sit back against the pillows. Situated with the drink in her hand, she sipped and sighed, unsurprised when Shepherd moved the curtain of her hair over her shoulder to reveal her breasts for his gaze.

"Are you enjoying your coffee?"

Shepherd had never woken her unless it was for sex, and certainly not with coffee in bed. Claire did not trust him for a moment. "I am not going to thank you." But she did take another sip and melted… hating to admit that the drink was really fucking good.

Though his expression did not change, Claire was certain he was satisfied with her reaction to his offering.

Elbow on his knee, Shepherd watched her savor her drink. "Maryanne Cauley is in the Citadel as we speak."

Cup rattled against saucer, and the moment of coffee-induced comfort was gone. "You promised me you would not hurt her."

"And I have not." Shepherd's eyebrow arched. "But I will if she is here in some attempt to steal you from me."

"Considering how you collected me, I doubt anyone even knows I am here." Claire turned belligerent. "I came with you willingly to respect my end of the bargain, and I will not attempt to leave so long as you respect yours."

The purr came and so did a pet down her hair. "That is all I wanted to hear."

Claire looked to one side, debating. "Could I speak with her?"

Of course Shepherd was going to deny the request, he knew she knew that. With a deep sigh he took her empty cup and saucer away. "I do not wish to argue with you."

"Then you may as well go back to torturing Thólos, and I will sit here like a good captive and stare at the walls."

He shifted, leaned closer while Claire pressed herself

further into the pillows. His lips brushed hers as he asked, "What is your connection to Miss Cauley?"

So close, Claire felt… torn. "Maryanne was my best friend when we were children."

He stroked her arm as if rewarding good behavior. "I find that difficult to believe. The woman is a thief and a prostitute."

"Like you," Claire said, frowning, "she too was once innocent… Though, unlike you, I think she is trying to be good now. She is just not very confident in the pursuit."

"You are the one to hold all the goodness, and I will hold all the power," Shepherd purred, leaving a lingering, and ignored, kiss on her slack lips.

"As you say," Claire responded, her voice flat once he disengaged.

"Are you sore"—his fingers dipped under the covers to brush over her mound—"here?"

Any second he would make the growl and she would be spread under his rutting body. "Does it matter?"

The hand left her. Shepherd brushed the pout on her lips. "You will rest today. Food will be sent. If I find out you have not eaten, one of your forty-three will pay for it."

"You do not need to threaten them." Claire did not want to play such games. "I gave you my word."

"That pleases me, little one." Shepherd was so damn confident as he shifted from the bed.

He gave her a long look while she slipped back under the covers for more rest, then left silently, turning off the light.

The next time she woke, food was waiting on the table.

She showered and dressed in one of the feminine dresses Shepherd seemed to think she should wear, and looked at eggs benedict. He had a chef somewhere in the compound just to make her food. She wanted to roll her eyes at the strangeness of the long ignored gesture, but had noticed it almost from the start. Canned veggies and mass-produced meat products had transformed into satisfying cuisine only a week or so after she had first arrived. The confirmation should not have mattered, but it bothered her that he had mentioned it, and now it had to be addressed.

What bothered her more was that the chef was probably safer down there than above ground. Claire even suspected he or she had been taken from the Premier's mansion. Shepherd was a thorough man. He would only take someone renowned… a celebrity. And he had done it to please her.

Claire ate every bite of that food, though it was too rich and her stomach was bound to rebel. The vitamin followed, and all the milk was drunk. Of course she threw it all up about thirty minutes later, but that could not be helped.

Customary pacing came next, her only form of exercise. Matters needed to be sorted now that her thinking had grown sharper. Shepherd knew of the Omegas, of Corday, and of Maryanne—the Alpha female having been the only one on her list that he was not previously aware of. The real question was how had Shepherd found her, which part of the branch had been first observed? Considering when he had come, it seemed that the answer was Corday. Which meant Shepherd would undermine every move of the resistance.

The supreme art of war is to subdue the enemy without fighting. - Sun Tzu

Shepherd had infiltrated the Enforcers… but it would have had to have been very recently. Otherwise she would have been collected that very first night.

Claire's bare feet stopped their limping shuffle, and she stood there, worrying her lip. The grate of the deadbolt drew her attention. The door swung in and Jules, bearing a tray, entered.

The blue-eyed Beta did not seem interested in acknowledging her presence, so she spoke instead. "Hello, Jules."

The trays were swapped and he grunted, "You did well outside the Undercroft."

Surprised he was engaging, even if he was not looking at her, she grumbled, "Not well enough if I'm back here."

The male did not respond, simply walked towards the door.

From her lips came a name synonymous with Satan in her mind. "Svana. That woman will ruin you all… You know that."

The man halted and turned his head enough so that she might see his profile. "It would be wise for you to choose your topics of conversation with greater restraint."

Claire scoffed and looked at the suddenly still Beta. "You follow a madwoman."

"I follow Shepherd."

Claire actually smiled, a little wicked, and laughed at the man. "And he loves her. Your point is invalid."

"The future is what matters, and your ignorant opinion matters little."

"A fact of which I am well aware."

At the door, he spoke over his shoulder. "Do not measure your worth by one minor success, Miss O'Donnell."

"I agree. I measure it by my countless failures instead."

"You fight for what you believe in, yet when you grew fragile, your answer was to seek out a meaningless death. Mine is to spend what years I have left working for a greater purpose. I will see the world altered, improved. You and I are not that different. I simply chose to be stronger and was willing to pay the price to enact change."

She had no idea where the words were coming from or why they seemed so important. "Your logic is corrupted. I chose to die before I became like you. That makes me stronger than you are."

The man faced her one last time, those striking eyes unsettling. "It does not make you stronger. It makes you a coward."

Claire felt as if he had struck her, the storm in her words unleashing nothing more than a pointless whispering breeze… because there was an undeniable fragment of truth in his words.

There was nothing else to be said between them, the man dismissing her as if she were nothing. The door closed with a thud. She must have stood there for ages, staring at the metal, half numb. Eventually, she moved towards the food, chewed and swallowed with no idea of what she ate, nor did she notice that she did not get sick.

Thinking of that stupid book, *The Art of War*, of Sun Tzu and all he seemed to have accomplished, Claire remembered: *Thus the expert in battle moves the enemy, and is not moved by him.*

Jules had just done that to her.

So, how does one move a mountain? Her words were nothing to Shepherd, arguments ended in sex, but her actions had affected him more than once. On occasion she must have caused distraction in his pursuit. The monster even said he loved her, in his own twisted fashion. That gave her influence of a sort, now she just needed to learn how to wield it.

Her green eyes went to the watercolor of poppies still resting against the wall—a mindless project that had once made her cell a little more bearable. The unwelcome cord in her chest pulsed. She needed a reaction, something small, a place to begin.

Absently, she prepared her paints, her mind full of one image, one hard truth. There was no need for much color, the world was nothing but shades of grey under a bruised sky.

9

While still deep in her work, the door's hinges whined. Claire ignored the giant's entrance and approach, even his large hand once it rested on the table alongside her painting.

The beast leaned down with a low, displeased growl. "Throw it away."

Claire was focused on finishing the last details, the little flicks of her brush exaggerating the cracks in the Dome. "Why would I throw it away?"

She had painted her final morning of freedom; the moment denied her out on the ice.

It was stark and horrific in its implication.

His lips were at her ear, his breath fluttering her hair. "Have you done this to upset me, little one?"

The brush tip was dipped again until drenched in black paint. "No."

She felt his hand gather up her hair so he might pull her head back from where it hung over her project. Shepherd was not hurting her, or yanking, he simply unfolded the Omega, forcing her to meet his narrowed gaze.

He was stern as he searched her expression. "You will paint something else."

Claire set the brush on the table and furrowed her brow. "I like this one."

"*I* dislike what it suggests." He released her hair to take the offensive piece of paper, staring with rancor where Claire had painted her last moments of freedom… only to have changed the story to show the ice cracked open in a gaping hole—alluding that she had fallen through to her death.

"Fine," Claire challenged him, "I'll paint you instead."

Crushing the wet paper in his hands, Shepherd snorted. Once the painting had been thoroughly balled up and ruined, he threw it in the bin, found she still was willingly meeting his gaze, and slowly took the seat across from his mate.

He'd yet to strip off his coat or armor, looking just as he'd looked when Claire had first seen him in the Citadel—namely, intimidating and angry.

The hazy dreamlike high of estrous had made her find him attractive. Seeing Shepherd now, seeing him through her anger, disgust, and the effect of their re-established bond… it was different on every level. Already reaching for a fresh piece of paper, looking objectively at the subject of her nightmares, Claire's eyes darted over the Da'rin marks creeping up his neck and a lifetime of collected scars.

The silver of his eyes never wavered as he watched her

take him in, though they grew a little hard when she squinted and leaned closer. Then her attention went to the paper and, like magic, the lines of his face began to appear.

Every few seconds, inquisitive eyes would glance back at the motionless Alpha, run over whatever part of the outline she needed to adjust, and then go back to the paper. Quickly, the line of his jaw, his closely shorn hair, were captured in shades of black. Concentrating on her work, Claire began to create his mouth, with the scar she had once called beautiful slashed across it. Had they not been marred, Claire would even admit Shepherd's lips would have been considered handsome—their fullness almost pretty. His nose, now that she looked far more closely, was not straight; there were places, small deviations, where it had been broken and reset more than once.

Tiny scars were in his stubble, all over his hairline and forehead.

Picture nearing completion, only one key feature neglected, Claire took a deep breath and made herself look into Shepherd's eyes. The silver was so familiar to her, she could have painted them a thousand times without looking, but every study would have been eyes focused on intimidation, on drawing out fear. At that moment his eyes were almost complacent, the animal aggression, the focus of a predator, contained.

As he was, it seemed to take ages to translate such an expression onto the paper. She tried, but her interpretation was never quite right.

How could anyone capture eyes like that?

"You are growing agitated," Shepherd commented, displeased when she began to glare down at the painting.

Again she tried to capture his expression. "I can't get the eyes right."

Slowly, his hand reached out and took the paintbrush from her stained fingers. The portrait was turned, Shepherd asking, "Is this how you see me?"

It seemed a strange question. Of course that was how she saw him, that was why she'd painted him that way. "I am better at painting landscapes."

His voice was odd. "You made me different."

"The eyes are wrong." Gathering up her supplies, she stood and rounded the table so she might clean her brushes. A large hand stopped her progress, pulling her closer. The paints were taken and set back on the table, his arm snaking around her middle.

Shepherd just looked up at her, regarded the dark-haired woman who'd painted him.

Holding her messy hands away so as not to smear his coat, she stood awkwardly, unsure why he was looking at her with such an expression. She had done nothing to soften him in the picture; every mar, every scar, every part of him was on that paper.

Shepherd pulled her to his lap.

Watching him as one watches a snake, Claire sat stiffly. He began to touch her face, to thread his fingers in her hair, and then those lips, the full lips she had translated perfectly, came to hers.

He was insistent even in a languorous slow kiss, even

when she complained against his mouth, "I'm going to get paint on you."

Smiling into his answer, brushing his lips over hers he whispered, "Then get paint on me."

A warm tongue slipped in her mouth, Shepherd held her tightly… but she did not kiss him back.

His lips traced her jaw, tasted her neck, nibbled at her ear while her eyes were on the portrait on the table.

"Kiss me, little one," he murmured against her skin, smirking as he purred.

"No."

The monster softly laughed and retook her mouth with passion, bowing her body until the table met her back. The paints were under her, their color seeping into her dress. Shepherd didn't care; all he wanted was his mouth on her body.

Fabric tore under his hands, her dress split down the middle.

"The paints," Claire gasped, worried they were being ruined, trying to wriggle off her things.

"Are nothing compared to this." The man fumbled with his zipper, groaning as he nosed her breast.

Lips were at her nipple, his tongue flicking the bud before he moved lower and pressed his mouth to her mound. He attacked her there, tasting a place he had not enjoyed since he'd collected her from the Omegas. Claire tried to push him off, squealed as her legs kicked, but Shepherd held firm.

Leaning up on her elbows, Claire's jaw dropped, her hips jerking to escape something so intimate. He watched her every expression, all the while thrashing his tongue in her pussy and releasing his cock from his pants.

When her legs began to twitch, her breaths nothing but stifled gasps of air, he drank her up, seeming to know just where to move that tongue until Claire's face grew pained and she began to come. A shriek, short and stuttering, passed her lips as the tight winding coil the man had fostered snapped apart. In answer, Shepherd grunted into her, wove his tongue deep, stroking himself madly under the table.

Her groans grew rabid, his fist tightly gripping his burgeoning knot until seed splattered the floor. Air ripe with the smell of semen, he rode the high, tenderly kissing Claire's inner thighs and mumbling that she tasted delicious.

Falling back against the table, Claire stared blankly at the memorized grey ceiling, trying to ignore that her thighs were on his shoulders, that he was licking her clean, and that he had, once again, expertly commanded her body's response… as Svana had claimed the two of them had done to other Omegas.

That thought brought blistering heat to her chest, the painful knowledge inspiring instant anguish.

"What is wrong, little one?" Shepherd pulled his tongue from her slit. "I did not mount you. That should not have caused you pain."

Claire answered robotically. "It didn't hurt."

More soft kisses to her inner thigh and a strong purr preceded the promise, "I will replace your paints. You need not feel distressed."

To win the war, she would have to wage a battle. Closing

her eyes tight, she told herself that she could do this. "It's not the paints. I was thinking of the Omegas."

"They are safe, as per our agreement. My men watch over them from a distance." Again he tasted her center, enjoying how she bowed from even a simple kiss over her pert nub.

Gasping, Claire answered, "Not those Omegas. The ones you shared with Svana."

The man froze, hesitating before he spoke. "Why would you think of them?"

Claire forced her eyes open, lifted her head, and found Shepherd watching her very carefully. "I wonder if they were frightened or ashamed."

Each word was growled. "They were all willing."

"Somehow I think you misunderstand the meaning of that word. Estrous bends the mind." She knew that better than anyone. "Did you speak to them before or after?"

"No."

Then they were probably dead. "That makes me sad."

Large hands accompanied an almost unsteady purr, Shepherd stroking her from her knee to hip. "Do not be sad, little one."

Claire lay back, eyes once again on the ceiling. "I do not remember how to be happy."

LESLIE WAS ON HIS COUCH, working on a COMscreen when Corday returned.

Her mouth was set and she was clearly displeased. “Another rendezvous with your Claire?”

“No.” Corday stripped his coat, his back to the Alpha female.

“Yet you smell of her.” Leslie scooted a little closer, her tone instantly light. “How is the Omega faring?”

Tired eyes, his face lined in disappointment, Corday could not muster any enthusiasm for Leslie. “Claire has—”

A knock sounded at the door, not Claire’s timid scratches but an arrogant bang. Gun already in hand, Corday motioned for Leslie to move out of sight.

“I hear you breathing on the other side of that thing, Enforcer.” The tiny view through the peephole showed an unwelcome woman. “Open up or I will simply turn the knob of the door I’ve already unlocked.” Maryanne smirked. “I am trying to be civil.”

Corday turned the knob, finding it was indeed unlocked, and opened the door far enough to point his gun at Maryanne’s face.

Maryanne sniffed and waved her hand at his petty threat. “I saw you skulking around the Omega’s trash heap. Low and behold, it *was* Enforcer stink she was wearing when she came to me. Now that I smell her on you, I see that I was right, as usual. Let me in, I want to talk to Claire.”

Teeth clenched, Corday hissed, “She isn’t here.”

“Bullshit,” the woman spat, looking over Corday’s shoulder to peer into the apartment.

“You have three seconds to tell me who you are before I shoot you.”

"Oh, shut up." The blonde pushed past him. "I'm here to see my friend."

"Claire O'Donnell is not your friend." But he felt a spark of hope that maybe they were… because he could smell traces of the Omega on the strange woman's clothing.

He closed the door and watched the woman look around, frowning when she saw no sign of Claire.

Maryanne dumped the bundle in her hands on the floor. "She left these clothes at my place. Feel free to thank me for returning your crap to you." Moving deeper into the apartment, her chocolate brown eyes looked straight at the pretty Alpha standing in the corner watching her like a hawk. "And what do we have here?"

Running a hand through his hair, Corday said, "That's my girlfriend, Monica."

"Nice try, Enforcer." Maryanne rolled her eyes. "But anyone paying attention knows Leslie Kantor's heart is pining for Premier Callas." Smirking meanly, the blonde looked at the woman and teased, "I slept with him twice to get out of jail time. He was awful… You dodged a bullet when he shot down your marriage proposal."

Leslie's expression grew dark. "Who are you?"

Turning her attention back to Corday and ignoring the spoiled niece of Senator Kantor, Maryanne growled, "I smelled you in her apartment, I smelled you on her clothes, this room is saturated in her, but she is not here or with her pack… so where is Claire?"

Corday showed his teeth. "What do you know of the Omegas?"

"Who do you think chose the location of their cozy new home? Claire?" Maryanne rolled her eyes when the man glowered. "Goddess save us, you really did think she broke them out all by herself…"

Aggressive Alpha females and dominant Beta males did not mix well, leaving the air full of tension and mistrust.

Maryanne had not come all that way to be disappointed. "I want to talk to her crazy ass. One last time, *Enforcer Corday*—that's right, I know who you are—where is Claire?"

Lip curled, shoulders tense, Corday hissed, "Claire is missing, okay? I don't know where she is!"

For a moment Maryanne looked worried, studied him as if there was more to the man's outburst. "I don't think you are lying." That left the most likely outcome. "Then she is probably dead… or Shepherd has her again."

And that was exactly why Corday felt such desolation. "I don't think Shepherd has her." If Shepherd had her, then the tyrant would know of his own location, the Omegas would be gone, and Leslie's access to their communications would have been terminated.

"You make a good point"—Maryanne covered her doubt with a cocky smirk—"because if he did, you and I would both be strung up from the Citadel… Unless, of course, we and her little pack of Omegas were offered in trade for compliant behavior. The little twit is stupid enough to fall for that, you know."

"She wouldn't go back to him." There was no way. Every feeling inside Corday knew better. He'd seen what the monster had done to her… what she had been forced to live through. Touching where her ring circled his pinky he walked back to the door, opening it so his *guest* might take a hint.

Before she left, Maryanne faced Corday one last time. “I know her better than anyone else in the world. I also know she wanted to kill herself… That’s why I am going to pray that she did instead of considering the horrible alternative. Thank you for *nothing*, Enforcer Corday.”

He slammed the door.

Corday turned towards Leslie, found the outspoken woman awfully quiet.

The strange woman’s warning scratched at his composure. “If Claire is in Shepherd’s possession, if she struck some reckless exchange for our lives, then he knows about you. If all this is true, then every piece of information you’ve uncovered is compromised… useless.”

Leslie looked about ready to break something.

10

Claire was still sleeping, restless under the covers on the bed beside him. It had taken a great deal of effort to get her comfortable after Shepherd had found her holed up in the bathroom vomiting upon his return. Hours of soft touches, bland broth, and her agitated growls eventually turned to snores. Once Claire had finally lost consciousness the thread seemed to harmonize, leaving Shepherd able to work as he lay at her side.

Reports on Enforcer Corday's movements were less than pleasing. Svana was still holed up in his apartment, and irksome Maryanne Cauley had come calling, looking for Claire.

Neither woman's agenda was clear. Svana was toying with the resistance, for what purpose Shepherd was uncertain, but she was up to something.

In the years of their relationship, there had been no

secrets, no dividing line between them. Ordering Jules to continue with her constant surveillance had been… difficult. Studying her motives as he'd studied the Senators, their families, their work, for years, troubled Shepherd greatly.

This woman was not that same revolutionary he'd loved with every last fiber of his being. Worse, not knowing where she'd stashed the contagion, having had all the usual places searched, made him uneasy.

She wanted to remind Shepherd that she had the power. Knowing he was watching her flit around the Beta's apartment was her less than subtle way of reminding him she was in control.

She played her games with the resistance. Leslie Kantor wanted them to find her valuable, even passing fragmented information that could potentially undermine Shepherd's control.

Svana was taunting him.

Why?

There was more to this than her anger over Claire.

So far just Maryanne Cauley had thrown the only wrench into her plans.

…when he shot down your marriage proposal.

How did a woman like Maryanne possess information even Shepherd had never heard whispers of? Why did Svana just about reach out and break the blonde's neck?

Most importantly, why hadn't Svana noticed the immediate look of suspicion the Beta Enforcer had shot her way once those words were out in the open?

Challenging was not the right word to describe the feelings embedded in the problem. Deeply, Shepherd wanted to trust Svana as he always had. But the little black-haired Omega curled up at his side… one look at her, and Shepherd was at a loss.

Never would he trust Svana anywhere near Claire. That fact gave him pain.

And that, at its essence, was why Svana remained with the Enforcer. She knew Shepherd's abiding loyalty had been shaken, and she taunted him by fostering a new champion, lightly touching the Beta at every turn, keeping herself beautiful and engaging.

Was she trying to seduce Corday, to flaunt her conquest?

Never before in his life had Shepherd struggled with so many questions. Answers had always been obvious, his course steadfast.

Now he knew he had to greatly alter the plan. He had to find the contagion and make sure it was beyond Svana's control. Stripped of her greatest advantage, he could reason with his beloved, maybe find her an Omega male so she, too, could be enlightened.

Their partnership, their rich history, need not be tarnished by his natural devotion to such a pleasing mate.

Reassured, Shepherd read the latest update again. There was something in the transcript that was intriguing. Just as Claire had explained, the once disposable minion, Maryanne Cauley, *was* fond of his mate.

In Shepherd's experience, Maryanne Cauley was very easy to control, a creature inundated in self-preservation. Shepherd could use her again, augment Jules' initial plan to win more than just Claire's complacence. She could be a valuable tool, and the selfish Alpha female would even be willing for the right price.

As Shepherd's plot developed, Claire grew restless in her dreams. Absently, Shepherd began purring, lightly tracing the furrow between the Omega's brows until it softened.

Before all could be made right, there was a list of issues that had to be remedied. The Omega was not showing any of signs of the affection she had displayed before their recent… complication. In her waking hours, there were no activities of nesting, not like before. Normal habits of a pregnant Omega must be encouraged, but she no longer touched her belly like she should—never acknowledged the child he'd placed in her womb, even though it was the cause of her almost constant nausea. Only in her sleep would her hand rest above the baby, and even then she looked… troubled.

Claire also was incredibly disinterested in being touched, yet if he initiated, highly responsive to sex.

They were at square one.

Shepherd kept her in a constant state of the mating high, took her so many times her eyes remained half-dilated, almost as if in the first stages of estrous. It was necessary to keep her mending, to keep the bond fresh and unchallenged, and it soothed her. But she no longer whispered or called out his name, seemed half involved but eager for pleasure.

Pure escapism…

When the sleeping woman quieted, Shepherd went back to the latest reports. With only eight weeks before transport would carry those who'd chosen loyalty to his cause to seize

Greth Dome, his new life was soon to begin. Svana's lineage and title would place her as the savior queen of what all intel confirmed was a highly repressed population. Transition would be relatively seamless. Of course, there would be turmoil and battles in those first weeks as the usurper regime was decimated, but Shepherd had a worthy supply of Followers to raise his standard, and the Greth government had no indication a nightmare would soon be crashing down upon them.

Best of all, as Shepherd thrived, as he gave Claire the things that would bring her happiness, nothing but corpses and rot would be left in a place he hated with all his heart.

Everyone left in Thólos would succumb to plague.

Toying with a strand of Claire's hair, Shepherd grinned—vindicated, in perfect alignment with the universe, until he heard her call out.

It had been only a little noise in the dark, a voice laced with fear… a call for him to help her.

Mechanically he moved, swift to gather her close. "I am here, little one."

Shepherd could see she was not quite awake when, instead of tensing up at his touch, she gripped the fabric of his shirt and pulled him closer, urging him to surround her in his heat and strength.

Swallowing, trying to catch her breath, Claire tried not to think of the sound of screaming convicts and lingering echoed flashes of men lining up to hurt her in her dream. It had been another horrible nightmare of the Undercroft Shepherd had described from his childhood; a prison that gave birth to monsters, inhabited by demons even Maryanne had once warned still lurked down below.

Brushing the hair from her face, Shepherd encouraged her to calm. “You are allowing your brooding to affect your dreams.”

Claire released her grip on the nightmare-inducing monster at once. “I’m fine.”

“You would not call out for your mate if something had not frightened you.”

Shepherd rolled them, holding her to his chest so Claire might rest atop him as she had slept before the complications of the last few weeks. In that position his vibrations would pass far more noticeably into her, and the hatred in her eyes would go back to the faraway stare of complacence.

“What time is it?”

Shepherd did not let her budge, but answered the question. “A little after 16:00.”

God, she was so tired even after all that sleep. Too tired to protest the thick arms that came to embrace and stroke, feeling guilt she was experiencing comfort from such a thing, she complained, “I hate the hours down here… everything is backwards.”

“If you had slept during the evening instead of fighting the rest you require, then you would have settled into regular rhythms.”

Claire gave an annoyed groan at his pointless lecture. It was his fault she could not sleep, his fault her mind was *unstable*, his fault she’d had the nightmare, his fault she could feel again and that everything felt horrible. Unsure if she spoke simply to annoy him, or to test him, or because it was what she actually needed, Claire muttered against the fabric of his shirt, "I want to go outside."

The purring stopped.

A moment of time hung between them, the air tangible with mutual dissatisfaction. Trilling her fingers on his chest, she made it clear she was waiting for an answer and that there was only one right one.

Everything about his reply was displeased and growled with great annoyance. "You will eat and bathe first. After we have mated… I will escort you to see your sky."

How fucking romantic.

In the mood to continue being difficult, Claire said, "I want to eat fried potatoes with mayonnaise."

He threaded his fingers in her hair. "No."

"And a chocolate shake."

"No." Shepherd stroked her spine in an attempt to urge her to fall back asleep and forget her expectation of the sky.

"Raspberries, lots of raspberries."

"That you may have."

Aware he was trying to make her melt until she forgot her request, and conscious Shepherd was about to achieve his goal, Claire began to wriggle away, stretching like a cat and cracking her spine. He made her work for her escape. Even with his arm just lying across her, the damn thing weighed a ton, and he seemed far more interested in groping her ass than letting her up. In the end, she bit him and slipped out of reach.

Shepherd found it funny.

She moved into the bathroom, ignoring the light laughter coming from the giant splayed on the bed. A long shower that was blissfully alone helped to clear away the remnants of her nightmare. It was not the first time she'd dreamed she was locked in a cell, her upper body pressed to a stinking cot while a devil rutted her painfully. Beyond the bars, masses of Alphas watched and waited. Their faces contorted, they snarled and snapped, reaching through the metal bars, stretching inhumanly until they could almost touch her.

Claire did not want to think of the Undercroft, of the things that were locked in it, but the feelings of the dream seemed to linger like a stain even a scalding shower could not wash off.

She turned off the water, combed her hair before the foggy glass, and felt the woman in the blurred reflection was a ghost.

Shutting off the light, she went back into the main room of her cage and found Shepherd had created daytime by switching on every light. Once she was clothed, he left to retrieve her food. Her paints had been cleaned up days ago, his ejaculate from the floor as well, but the portrait remained on the table. She was not exactly sure why he had left it there, and she had tried to ignore it as she ignored him, but it seemed the incorrect eyes were always watching her.

Studying the thing, the rugged face of the man who hurt so many people, she could not find what about the painting had seemed to please him. Of course, she may have completely misread his reaction—the Alpha was layered in half-truths, and had no qualms about deceit if it meant he would attain his goal. But something in the cord, something on his end, had been so very satisfied at what she'd done.

Claire had wanted a reaction, she had got one. Now she had no idea what it meant or how to use it.

Absorbed in the flawed eyes, she listed the mistakes in her rendition. They were not hard enough; the silver did not hold back a tidal wave of twisted history. Shepherd just looked like a man. And how would she look if someone were to paint her? Would it be the ghostly blurred image from the mirror, or somebody completely different? Had her eyes become infected with the same thing that lingered in his?

How much time would it take for her to wake up and no longer care about the forty-three lives he held over her head, or the millions in Thólos she had to find a way to fight for? Why had she not just stomped her foot against the ice and cracked it so powerfully that they both were sucked under?

Her slender hold on composure began to slip just as the bolt on the door hissed its metallic warning. Shepherd had returned. Quickly scrubbing her face of tears, Claire sat straight and prepared for the next round.

The man came in with a tray and set it down before her, noticing the redness around the eyes of the woman sitting ramrod straight.

When she saw what he had brought her, Claire began to sniff. She reached for a steaming fried potato wedge, dipped it in mayo, then dunked it again in the chocolate shake. Shoving it in her mouth, tears began to fall, her acknowledgment pathetic. "They're really good."

"There are no raspberries on premises. They will be

acquired shortly," Shepherd explained, assuming she was, at last, having some sort of pregnancy moment.

Sniveling, Claire dumped the chocolate shake over the hot fries, smearing into the mess. She gorged, sniffing and frowning, devouring what to Shepherd looked absolutely disgusting as if it were manna from the heavens. By the time she had finished what had to be the unhealthiest thing on the planet, her brief blubbering was over and she felt much better.

Wiping her mouth, Claire looked to the man who'd observed her meal. It was obvious Shepherd wanted her to thank him—he had done something *nice* for her, something apparent and obvious that she had requested specifically. All those other months, she had defiantly used none of his things outside of mere necessity, never made requests aside from demands of freedom… simply to make the point that she was refusing his *hospitality*. But this meal she had blatantly stated she desired, and he had delivered it, though it was clearly something he had not thought was best for her. In his strange language it was almost as if, again, he was affirming there was a new precedent and that he was making an effort.

Looking down at the remaining melted mess on her plate, Claire took a deep breath and breathed it out. "Thank you."

The tray was scooted aside before a large hand came to her face and turned it up. His thumb rubbed away a missed smear of chocolate, Shepherd very pleased. "You are welcome."

She did not want to look into those impossible eyes, but he held her in thrall. Claire was lost as she measured how many deaths stuck to him, how many appalling things he'd done of which she hoped never to learn. Why did he have to have a tragic history that haunted her sleep, and how had he become so distorted he'd developed into the harbinger of Thólos' apocalypse?

Why was she even thinking of all that shit?

Shepherd gave her time, taking in her confused expression as she confessed, "I dreamed of your Undercroft, and I was trapped with the prisoners reaching for me through the bars… while I was being raped like you said."

Elbow resting on the table, he cupped her cheek and purred, "It was only a dream. You are safe here and will never endure the Undercroft."

She sniffed, lost in the quicksilver changefulness of those damn eyes. "What's it like?"

Unsure exactly how much he should disclose, Shepherd said, "Dark, cold. The prisoners eat the mold on the walls. There is no sewage system. In the tunnels it is easy to get lost… many go missing. As a child, an inmate told me those tunnels span the entire continent of Antarctica. They go on for ages; you walk and walk, and never find a way out. But you do find the bones of others who've gone mad searching the paths only to die from lack of water or starvation."

"I dislike that I feel pity," Claire breathed, eyes full of sorrow, "for you."

The way he watched her, the slow move of his analyzing gaze, it was if he already knew everything she confessed. "Little one, it is merely an indication of your nature to feel compassion—even for me."

Her brows lowered, that little line forming between them. "Is this where you call me a coward or a fool?"

Shepherd smirked. "You are somewhat foolish, but you are not a coward—simply naïve. What you are is innocent."

But that was not true. Disappointed in his answer, she rose from her chair, hands tugging the straps of her dress so the fabric could whisper down her body. Eager to finish the final requirement to leave the room, she moved, naked and expressionless, to stand before the Alpha.

He took in the secret places of her body, but did not touch.

Voice harsh, Claire felt the guilt, the anger, the fear eat her up. "What do you see now?"

Slowly, Shepherd met her indignant expression, softly purring, "My mate."

The thrum was deep in her chest, something it took a great deal of focus to recall was unwelcome. Confused, she watched him, unsure why he wasn't touching her. Unsure why they were not already on the bed, or table, or floor?

The moment was growing into something it was not meant to be.

Just as she was about to turn, to just walk away from him, the growl was made. It was loud, expectant, and brought with it a small pleasurable cramp as her body instinctively responded.

Slick came thick and copious at such a call, dripping down her leg. Shepherd watched the little trickle, captivated.

Rising slowly, he pulled his clothing over his head, stripping down to only flesh until he stood before her in an equal state. He was beautiful and grand, all the glorious epitome of Alpha physique in the control of a man who used such strength ruthlessly. Claire had to crane her neck to look up, to keep her eyes off his marked body where she could focus on his face and those hated eyes.

"What do you see when you look at me, little one?"

A monster, the man who had ruined her life, the little boy raised in hell whose mother had performed unspeakable acts just to secure him a knife, a former prisoner who had dedicated his love to Svana, a man with twisted faith, the male who had betrayed their pair-bond and caused her great pain, her jailor, the father of the life growing inside her, a creature she could not trust… Claire drew a deep breath and said the only thing she could. "I see the Alpha pair-bonded to me."

"Can you not see more?" Shepherd hinted, trying to draw out the proper words.

Her reply twisted in the thread and tore out her heart, but Claire stood still, her face a mask, and spoke the hated truth, "I see my mate."

"You are doing exceptionally well today," the Alpha claimed, but still he did not move.

And Claire understood. Shepherd wanted her to initiate sex, he was pushing her boundaries, seeing how much she was willing to exchange for what she wanted.

She let out in a low whisper. "I can't."

"You can." Shepherd was confident, nodding for her to try.

Already half-high, drugged in scent and the call, Claire knew in truth she wanted it. She wanted him to fuck her so hard that she forgot herself, that *Claire* disappeared. It had been her only respite since their deal had been struck, her only succor the distraction of sex. In a sick way she almost longed for a heat cycle, a mindless source of existence that shut off her thinking until all that mattered was physical gratification. But she could not allow herself such a thing if Shepherd didn't force it or take it. It would make the act of mating something she could not bear.

Clenching her fists, she glanced to the side and shook her head belligerently. "I. Can't."

Another of those powerful growls, so loud it was almost a roar, and her pussy clenched, more of that damn slick spilling down her leg.

Shepherd persisted. "You can."

She knew how very easy it could be, how falsely fulfilling his arms would feel—the decadence of fornicating with such a creature, to hear his whispered words at her ear… the culmination of the moment when her world burst apart and everything bad was forgotten. Had she not felt it a hundred times? But Shepherd had to inflict it, if she took that fateful step and admitted that she desired such a thing, it would ruin her.

Crumbling, she closed her eyes and rested her forehead on his chest, doing nothing more than pulling in deep breaths of what nature told her was hers, but what experience had taught her was far from the case. Lightly, her fingertips came to his torso, running upward, delicately tracing over his nipples in their journey to reach around his neck.

Claire froze. She could not sell herself for the sky or oblivion.

"What more do you want from me, Shepherd?" Frustrated, desperate, she whined, "Just fuck me already!"

She felt him bend to reach her ear, knew the press of scarred lips. "I want everything."

The massive male tugged her towards the bed. Claire was spun about and pressed down on her belly, her legs left dangling towards the floor. A hand raked almost too hard down her spine, the pulsing head of his cock positioned at her folds. He did not press in. Instead, Shepherd slapped her; his palm met the full roundness of her ass and left it red and stinging as she cried out in surprise. His hips surged, and in the midst of her yelp he speared her with the entirety of his girth.

"You are so fucking wet, yet still dare to pretend that you don't want this? That you need to be forced?" he roared, gripping her hips even as she presented, arching her back in instinctual invitation. Roughly, he pulled her back to meet each thrust, Claire mewling into the covers, falling into the drugged delirium where she could fade away and forget.

The second her mind grew free of petty feeling and thought, Shepherd took his cock away, flipping her over.

Blazing silver eyes met hers. "Do you want me to continue to fuck you?"

Her eyes glued to the shining, throbbing thickness that he should be burying inside her again and again and again, she snarled, "Yes!"

The man stood there, panting, eyes blazing, with her slick all over his groin… and simply did nothing.

Claire pounded her fist against the mattress and looked up with furious, half-dilated eyes. There was a snarl, her own version of the growl, and she launched herself at him to take back the only thing she had left to ease the pain. The sound of her demand inspired the man manipulating the situation to his liking. Shepherd took her in his arms, plunging his cock slow and deep where she ached, and watched Claire's silent pleas for more.

Kept just at the border of the insensibility she craved, like he knew her game, Shepherd moved with decided cunning in the dissection of her avoidance of what they were and why he mated her—forcing Claire to recognize who offered her carnal satisfaction, what he felt like against her, and how much she loved it.

Without the frenzy, there was no void, there was no loss of self. Claire knew in her bones that he was knowingly denying her the only escape she had left by making love when she only wanted to fuck.

Shepherd smiled like a man standing in the bliss of heaven, whispered to her so she had to recognize his voice, and controlled every thrust no matter how she squirmed or rocked her hips. There was no escaping him or the pleasure.

Her mind grasped the irony with each tender stroke that the one thing she'd fought to preserve when Shepherd first took her had been her sense of self… until he broke her. Now all she wanted, now that her world was so dark, was to forget that identity and waste away.

"Faster," she breathed on a lengthy moan.

There was such pleasure in his voice, Shepherd gently rocking his hips to fill her cunt in slow measure. "No, little one."

It went on for hours, until she was shuddering and cooing small sounds of pleasure. This was how it had been in those first weeks, but the underlying distress was different. She was no longer afraid of what he could do to her; she was far more afraid of her mutilated sense of self and what she very much wanted from him.

A warm hand stroked from hip to breast, over and over, leaving a trail of soft tingles and ending with a little squeeze of her tight nipple until she whimpered for more and spread wider in invitation.

"Open your eyes."

How many times had he already commanded her to do so? Why did he have to make her look? Complying, her green eyes met beautiful silver. She saw her palm cradle his cheek, she saw him kiss the tip of her thumb.

A catch of breath and a long shuddering sigh came from the Omega. "I can't… I need…"

The purr built from deep within Shepherd's chest, the Alpha observing each minute reaction of pleasure on her face. "Soften, little one. Let it happen this way. There is no more need to fight what we are."

He wove his fingers into hers, his sweat-slicked muscles moving over her entire body. Each time he had her stuffed full, he'd grind his groin in a tight circle to tease at her clit, drawing sounds from the Omega that made his balls tighten.

Shepherd's name came to her lips when she felt that first fluttering of the hour's long building climax, a name she never wanted to call out in passion again.

There was not even a hint of a veiling fog in her mind when she felt tears leak from her eyes and her cunt squeezed like a fist around his swelling knot. Claire orgasmed completely, powerfully aware of Shepherd, her insides vigorously milking his cock, drawing out every last drop of his come as the man groaned in his own ecstasy.

Boneless, vibrating from the humming thread, Claire didn't know what to do. The feeling of his cheek slipped past her palm, the Omega wilting against the mattress.

"That was perfect." He kissed her slack lips, nuzzled her cheek. "You, Claire, are superior to any sky."

Her contentment shattered. With a growl guttural and vicious, Claire threatened the man still deeply knotted. "Do not *ever* call me that name!"

11

The knot was fresh, the male's cock still filling her with a steady trickle of semen, his fingers still warmly enfolded with hers. Yet whatever tenderness the Omega had displayed as he led her down the path to orgasm had evaporated. Her small body was stiff, Claire's hips moving just enough to communicate her desire to reject his knot, even if trapped by it.

If Shepherd was angry, he hid it well. Looking at her with deceptive calm he spoke her name again. "Claire."

Her building rage blended with disgust, yet she mirrored his move on the board. In a tone so calm it was chilling, she explained, "Every time I hear you speak that name, I feel your Alpha *beloved's* hand crushing my throat. I feel her fingers scratching my insides. I see you, a monster who has the audacity to call himself my mate, stand by and watch. I hear you order me into the bathroom saying *Claire*… a name you refused to acknowledge up until that enlightening moment."

Shepherd had to make use of this opportunity; he had to reason with her. "I did not witness her touching you sexually and only learned of it later. It will *never* happen again."

Incredulous, Claire's eyes went wide at his nerve. "And that makes it okay?"

The man tried again. "I am aware you harbor great anger towards me, hatred even, for what was done."

"I do hate you. I hate her. But most of all I hate myself."

Rocking his hips, pressing the knot deeper, he insisted, "Tell me the reason you hate yourself."

She held his eyes, hers violently raging. "We both know why."

But it needed to be said aloud. "Claire, your self-hatred stems from the fact that you recognized you had affection for me before circumstances caused you pain."

"Circumstances?" Claire laughed meanly, not at all impressed. "She has a name. It's Svana. What you did to me has a name. It's called betrayal."

Odd remorse burning in his consternation, Shepherd pressed his forehead to hers. "You have my fidelity now. I gave you my word. We could be content in one another if you would forget, and try again."

Claire saturated her reply with every ounce of disgust she could muster. "You are a very smart man with the skill to inspire others to follow you into evil, Shepherd, but your understanding of people is so primordial. You claim to love me, so answer this: had I fucked Corday while you were watching me in the warehouse, would it be something you would ever forget?"

The man's entire body went rigid. "No."

"So you see, it is impossible."

His eyes were full of a hundred things. "You will forgive me."

Her black brow arched. "Forgive what you can only call the *circumstances* that caused me pain?"

He knew what she wanted. Growling like a beast, Shepherd gave it. "I mated with Svana and dishonored you."

"You did."

"I did it to save your life."

Claire arched beneath him, wanting to get away. "You are lying."

His hands squeezed her fingers so hard it hurt. "I did it because I could not harm her. She is my only family… Because I was concerned she would take you from me. I gave her the attention she came for to distract her, so you would not be considered a threat." Almost frantically he admitted, "The whole time, I was thinking of you."

"That is disgusting."

Shepherd did not know how to answer such a thing, so he chose silence. While the knot persisted, he held her unwilling hands, he purred and nuzzled, but Claire had lost all traces of softness… In fact, she only looked sad.

When at last his knot diminished enough for him to pull out, he did. "Get dressed." Shepherd stood with grace a man of his size did not deserve. "I will take you to see your sky now."

Claire had lost interest in going outside. She wanted nothing but sleep. "You don't need to waste the effort. I no longer want to see it."

Shepherd gripped her arm and pulled her to stand when she began to roll over. "You will put on a dress at once."

After cleaning up the expected river of semen that came from her womb, Claire grabbed her dress from the floor and pulled it over her head. The giant clothed himself and returned to her, holding out a blanket, waiting for her so that he could wrap her shoulders with it in place of a coat. There were still no shoes.

"Give me your hand," he grunted.

Claire complied and his massive paw closed over her small wrist, leaving cold metal and a grating sound of cuffs being fitted. The opposite end he fixed to his own wrist, Shepherd warning, "You will behave."

"I don't take forty-three lives lightly."

He lifted her into his arms. "Your recent effort has not gone unnoticed."

Once she was settled against his chest, they left the room.

Shepherd took her down an alternate path that ended at a service elevator stinking of his men. The door closed, the contraption jerked, and the long ride began.

He was taking her to the upper levels, a region she had only ever visited once a year as a girl. Or at least that's what she thought. When the door opened, a decadently decorated hall appeared. The walls were well-appointed, clean, and filled with soft crystal lights. There were no windows, and when Shepherd began to approach a sinister looking door, Claire began to think the male had tricked her.

He was going to punish her again.

He tapped a code into the door's console, the hiss of decompression letting them know it had unlocked. Shouldering it open, Shepherd took her inside. The vault closed, bolted, its click exceedingly final.

He set her down. Claire's feet were touching plush carpet that looked like it was out of an old-world picture book. There was golden wallpaper, paneling made from actual wood.

Mostly, there was glowing light.

Eager to reach the window, she stepped forward only to find her arm still chained to the man behind her. Claire was confused. "This is not outside."

Shepherd escorted her forward, his torso warm on her back. "I never agreed to allow you outside. I believe the arrangement was that I would allow for you to see your sky."

Technically he was right, and Claire knew there was absolutely no point in arguing.

The prospect the small room afforded was unlike anything she'd seen in a house: a vast display of rugged tundra. The window was an actual part of the Dome; if she touched the glass, she would be touching the only thing between her and hundreds of miles of snow—a thing forbidden.

Reaching forward, ignoring the uncomfortable handcuff and arm that followed to allow her movement, Claire put her hand to the glass and felt its chill. Wild nature was her view, in a warm room, where she was chained to an Alpha to ensure good behavior.

The room's furnishings had been removed, leaving only that beautiful rug and a single large chair. It was angled at the window, filled with a man who drew Claire into his lap. With the lights on, Shepherd's looming presence at her back was reflected in the glass, his attention acute.

Meeting his stare in the reflection, Claire admitted, "Men have been put to death for touching the Dome."

Shepherd answered, "Or they are thrown in the Undercroft for daring to look outside."

Why would they look, there was nothing but snow outside. Yet Claire found herself taken with the view, all that white, of distant mountains and jutting ice. The land beyond the Dome was glorious.

Shepherd's body was warm, the purr soft and continuous, the perfect recipe for her to ignore him, relax, and just saturate herself in something other than four concrete walls.

The man did not ruin her comfort by speaking or making demands, and Claire was grateful for it. He was deep in thought, staring at the setting sun, his Omega held hostage on his lap.

The dark came, bright moonlight on glittering snow, and Claire fell into a dreamless slumber—the first she'd had in many weeks.

The whole night passed before intruding light set the backs of her eyelids glowing red. She woke comfortable with only beauty before her. It was almost as if Thólos did not exist. She could sit there and pretend. She could forget the man cuddling her was evil through and through.

But the truth could not be ignored. Though she was warm and safe, her people were waking up with nothing to eat, with no power, with no heat. Outside of that beautiful room, behind that grand view, the world was falling to pieces.

Shepherd stretched, his large hand cupped over the place where his child grew. "You enjoy this room and the view. You are comfortable here."

Looking away from the window, she surveyed the empty room. "Why did you have the furniture removed?"

"I did not want you to wrongly cultivate hope that I might allow you to remain."

There was logic to his rationale. Had there been a bed and other objects for comfort, she would have longed for more than just his lap on that oversized chair. She may have even grown upset when he'd demanded that they leave. "I see…"

"As I promised, I will bring you here." He took a breath of her hair, kissed a trail down her neck. "And as you promised, you will live as my willing mate."

WHEN THEY CAME BACK from her sky, Shepherd set her hand free. The handcuff had not been tight, but once he removed it, she felt an ache in its wake. He took her wrist and used his big thumbs to rub the skin, as if he understood the feeling and why she had cradled the offended limb in her hand.

Claire watched his caress, finding it peculiar that with

paws that could crush her, Shepherd seemed to know just how much pressure was appropriate. As the odd touching continued, she worried her lip and found him once again watching her carefully. When the silence stretched and his big thumb continued to rub, she grew nervous.

Unwilling to act without specific orders, unwilling to be tricked or manipulated, she thought to withdraw her hand.

Shepherd trapped her wrist in circling fingers that seemed far more binding than the handcuff had been. "How will you fill your hours while I am gone today?"

"Are you mocking me?"

"What did you do with your free time before I claimed you as my mate?"

That was easy to answer. "I spent every waking hour trying to find food for the Omegas."

The giant smirked, using his grip on her wrist to pull her nearer. "Before Thólos became mine."

"Thólos is not yours."

The bastard smiled at her. "Answer me, little one."

With a huff, she began to list off activities. "Aside from painting, I played my mom's old piano. I spent time with my friends… read stories, took cooking classes when I could afford to."

Her response satisfied the man. Shepherd released her arm, the drag of his callused hands against her fingers extended.

Claire used the opportunity to put distance between them, heading towards the bathroom, a place where he generally left her in peace.

When she emerged from her shower, she found Shepherd had brought her tray of breakfast. Scrunching up her face at the offering, she made a noise that displayed her reluctance to eat it. Apparently the junk food of her last meal was off the menu. In its place was some kind of green fluid that smelled heavily of bitter ginger. She drank it, hating it, and then sat in stupefaction when after twenty minutes, nothing seemed eager to come back up.

The Alpha seemed pleased, then he left.

Alone, Claire chewed her lip and found again that the painting of Shepherd was watching her. It was still there, left out in such an obvious position, still waiting for someone to do something with it. Wiping her hands, she reached for it, aware that even in the hours she had been free of him, his face still plagued her.

It struck her then that the Alpha had hardly left her side in her waking hours, or even physically left her touch in days. Whatever had happened between her arrival and the night spent in slumber on his lap must have left him content that she was established back in his power completely.

He was right.

Claire would remain a slave—for Corday, for Nona, the Omegas… for Maryanne. She would do as he wished to give them all a chance, and she would continue to engage, stomach the bond, and play the good captive as she looked for a way to help Thólos by the singularity of her situation.

But it was strange to be alone in that cell, wide awake, and alone for more than just a fleeting hour. Looking back at that damn portrait, at the face of the man on the page, the hard set of his jaw, even the beauty of his lips, she grew uneasy at the apparent change in him. She had verbally attacked him when he could not use his normal recourse—already knotted, he could not fuck her, and had seemed astonished at the amount of malice he felt burning through the thread. Yet Shepherd had not yelled, or punished. Instead he had admitted his wrongdoing, and when their bodies were untied, the man had even supplied what she had demanded before she'd lost her temper—he took her to see her sky, let her wake in the sunshine… then asked her personal questions.

The thread hummed: *Is your mate not trying? Are you not pleased?*

She was not pleased, she was suspicious.

The wave of instant soothing reassurance was immediate from that warm, worming cord. It sang to her that there was no need to panic. Even Claire had to agree. The nightmare would end with his regime's demise before the baby was born, or she would go back on a hunger strike. Or she could break the mirror in the bathroom and slit her wrists. She could just refuse to breathe.

She still got to choose.

A wave of apathy broke, all good feelings from the view swept into ennui. Claire needed to think objectively, she needed to not feel. A finger began to trace the outline of the portrait's jaw. She made herself remember.

Svana… Shepherd's beloved.

Claire had accused him on the ice of being twisted by Svana, but that could not be completely accurate. They had twisted each other in their sick, unbalanced relationship. The man Svana sought out in the Undercroft had earned her attention because he already had darkness in him.

Shepherd had suffered; his mother had been raped until she died. How many children suffered, how many people had been raped in this siege? What did he really expect to accomplish here?

Furthermore, why had he captured her if he had a lover who had been his for ages? It was more than the legacy he claimed to desire from his mate. Otherwise Shepherd would have reproduced with Svana. Why not couple with his beloved?

There was some upheaval, some key beyond simply wanting a child that Shepherd had been unwilling to share. Recreating the timeline in her head, Claire worked through his actions, her reactions, and the consequences of her escape attempts. He had impregnated her as a result of her first escape, injected his fertility drugs into her before she had even regained consciousness. It was such an extreme response, and the more she allowed herself to think about it objectively, to see past her feelings, the clearer it became. It wasn't just the baby; he wanted her devotion, was willing to force it by any means he could. Shepherd had done everything in his power to keep her just for himself, obsessed over it, and hid her away to the point of paranoia. He even thought he loved her.

Shepherd didn't even know her, his love was based off something she could not put her finger on.

What more do you want from me, Shepherd?

I want everything.

The image of Svana, of the expression on her face and the subtle flaring of her frightening blue eyes… The Alpha female had been displeased with her existence, Claire was certain of that. The woman had also been surprised to find her pregnant. Yet to his face, Svana had numbly accepted that Shepherd would have a toy… one the crazy Alpha female thought should have looked like her, as if every Omega she claimed they shared had been facsimiles of her exotic beauty.

Why would his consort, one Shepherd admitted he loved, not know he'd taken a mate, or that he had created a baby? Why had those eyes looked at Claire almost as if she were a mere nuisance, an aggravating rebound?

Rebound…

Svana was my lover and I thought she was also equivalently my mate. I learned I was wrong.

Holy shit. Svana had been unfaithful to Shepherd's devotion.

Understanding dawned and Claire's jaw dropped; she *was* a rebound. Her skin began to buzz as if overstimulated, her mind flew into a thousand directions at once. Shepherd's whole world had been shaken and his mutilated reaction had been to take an Omega—to continue his dedication to the woman who'd freed him from the Undercroft, but ease his own troubled heartache by forcing another to love him as he longed for Svana to love him.

"Why are you crying?"

Startled, Claire looked up to see the blue-eyed Beta had come with a new tray. Turning the paper pinched in her fingers towards the intruder, she ignored his question and just showed him the rendition of Shepherd in watercolor.

With brows drawn low, Jules looked at her painting, then looked away immediately. "You do not lack talent."

"So I've been told," wiping tears off her face, Claire conceded. "Does he know that you talk to me?"

"No."

"I'm glad that you do."

Such startling eyes in such an expressionless face, it was an odd sort of imbalance. "I know."

With a sorry smile, Claire pushed the painting of Shepherd aside. "You asked why I was crying. I was crying because I just sorted out… why he took me. I am not sure if I feel worse for my own ruined life, or for a man who is so fucking clueless. Shepherd may think brushing aside his pain over Svana's infidelity will make it go away, that by taking a mate he might fill that void… but love does not work that way."

Jules stiffened. "Your assessment is incorrect; do not think of it again. Such thoughts are unhealthy for your son."

"Why do you say son? How do you know it's not a girl?"

He sniffed the air but did not alter his expression. "I had two sons once… the subtlety of the scent is specific."

She echoed, "Had two sons?"

His voice never wavered. "My children were murdered when my wife was taken from me."

Everything in his statement was exactly what was wrong with this whole damn situation. "Children are dying in Thólos now, others' sons and daughters!"

Jules answered blandly, “It is unfortunate your people prey on the weak, but what we allow is necessary.”

Claire stood, she railed at the Beta. “Necessary? Explain it to me, then! Explain yourself to the woman your master has ruined because he didn’t know how to handle his hurt feelings!”

“Discuss it with Shepherd.” Face blank, Jules left, locking her back in her cage.

Discuss what part with Shepherd? The part about how she was superfluous and he just had not figured it out yet, or the dead babies part? Lying back on her space of concrete, Claire stared at the ceiling and felt like she was drowning in all the fucked up mess of things, the twisted histories, and the pathetic chain that was forged by a man with the emotional intelligence of an adolescent.

She would talk to him all right. She would make him look straight at what a hypocrite he was. She would show Shepherd what she’d discovered, the truth of what he was doing through her eyes… not his distorted vision. The Gods had even directed her to the signpost of what a sad joke everything seemed to be. That boy. That curled up child she had rested on, the corpse with no name and nothing in his pockets. He would be her mascot, and Shepherd would have to look at him and answer to her.

Claire mixed her paints and began to recreate that lonely moment in the alley. There were hours to spend on the work, hours wherein she detailed the brick, the cold, the withered child, and herself… fast asleep against the cadaver’s stiffness.

She had never painted herself before, used the memory of her black hair on her cheek to mask most of her face, but it was her. The same curled up slender form, the bone structure that screamed Omega, all in the clothes she'd stolen from Maryanne.

Mindless tears were falling on the painting as she worked, mixing the colors as her hand moved in a frenzy. Shepherd was sitting across from her, she blithely recognized the fact that he had arrived, but ignored him in her fervor to remember her boy perfectly—to not miss a detail of the grotesqueness of his withered face and milky, shriveled eyes. It was not until the hand holding the brush started to shake that he reached forward and stilled her. The brush was taken from her fingers, the painting turned so Shepherd could see. With his hand encasing hers, he viewed what had eaten up the hours of her day.

His rich voice stated fact. "This is you."

Stuck in the artist's haze, that blurry moment where one knows they are creating something monstrous but still mentally indistinct, she muttered, "I was tired and alone. I had been wandering Thólos for hours because I needed to see what had happened, what had been taken when you locked me in this room. I found this boy who'd died alone and sat at his side, feeling as dead as he was… I couldn't go any further so I leaned against him and fell asleep."

Shepherd tightened his grip on her hand, growling, "You could have frozen to death."

Claire nodded. "As that child did. That boy died with no

one to care for him… alone and frightened in a trash strewn alley."

The hand on hers suddenly withdrew. The behemoth stood from the chair and moved something new into her line of sight. "You did not eat your lunch."

Claire looked at the cold plate of fish and knew better than to argue. Reaching for the fork, she started to push trout past her lips. After shoveling down half the meal without tasting what was probably a divine recipe, she looked at the looming Alpha. "I carried that boy's corpse on my back all the way to Lower Reaches… So I could bury him with the Omegas. So he would not have to be alone."

Shepherd sighed, fisted his hands at his sides. "You are upset over the child you carried back to the others."

With an open expression, Claire admitted, "I am confused as to how you went from a boy dedicated to a mother who loved you no matter the circumstances, to a terrorist who is the cause of the death of thousands of innocent children in Thólos. Why did you change? What justified this, Shepherd?"

He pulled her to stand, and moved them both towards the bed. "You are tired and I suspect you did not nap as your body requires. We will lie down."

Her words were not slung in cruelty, but curiosity. "Do you not have an answer? No long-winded explanation of legends and greatness to make up for the death of that nameless boy?"

He took her dress, put her in the bed, and followed as soon as his own clothing was shed. Pulling Claire above him, to the place she could feel the purr the strongest, a place that was minorly dominant for the Omega, Shepherd arranged her for sleep. "There is no answer I could give that you would find satisfactory."

But that in itself was an answer.

When her eyes were falling closed and the purr was moving her to stillness, the male shared his frustration. "Did you never wonder that I may have kept you segregated so that you would not have to be exposed to what is taking place outside these walls?"

Half asleep, Claire hummed. "I am a grown woman, pregnant with your son… a baby no different than that little boy who died because of what you inspired here."

Fingers rubbed her scalp and he reminded her, "A baby you almost murdered by attempting suicide. A baby you no longer nest for or touch."

Putting her chin to his chest, knowing the words were true, she did not balk. "After what I witnessed and learned of your nature… the things she said you've done… did *you* never wonder that I would rather kill myself and the unborn child than allow the likes of you and Svana to ruin him as you ruined one another?"

Shepherd's chest swelled, and it was clear from his expression that the man was incredibly pissed off. Rolling her onto her back, looming over her, his large hand closed over her lower belly. "I am not at all happy with your current mindset or accusations."

Placing her hand atop his, Claire held his angry gaze and

asked, "Do you suppose you are some paragon worthy of this child? You fucked Svana—"

His anger was growing dangerous. "I was trying to keep you safe."

"Stop lying to yourself. Have you ever told her no, or do you do anything she wants just to please her? You enable her… and she thinks of herself as beyond reproach… because you worship her. I saw it myself! And for that perversion, she crafted you into what you are. A thing she owns: her unquestioning disciple."

The villain roared right in her face. "Svana loves me!"

Claire was on some sort of high, past caring for the consequences of her words. "The same way you claim you love me… the kind of *love* that justifies infidelity and cruelty."

The pain did not register, not at first, and considering the size of the Alpha it could have been a thousand times worse. The grip he had on her arm, the way he bent it back to remove it from his body, Claire ignored, reaching for his shoulder again, wanting him to hurt her.

The room moved, and a great crushing weight made it difficult to draw breath. His grip on her forearms left her hands almost purple, but green eyes held silver as she fought for the short stuttering breaths his mass would allow.

Whatever possessed him was cold in its rage, calculating in speech. "You will never speak of such things again."

There was not enough breath to answer fully so she nodded her head and hissed the words, "It's the truth."

Shifting enough so she might breathe, Shepherd snarled, "You will be punished. Corday will die."

There was no anger or fear in her expression, simply unfathomable disappointment. "Look at me. Look at what you are doing."

Shepherd stared down at the woman he was hurting. When she brought her other hand up to cup his face, ignoring the black marks already blooming on her skin, he did not stop her, but neither did he enjoy her touch.

"I am only trying to help you see, to understand the point you are missing," Claire whispered, seeing that she had shaken him badly, hurt him.

He was unmoved. "You hate me."

Success in warfare is gained by carefully accommodating ourselves to the enemy's purpose. - Sun Tzu

"I am trying to be your mate. A woman you only took because Svana was unfaithful and you were in pain."

The furious ache in her other arm abated, Shepherd lessened his grip. "I took you because you were meant to be mine. I could smell it on you."

The warmth of her small hand slipped to his neck, to the ridge of muscles he once claimed hurt him, and she rubbed. "Had she remained faithful, would you have saved me from the mob?"

"What do you think you are doing?" Shepherd's nostrils flared, and though he was furious, his cock lay hard as a rock against her thigh.

Claire stopped her touch. "I was only trying to soothe you

as you do for me when I'm upset. When your emotions are calm, you will see that I am right."

Growling, he jammed himself inside her in one sharp thrust. Claire grimaced, and braced herself. Shepherd, heavy inside her, cupped her face, snarling as he touched his forehead to hers. "This is how you may soothe me."

He jerked and rocked her again, making her breath catch as she brought her aching arms up to embrace the raging Alpha. Overly rough, he snapped his hips, pounding away, practically howling when her slick eased his passage. "And you will scream my name every time I make you come!"

12

Her entire body ached, even with warm water pouring over the fresh bruises. Overly attentive, Shepherd washed away the dried semen that made her sticky, which matted her hair, holding her to him as he bathed his mate.

They had both slept, tangled and sweaty from hours of fucking like animals. Even as she was now, her eyes were half-dilated as if still in a mating high, which was probably the only thing keeping the Omega from hissing at the touch of his hands on tender skin his zealous possession had rubbed raw.

Shepherd took her chin, drawing her sleepy eyes to his face. “I will not harm Corday.”

Flatly, Claire answered, “I knew you wouldn’t.”

The giant hesitated, the creases by his eyes betraying a smirk. “Did you?”

"If you hurt him, I would punish you as severely as I could."

Shepherd's amusement faded. "You would kill yourself."

"Yes."

Each word was perfectly enunciated and lacked the bitterness the man felt sour his stomach. "His value to you is higher than the rest of your forty-three."

Claire licked her wet lips and thought about how best to answer, or if she should even answer at all. "I owe him."

Shepherd felt the rush of blood behind his eyes, fought to be gentle as he rinsed her hair. "It is more than that. I saw you together. You bear fondness for the Beta."

Inspiring any type of excessive hatred in Shepherd for Corday could be dangerous to her friend, and would serve no purpose except to pointlessly agitate the Alpha. "I do not love Corday, not in the way you imagine. But I owe him, as I said. I have lied to him, and drugged him. I deceived him…"

"To keep him safe," Shepherd purred, finishing her statement, somewhat mollified at the truth of her words and their echo in the bond. "Does that not sound familiar?"

"No." Her answer was harsh.

"Do not lie to me, little one. His situation mirrors yours."

"I said no because I meant no," Claire argued, grimacing at the stiffness in her hips when he began to rub. "You didn't drug me to keep me safe. You drugged me to create a baby."

He took her chin and turned her face up to force her full attention. "And that baby justifies your value to my men. It is keeping you alive."

Scowling, feeling cold even in the heat and steam of the

shower, apprehension crept over Claire. "What do you mean?"

Seeing his words had unsettled her, Shepherd spoke in a hard tone. "If you are not careful, if you do not begin to nest again and ensure that our offspring grows, should you miscarry… I would have to replace it immediately."

A look of horror twisted her face. "I don't understand."

"You don't need to. You simply need to be a mother." Shifting his mass, he pressed her back to the tiles. "You are mine, and I will do anything to ensure your continued survival. I would kill millions, I would lie to you, and I would rape you if I had to and fill you with child again should you lose this one."

How had she felt even a moment of power over this man? "You're scaring me."

"Good." He turned off the water and pulled her out. "It seems to be the only way to get through to you."

"What about your legacy?"

He smiled, a nasty thing, and pawed her belly. "It will be unparalleled."

Wilting, Claire muttered, "I have no urge to nest. Not in that bed. Not anymore."

As if the idea had not occurred to the Alpha, he narrowed his eyes and seemed to consider. "You wish for a new bed?"

"I do not wish for anything," Claire sighed, feeling again as if she was talking to a wall.

Shepherd continued, speaking to himself. "If I procured this new bed, you would nest."

Desperately uneasy, she growled. "You are not listening to me, Shepherd."

"And you would desire new materials, in that color you like…" He was running a towel over her skin as if insensible to her bruised skin.

She snarled and batted his hands away. "You're hurting me, you deaf jackass."

Snapped out of his tirade, he froze and looked at the small thing that had just barked at him. Snorting a caustic laugh, he grunted, "You have grown far more outspoken with pregnancy."

"I have grown far more outspoken because I no longer care if you kill me! I don't want a new bed. I want you to explain what the fuck you are talking about!"

Shepherd took her arm and gently turned her so that he might pat her hair dry. "You are only being difficult… you need a new bed."

"Okay, fine! Since you don't listen to a goddamn thing I say anyway, here goes. I want a new bed in a big room with carpet instead of concrete. A room with a wall of windows that overlook a garden I planted full of flowers—which would be a miracle, as every houseplant I ever had died. I want to move without restriction through this grand house I will be nesting in, and be free to go outside and sit on grass… And I want a pony too, Shepherd. No, forget that. I want a fucking unicorn."

Pulling her hair so that she had to look back at him, he scowled. "You may not have a pony, and unicorns don't exist."

She really didn't mean to, was so in knots inside she could not even begin to fathom where it came from, but just for a second, she giggled. Slapping a hand over her mouth, still stuck with her head leaning back at an unnatural angle, she forced her face into neutrality and continued to make her point. "What color is it that you are so certain I like?"

"You prefer green, the same shade as your eyes."

Was that why almost every single dress he'd provided was green? "What gave you that idea?"

He looked as if such a miscalculation was not possible. "That is not the color you favor?"

"Sure, it's a pretty color… but it's not my favorite color." Understanding, Claire narrowed her eyes and leveled a disapproving gaze at the man. "Let me guess, you got this information from your interrogations of the Omegas."

"Red, like your picture?" he tried again, letting go of her hair so she might turn and he could see her fully.

"No. Why didn't you just ask me if you wanted to know something so mundane?" But then it dawned on her. He wanted to provide things she was supposed to like without prompting… as a tactic of sorts because that was the only way he knew how to be.

Shepherd grew aggravated, standing naked and demanding rudely, "What is your favorite color?"

"Bird's egg blue." Mocking him, Claire cocked her head to the side and batted her lashes. "And, Shepherd, since we are being so congenial, what is yours?"

"Expressly, the exact color of your eyes." He wasn't flirting, he was annoyed, but even so the words were… something. They made her blush and he noticed it, his intense gaze losing its edge and gaining that unnerving calculation instead. "I also find the rich black of your hair to be incredibly fetching."

She was positively scarlet and clearly wanted him to look away. It had been months since she had tried to cover her nakedness and she did not know what led her to do it, but her arm came up to hide her flushed breasts.

Shepherd looked only amused, or fascinated might have been a better description. "And now you are shy…" he cooed, evilly. "This is nothing I have not said before."

But she had purposefully never listened… she had ignored it and hated the sound of his distorted raspy voice.

"You know I find you to be very beautiful," the monster continued, proudly prowling, trapping her against the sink. "You are, in fact, the most comely female I have ever seen."

Claire was sorely tempted to snap something nasty at him, to bring up Svana, or the Omegas, or anything to get him to stop looking at her that way. Instead she just stammered, "I… am cold."

"Well then, by all means, pretty little one"—Shepherd's thick arms encircled her—"let me warm you."

A stifled noise sputtered passed her lips as bulging muscle pulled her flush.

His lips came to her ear and the man growled in the most licentious voice she had ever heard, "And you have the most beautiful pussy I have ever known. It is *perfection.* Anytime you should ask, I would lick it, taste you until you screamed my name like you did four times last night."

"STOP!"

Stroking his touch up her body until Claire's jaw rested in his hand, he pulled the Omega from where she tried to hide her face against his chest. Their eyes mere inches apart, his hand delved between her legs to lightly swipe the gathering slick at her folds. Pulling slippery fingers away, he made a satisfied male noise and left her standing, panting, flushed, and aroused, while muttering, "Bird's egg blue," as he left.

THOSE MOMENTS… when one has a black bag over their head, when a body is being jostled, and you know, you just fucking know, your number is up… those moments just plain suck.

Feeling hands shove her back until her rear end made an uncomfortable connection with a hard chair, Maryanne prepared for her greatest performance. Or she did until the bag came off in a swoop and she was face to face again… with Shepherd.

The words caught in her throat, the typical sensual quality she knew how to use to manipulate failed, and all Maryanne could do was stare.

That man had decimated Thólos… ruined her city. That man stank of Claire's cooch. Ewww…

"Well," Maryanne let out a breath, "turns out I was right about just where Claire disappeared to. Guess that means I'm off limits, huh?"

The looming male leaned closer. "Shall we discuss the nuances of the agreement between my mate and myself? I only offered to spare your life. There was no mention of what I would do with said life. Technically, I could break every bone in your body, subject you to torture, take what little freedom you have left. So long as you continue breathing I will have fulfilled my end of the bargain." Shepherd's finger lightly tapped the table between them. "And Claire would never know…"

But he wanted something, otherwise she would not be there. He wanted something for Claire.

The terror was there, the slow rising panic that tainted her sweat and signaled to the much stronger Alpha that she was afraid. "You have a use for me."

"You will be coming back into my employ."

"What do you need me to steal?"

His mouth did not move in the slightest, but Maryanne was certain his expression displayed just how stupid he thought she was. "Your duty will be to bring information about the circumstances of the Omegas and the Beta, Enforcer Corday, to Claire. In these conversations, I advise that you make her happy, or you will be very unhappy when they conclude."

The thought of seeing Claire chased away a fraction of the dread. "Sure thing. I know exactly how to make her smile."

"You will not share detailed information, just the general wellbeing of the individuals I send you to photograph. You will not interact with these people or be seen. All images will be checked before Claire views them, and should I find anything unsettling, it would not bode well for you. You will speak of absolutely no one else."

Nodding, Maryanne signaled that she understood.

The last warning held the threat of great pain should she fail him. "And if she tries to pass you a note or does anything subversive, you will tell me privately. She will not be punished."

Claire might try, Maryanne knew it in her bones, and she already hated knowing full well she would hand anything over to Shepherd rather than face the consequences of being the go between in correspondences with Claire's little boyfriend. "She doesn't trust me."

"Let's not play games, Ms. Cauley."

"When do I begin?"

IT TOOK a few hours and another breakfast of the horrible green smoothie before her stomach settled from Shepherd's odd adoring behavior in the shower. He was gone again, a thing Claire was supremely grateful for so she could stretch and pace and formulate her next move.

Looking at the nasty bruising on her arm, Claire flexed the limb, certain it would ache for quite some time. *It was worth it.* Shepherd may have cornered her that morning, made her uncomfortable and bashful, but she'd had him with his back against the wall the night before, just long enough to expose that she had been correct. Pieces of it were coming together, Shepherd's mental need to keep her all to himself, using her to ease the grief Svana caused whether he recognized that fact or not, confirmed.

That was something; it was a place to start.

Shepherd's initial reaction had been violent, even the sex, but when they woke, he was only indulgent. It was as if the rage from the previous night, the force that had compelled him to fuck her so roughly and so long she'd become boneless, was just gone.

The man had exorcised a demon.

Even at his most dangerous, he had never looked from her face, kept much of his skin pressed to hers, ordered her to call out his name, his burning eyes almost rolling back in his skull each time she did. He communicated to her with his driving need, with the force in which he urged her climax. His fiery expressions used to frighten her, the set of his jaw, the glares… now she was beginning to understand. It was longing.

Shepherd was always watching her reaction, looking for something, some small hint as he coaxed out her sordid urges. He had some need that had been neglected. When coupled, she was tender and would stroke him, draw in his scent and smile. Perhaps that was why he mated her so often. He had a base craving for such affection. Shepherd wanted her to love him and was confused as to how to foster such a thing when she did not automatically fall into what he assumed was proper Omega behavior.

Claire did not love him, but she had offered him comfort when his side of the cord displayed the turmoil her words had stirred up. That had been instinctive, and even though she despised Shepherd, it was the right thing to do in the war she was waging. Progress would require her to serve her position as mate if she was to stand even a chance of edifying him, and petty tactics such as seduction or dishonesty would never serve her.

Claire was not foolish enough to believe she could fix him. After all, Shepherd's thinking was warped far beyond anything she could untwist. But she could chip away at the wrongness; she could expose weakness in a man who seemed to have none.

Claire was going to bare him to himself piece by piece if it killed her.

It probably would.

The door opened and the dead-eyed, dangerous Beta entered. He ran a quick appraisal over her and then went to switch the trays. "Your arm," Jules grunted, "do you require pain relief?"

The absolute disinterest in the man's expression made the question completely strange. Edging nearer, circling around to face the male, Claire tucked her hair behind her ear. "That would bely the effects of the punishment."

Aware of what the Omega had done to earn such bruises, Jules mocked, "You believe that to be a punishment? I thought you were supposed to be clever."

Cocking her head, Claire felt something odd in their exchange but could not put her finger on it. "You find Shepherd's actions intriguing?"

"He was gentle with you."

Looking down at her arm, at the black marring blotches,

she frowned. “And here I thought *you* were supposed to be clever, Jules.”

The male was not interested in further communication and gave her his back.

Slipping the straps of her dress off her arms, she asked in a voice devoid of feeling, “Does this look gentle to you?”

Glancing over his shoulder at the woman decorated in the bruises of rough sex, Jules turned quickly to the wall and barked, “Put your dress back on!”

“This is what confuses me about the lot of you.” Claire continued, unmoved by his *morality*. “You won’t look because you find my nudity inappropriate, yet you created a city full of rape that you do not even blink an eye at. You are all walking contradictions.”

“You are my leader’s mate. PUT ON YOUR DRESS.”

It was strange to see the man who always appeared unaffected grow agitated. Smirking, Claire pulled the fabric over tender skin. “I think we both made our point.”

Once certain she was decent, the man leveled her with a glare that almost held the same power as Shepherd’s. “You are playing a very dangerous game.”

Standing her ground, Claire said, “Not everyone is playing a game. I am simply trying to communicate, and I do not speak your language.”

“You speak it better than you know.”

Was that actual praise? “Then speak to me. How old were your sons when you lost them?”

The man was not thrown by her sudden shift in the conversation. “Bertrand was four; Joseph just under a year.”

Claire smoothed her skirt, felt sadness. "Why were they killed?"

"My wife was Omega." The sharpness of his gaze was frightening. "An Alpha wanted her. Before I even learned of what had happened, she had been pair-bonded to a friend of Premier Callas'. The same Alpha who'd murdered our boys."

"What was her name?"

"Rebecca."

Somehow she just knew, Claire whispering, "And you killed her when Shepherd led you from the Undercroft."

"Yes, almost a decade ago—at her request."

Claire understood. Even after the man had found her and taken her back, his Rebecca would have been gutted by the power of a pair-bond she must have hated more than Claire hated her own. Her lip began to tremble. "I am very sorry for what happened to your family, but I don't understand how it led you here to do what you are doing now."

"Every member of this army is here for the same reason I am."

It felt like Shepherd had told her a thousand times. "Revenge."

"Call it cultural enlightenment."

Her green eyes, wide and eager, sat in a face bearing an urgent expression. "How do you not see the flaws in your own argument? Do you want the human race to end?"

"How do you continue to deny yourself the truth? I overheard your conversation with Enforcer Corday. You admitted freely that Thólos has done this to itself." Jules approached her, unblinking. "Even before the breach, this very degradation infected all life under the Dome… Do not waste our time by pretending that you did not live a lie just to feel safe."

It wasn't that simple. "Shepherd took me. I had a life before. I had a career. I could have had a future if I'd met the right Alpha."

"Shepherd choosing you as a mate was the best possible outcome for you, though you are incapable of accepting that fact in your ignorance and resentment."

Before she could offer a cutting retort, Jules opened the door and left.

Glaring at the door as if the man were still standing before it, Claire clenched her jaw so hard it hurt. In a few moments and a few carefully selected phrases, the Beta had shared more than Shepherd had in the first five weeks she had known him. Jules was a villain, of that she was certain, but a part of Claire could understand his rage.

Rage, it seemed, was all she was made of most days.

These men were not simply the psychopaths Claire had assumed. They were all on a mission. Jules claimed every member of Shepherd's army carried the burden of a painful past. If that was what it took to distort the psyche, to perpetuate evil in an attempt to do good, how far behind could she be?

Picking at her food, focusing again on the painting of Shepherd that served as companion during meals, Claire did not register the opening of the door.

The giant was pleased to find her admiring his portrait again, rounding the table to brush back her hair.

"I have brought you medicine to dull any pain," Shepherd explained once he had her attention. "Open your mouth."

Between her parted lips, two tablets were placed on her tongue, Claire sitting stupidly as Shepherd held her glass, pouring carefully so she could swallow. She obeyed, and his large thumb wiped away a small drip of milk.

Soaking in her surprised expression, he asked, "Have you been ill today?"

"No. Whatever is in that disgusting green drink seems to settle my stomach."

"But you are in pain and I was notified that you required relief," the male grunted, his concern obvious. "You also look tired."

"I didn't ask him for medicine and you already knew I was sore. You are physically demanding and my body is not always up to the challenge." Claire *was* tired. Very tired. "Besides, wasn't that the point of your punishment?"

Crouching to be nearer her eye level, Shepherd burrowed his hands in her hair and cradled her skull. "There was no punishment." The male began to work his fingers over her scalp. "These bruises… You should know that I was incredibly restrained. Antagonizing your mate to such a point is dangerous, as you are fragile, little one, and I am very strong. Yet in the anger you purposefully fostered, I fought myself. I did not strike you. I could have easily damaged you beyond repair."

The purr was so loud and his fingers felt incredibly comforting tugging her hair… even if his words were disturbing. "It was worth it," she muttered.

The man was oozing patience, still in that seeming calm he'd woken with. "Explain such a statement."

This version of Shepherd was never quite what it seemed. Cautiously, Claire answered, "It is the only way I know of to communicate with you."

He seemed intrigued, eyes shining as Shepherd dissected her stratagem. "You long for more conversation?"

If you know the enemy and know yourself, you need not fear the result of a hundred battles. If you know yourself but not the enemy, for every victory gained you will also suffer a defeat. If you know neither the enemy nor yourself, you will succumb in every battle. - Sun Tzu

Claire needed to know Shepherd. She could no longer afford to ignore him as she had done before. She needed to know his Followers. More so, she needed to make sure she knew herself, and did not lose sight of what she was should he hurt her again.

Thinking over how best to answer, she sighed. "It would be normal to feel that I could trust you to simply sit down and talk with me. But you seem incapable of the restraint of listening to what you might not like—and feeling unheard makes me frustrated and unhappy."

"Do you not place some of the blame on yourself, little one? Your effort to ignore my presence is apparent."

"Why would I pay any attention to a man who doesn't listen to me or respect how I feel?"

"Because I am older and wiser. I know what is best."

Claire snorted, a small twitch in her lip. "What you are is

a fanatic and a despot. And I don't really think you know me at all, *Mr. green is your favorite color*."

He made no answer. Instead, Shepherd reached forward and the arms he slid around her felt… reassuring. Yawning, wanting to lie down, Claire did not fuss when he carried her to bed.

The Alpha sat on the edge of the mattress, played with her hair, and commanded she close her eyes. "You will sleep now. If I find you in an acceptable state when I return, we will converse."

When she woke in the dim room, it was the best Claire had felt in some weeks. It wasn't just the nap or the painkillers, it was a small sense of purpose, a deeper feeling that her progress was positive. Good feelings were dangerous and easy to lose in her prison, so she carefully cherished it alone in the dark before putting it away—burying it deep so Shepherd could not take it from her.

The male had claimed he would talk to her. Tthat gave her an arena she could prepare.

It had been fruitful to start a dialogue with him over her painting the day prior, so she would begin simply and try what she knew. Claire mixed up her paints and began detailing the image she had seen through the security feed before she broke the Omegas out of prison. She painted little sixteen-year-old Shanice being rutted by one of Shepherd's Followers.

Everything was as she remembered: nothing embellished, nothing altered.

Shepherd ripped it out from under her brush the second he returned and saw it. Balling it up, his eyes flared in fury, as he breathed so deep it stretched his chest like a dragon about to spit flames.

Claire did not react; she just let out a sigh and set her brush aside.

Speaking inoffensively about a very offensive subject, Claire began. “Her name is Shanice. She is sixteen years old. That was her first heat and I can guarantee that she was not willing. She’s cried herself to sleep each night since estrous ended.”

“Had my officer been able to pair-bond, she would have been as content as all the others!” Shepherd leaned his weight on the table, aggressively irritated to find what was not the ideal he expected to return to. “You are the only one unsettled.”

Claire put her hand over his, not to comfort, but to make it clear she understood the consequences. “That man could not be a day younger than forty-five. That girl is still in school.”

“I am much older than you,” Shepherd countered hotly.

“Maybe by a decade, perhaps a little more. Not old enough to be my father. I am also a fully grown woman, Shepherd. I am not a child.”

Flexing the fist under her small hand, Shepherd growled, “I am aware of what you are doing.”

“I am trying to communicate with you about things I

don't understand," Claire countered. Small fingers squeezed his hand again, and she let her feelings show on her face. "Considering your mother… explain to me where the line blurs and this becomes acceptable?"

Shepherd took the seat across from her, agitated but growing forcedly composed. "Arranged Alpha-Omega pairings are common throughout history, and are statistically successful."

"If the baby I am carrying were an Omega, would you want that for your child?"

"Under these circumstances, yes. The bonded Omegas are sheltered and protected by worthy Alphas. All are fed; they are safe… they are not mistreated. You are the one who would expose them to Thólos in your foolish misunderstanding of freedom." Twisting his hand, Shepherd captured her fingers, toyed with them, even though his words were harsh. "You never had it, Claire. You were never once free in this city… You have never once been free a day in your life."

She truly hated the sound of him speaking her name, knew that the unpleasant feelings it stirred up showed on her face, and felt her fortification slipping. Furthermore, she hated how Shepherd was holding her hand as if they were lovers, as if he had a right to—even if she had initiated contact. "*You* mistreated *me*. And I do not know what I hate more: your assumptions, or the fact that you just spoke my name simply because you know I dislike it."

A large thumb circled the flat of her palm. "Which makes this discourse the perfect time to begin adjusting you to the sound of it on my lips, little one."

Holding his gaze, forcing herself not to snatch back her hand, Claire admitted, "So we both have an agenda."

Pulling her arm nearer, Shepherd purred, "We will not have a repeat of yesterday's argument."

"That topic was already addressed. I know my feelings, I know what was done, and I know why… even if you will not admit it. It is up to you whether or not you face what is fact." After a breath, Claire looked up from where their hands were joined and tried a different approach. "Are the mated Omegas really settled?"

The word was hard and judgmental. "Yes."

She stared blankly. "You must wish you had chosen with less impulsiveness."

"I have never once questioned claiming you." Almost musically he explained his truth, "And in answer to your question yesterday; yes, I would have still fought the mob and claimed you had Svana not diverted. You were born to be mine."

Sarcastic, Claire cocked a brow and grumbled at the obtuse fool. "And were you always meant to be mine?"

He took her jaw and leaned forward. "Yes."

"Then I must admit I see the irony that, like my father, I received a mate who really wishes to be with someone else. That certainly is cruel of the Gods."

Shepherd did not hesitate to counter, "I only want you, Claire."

She let out a breath. "The first time I saw you at the Citadel, the first time I smelled you, I did not see you as my mate. All I felt was fear. It was very hard to stand my ground and not run."

Running his thumb over her frowning lips, Shepherd forced a question that tightened his mouth and squared his shoulders. "Because of my Da'rin Markings?"

Claire shook her head, her brows drawing together. "No. Because of what you'd done, where you were, how big you are… the violence. My father was a very nice man—funny and kind. That is the epitome of Alpha to me. That is a suiting mate. You are none of those things. Since you forced the bond, I feel controlled, manipulated, you have caused me grief, I cannot trust you, and you only treat me nicely to get your way."

"I will take responsibility for the grief, but as for the rest, much of it is your own fault. You have made little effort to be a contented mate. Your resistance and continued subversion requires a firm hand to ensure your safety. I would be cruel to you to keep you safe, and I freely manipulate you as there is no other recourse to draw you nearer. Had you settled as the other Omegas had settled, your life would be happy. *And I am careful of your wellbeing.* I bring you things you never thank me for. I offer you the best foods. I stroke and purr and please you physically for hours."

Claire had intended the conversation to highlight her concerns with Thólos, not nitpick at the major issues as to why, aside from his many transgressions, their pair-bond was madness. Gritting her teeth at his list of ridiculous accusations, she took a deep breath and tried to control her temper.

"When you were in the Undercroft, did you thank your jailors for what they brought you?"

Shepherd's eyes went fractionally wider, the man incredibly insulted. "Thank me for the paints."

Claire snarled, "Thank me for all the hours I have spent cleaning this room."

"Little one." The shift in him was unsettling. The male purred and squeezed her hand gently. "Your domestic behavior in our shared den is nothing but pleasing to me. Thank you."

Scowling, Claire lost ground. "I am concerned that if I thank you for the paints, you will know how much I like them and take them away."

"I will not take your paints. I understand that you need them and that there is little outlet for you when I am not here."

She did not believe him, but it didn't matter. Her lower lip trembled. Feeling her eyes grow damp she whispered, "Thank you for the paints."

"Do you wish to continue talking, or would you prefer to go see the sky now?"

She had made no ground in her agenda, had wasted the opportunity and learned little. The whole fucking conversation had been imperceptibly moved to the tension between them by a man far more gifted in discourse. That was not her goal; that was not her purpose.

Taking a mental step back, needing to reformulate, Claire nodded, disengaged from the ordeal. "The sky."

13

Entering the room with her window, Claire was wary the second her feet touched the floor. The setup had changed; a small table held two trays of food… as if Shepherd were going to eat with her—which would not only be odd, but a domestic act she was in no mood to engage in with him.

Like an iron bar around her waist, Shepherd's arm held her flush to his body, the uncomfortable handcuff still in place. They were not moving deeper into the room, just standing awkwardly as he leaned down to possessively sniff her.

"I would have preferred to mate you before this, yet forewent the experience because you desired to converse. I am also going to allow you a short time without the handcuffs," Shepherd said, unlocking the metal at her wrist while still maintaining a stiff hold on her body. "Should you disappoint my trust, this coming moment will not happen again. It would be in your best interest to behave."

Before Claire could reply, the numerous locks on the door began to hiss and her body was shifted so there was no view but that of Shepherd's chest. The door was opened and closed, and only then did Shepherd turn them so that she might see.

Instantly panicked, Claire eyeballed the stunning blonde and rushed to throw her body between Maryanne and Shepherd. "What the fuck is she doing here? You promised me!"

"Claire, calm down before you give yourself an aneurism," Maryanne teased, throwing an arm around her shoulders. "I was invited for dinner."

Bull-Fucking-Shit. There was a catch, there was always a catch, and cold dread settled over the Omega. Her attention darted towards the folding table, back to her massive mate, then over her shoulder towards Maryanne.

Claire was scared.

The Alpha female herded her forward, smiling and bouncing her eyebrows as if possessing no care in the world. "It was impossible to say no once he told me steak was on the menu… Don't think for a moment that I came to see you."

Claire's nervous laugh did not sound the least bit reassured. The women sat, Shepherd moved towards a third chair in the corner to watch like a warden observing a convict's last meal.

Enthusiastic, Maryanne dug into the food, made pointless inane chatter, smiling as Claire worked through the knot in her stomach and prayed the food would stay down. With the passing of half an hour, the tense situation calmed. Shepherd's soft purr from the corner, and the approving look in his eye every time Claire looked over at him, helped to settle her.

Just having Maryanne near was extraordinary, and for a moment, Claire felt… comfortable.

"Maryanne," swallowing the last bite of steak, Claire looked at her pretty friend and teased, "I think you may be the only woman in Thólos who's still wearing lipstick."

Full red lips curved up in a decedent smirk, Maryanne was proud as a peacock. "I have standards." The woman eyeballed Claire's hair, frowning. "And you have been slack in yours. You need a haircut."

"As you must have noticed from the pre-cut steak, I'm not allowed access to sharp objects. I am also pretty certain salon services are not part of Shepherd's philosophy."

Maryanne cocked a snarky eyebrow and purred, "But gourmet food is?"

Claire looked down at their finished plates, frowning.

Maryanne ran a pet down Claire's hair so she might show her the ragged ends. "You know, Claire, if it comes to girly things, you're going to have to outright tell him if you need something. Your Alpha seems dense as a boulder in regards to women."

Before she could stop it, the Omega burst into uproarious laughter. Hand pressed to her mouth, she imagined Shepherd's expression behind her, and laughed even harder.

It took a minute before she could chide her cocky, smirking friend. "For fuck's sake, Maryanne. He's never going to let you come back now."

"Oh." Maryanne lounged back in her chair like a well-fed cat. "I think he will."

While Claire composed herself, Maryanne began her duty. "I have visited your Omegas. They are blissfully unaware of your situation."

And that was why Maryanne had come. Claire ran a hand through her hair, worried. "Do they think I killed myself?"

"Yes."

"That's good. They would fret if they thought I was still alive."

"Only because they'd fear you might cause them trouble."

"Maryanne…" Claire warned, "that is not fair."

With an arrogant smirk, Maryanne waggled a finger. "Life ain't fair, sugar pie."

"Life is what we make it."

"Says the woman with scraggly hair and chapped lips. You clearly have not been making yours that great."

Irritated that Maryanne thought to scold, Claire leaned forward and snarled, "And what the fuck is your point?"

"That after one good look at you, I can see you've been playing the victim instead of trying *to live*." There was no more frisky tone in Maryanne's voice, no more playful looks. "Yeah your situation sucks; yeah it's not what you wanted. But it is what it is. And I know you… I can just see you stagnating instead of adapting, all stubborn to the point it hurts. He might not be Prince Charming, but it's safe here. He feeds you. You have it better than almost everyone else under the Dome."

Looking to be near the brink of ripping off her guest's head, Claire hissed, "Did he tell you to say that?"

"Do I look like I'd do anything he tells me to?"

"Of course you do." Narrowing her eyes, Claire mouthed, "You needed friends once… that's your *friend* sitting in the corner now."

For a second Maryanne looked stricken, and then grew coldly composed. "You don't know what it was like down there, Claire. Even you would have done *anything* to get out. And no, he didn't tell me to say that. It's my own opinion."

"Well, from your life decisions, it's clear your judgment isn't always the best."

"That look in your eye"—the blonde settled back, just as unhappy as her friend—"I know what it means. You know I'm right. And yeah, I've fucked up. I am what I am. But you still love me."

"I do, you cunt."

Sudden heavy warmth settled on Claire's nape. She tensed, unaware Shepherd had silently come up behind her. His thumb stroking her spine, he spoke, "That will be enough for today."

Claire stood to say goodbye, Shepherd maintaining his hold on her neck. "I'm sorry I snapped at you, Maryanne."

"You shouldn't be." Maryanne smiled softly. "You're allowed to be bitchy; you're pregnant. Before you know it, you'll also be fat."

And just like that, Claire was chuckling again, stepping out from under Shepherd's shadow to embrace her friend.

Standing on tiptoe, Claire pecked Maryanne's lips, the close friends' customary goodbye.

And it had been a mistake.

Shepherd snarled, Claire darting back against him, begging, "Don't hurt her!"

"She's like my sister, Shepherd," Maryanne tried to pacify, failing to hide the fear in her voice. "Get your mind out of the gutter."

"You will not kiss her again." An arm came around Claire's waist, keeping her locked to his side as Shepherd shouted a stream of foreign words towards the door.

The bolts were thrown and the door opened so Ms. Cauley could be escorted out by a parade of armed Followers. Even as the door was closing, Shepherd pressed Claire to the wall. She heard his zipper, the impatience of Shepherd's growl as he lifted her skirt, and he was inside her in a quick thrust.

It was nothing but an animal claiming, both of them still dressed, but his grunts were loud, and Claire knew that Maryanne, anyone, in the halls could hear them. And that, of course, was his point. Shepherd was loudly broadcasting that she was his. She wanted to be shamed, but found her body glorying in it, her mind already slipping into the haze. It was a quick pairing, especially satisfying when he spun her about just before she came. Face to face, the knot formed, her legs around his waist, his strength supporting her fully when so much pleasure bloomed.

"You didn't say my name," he panted, eyes like molten iron.

She said it, just so he would shut up and let her enjoy the aftereffects. "Shepherd."

There was a smear of red lipstick on Claire's mouth. Holding her still, Shepherd went to rub it off. His finger hesitated, changed course, and instead spread it around until her lips took on a rosy hue. "Was Ms. Cauley's assessment correct? Are cosmetics something that you require?"

The man had just knotted, was still spilling, and he was asking stupid questions. Looking at him as if he were nuts, Claire scowled. "Nobody requires cosmetics."

"I see no problem with the length of your hair, nor is it ragged," he grumbled next, stroking in the exact same place Maryanne had, as if erasing the other Alpha's touch.

Claire rolled her eyes to the heavens and leaned her head back to the wall.

His lips went to her cheek, her ear, her neck. "I have never heard you laugh in that manner."

There was nothing she could say that would not be inflammatory, but it was clear he expected some sort of answer. "She's funny. Always has been."

Shepherd understood that it was less Maryanne's comment, and more the fact that Claire absolutely agreed with her friend's assessment. Svana had never found him wanting when it came to understanding her or her needs. She was easy to please, loved the gifts he brought her, and always thanked him profusely. Claire was disinterested in almost everything he had provided, never glanced twice at new clothing, jewels tucked into her drawer, or fine things he put in the room. He knew she enjoyed the food, though her pride kept her from expressing it… and she found pleasure in her paints. Nothing else had ever drawn a reaction.

He had hated every moment of the women's conversation, save Maryanne's wise reprimand to her friend. It was the only thing that might induce him to allow such a meeting again.

Stranger still, Claire had grown hostile, they had argued, and then it was over. No hard feelings on either side.

The Omega was growing limp, falling asleep in his arms. Still knotted, Shepherd carried her to the lounge chair and arranged them both while he waited for his member to soften. When her nose went to his neck and she began to draw in his scent, the Alpha encouraged her behavior, played with her hair, and listened to her strange musical hum—an Omega noise she had not made since… since Svana.

He had pleased his mate. She was even smiling against the flesh of his neck, Shepherd certain she was unaware he could enjoy such a sight by their reflection in the window. The purr deepened, her eyelashes fluttered, her fingers toying with the fabric of his shirt.

"I would provide female things if you asked for them," the man grumbled, oddly relaxed considering how annoyed he'd been only minutes earlier.

She took a deep breath, and pushed up to look him in the eye. After their conversation downstairs, she knew what was in order. "I don't know why you did it, and can only assume there was some ulterior, self-serving purpose, but at this moment I appreciate it. Thank you for arranging for me to spend time with Maryanne."

He could be so gentle, so different. Cupping her face, he looked at her with a soft expression. "My motive was simply to show you that I am keeping my end of the bargain and for you to enjoy yourself."

Shepherd was behaving properly, he was making concessions… and he wanted her to acknowledge it. Sucking her lower lip into her mouth, she allowed herself a moment to study him up close; raised up so that his softening member slipped out, they were eye to eye. Claire touched where his neck swirled with Da'rin parasites, the arch of his eyebrows, the various scars over his face, collected over decades of brawls.

This man was her enemy.

Shepherd sought to encourage her. "You're curious…"

Having the male speak snapped her from her abstract regard. What had been a subject became a person, and Claire shrank back. "Senator Kantor told me your Da'rin marks symbolize the men you killed."

"It is a common thing underground, to threaten potential adversaries."

"He said they hurt…"

"In sunlight, yes."

They were sitting in a pool of sunlight, and though he wore long sleeves, the marks on his neck were exposed. He seemed so calm, his eyes focused but soft, that Claire doubted. "But you don't cover them."

Shepherd smirked, tried to kiss her unresponsive lips. "I can bear the pain."

Crooking a finger under his chin, eager to distract the

man's more amorous intentions, Claire urged him to stretch so she could see his neck in the light. Nail scraping over the branching marks, she explored, she counted lives. "How many?"

The male began to purr, stretching, luxuriating, when Claire traced over the patterns. "Many."

Eyes sad, she confessed, "I have tried to tally them, over and over. I always lose count…"

He wanted her cuddly and content, not frightened and eager to quarrel. "This is tradition underground. You have traditions, too. Most men are in the Undercroft for a few years, maybe a decade if they are strong. I was born there. Before I gave prisoners purpose and will to survive, few lived long enough for Da'rin to spread as extensively as mine. My marks were hope to many that they, too, might endure."

For men who had been thrown into darkness in innocence, for men who had been cast down there for small infractions… for Maryanne… Claire could let herself understand. "The Dome is not what I thought it was, but it's not what you think it is, either."

Running his fingers through her hair, he teased, "You know so little, yet talk so big."

"Don't minimize my life." She ran a hand over her eyes. "An Alpha cannot imagine what it's like growing up Omega. Of course, dynamic is not confirmed until twelve or thirteen, but that fear, to know all your childhood prayers to be Beta went unanswered. To know you would never amount to more than an Alpha's prized possession. I had broken that circle. I'd taken such care."

The man slid his arms around her, as if they were sharing a tender moment. He even kissed her forehead. "Someday, you will thank me—surrounded by our children, happy in the life I've provided."

"You want my thanks? Well, there is something I want."

Wary, pinching down her spine vertebrae by vertebrae, he made the question a warning. "Yes?"

Hand to his chest, her warm breath at his neck, she sighed. "When I wandered Thólos, I saw Lilian and the other Omegas dangling outside the Citadel. Would you bury them properly if I asked you to?"

The tilt of his head let her know he was intrigued, that he was weighing the pros of performing such a thing for her. Turning her chin, Shepherd's eyes glittered, his strategy to get the upper hand developing. "I would be willing to grant your concession, if one was made for me in return."

Claire had been disillusioned by this man long ago. Of course he'd want something. "What do you want?"

His gaze grew liquid, like molten iron. "I think we both know what I want."

"I am not going to be tricked into something. Either be exact, or forget my request."

A soft chuckle and Shepherd said, "You have grown even cleverer, my little Omega. Kiss me and I will give you what you want."

"You would have to offer something far greater to entice me to kiss you. Instead, I will offer," Claire pursed her lips and tried to consider, ignoring the way he was moving his warm hand in small circles against her lower back, encouraging negotiation. "I will offer…" She did not really have anything to offer. "I will sing for you."

"No."

"I will paint you whatever you wish."

"No."

She had failed so many; she could at least do one thing for the dead women. Moving her hand to hover over his exposed dick, she faked resolve but her unsteady voice betrayed her. "I will initiate sex at a time of your choosing."

Shepherd looked down between them where her hand was so close, but not near enough. Enticed, he purred, eyes ready to devour her. "That is a far more interesting offer. I choose all three."

Fine, then that was what he would get. "I want proof it was done."

The Alpha grinned, thoroughly smug. "Sing something now, in good faith."

She could do this. "What song would you like to hear?"

Moving her hair behind her ears, Shepherd ensured his view would be unobstructed. "The song you first sang, but no crying this time. You must also look me in the eye as you sing to me."

The ballad began and she sang it the whole way through, Shepherd caressing, purring, seemingly well-satisfied with the arrangement. Claire did not cry, far too eager to have her way.

When she had finished, he was tame… looking at her as he'd looked at Svana. "It could be like this all the time, little one."

She put a hand to his cheek and said softly with a heart hard as stone, "No, Shepherd, it couldn't."

"You will see…" Placid, Shepherd drew her back down to rest. "I will show you."

EVERYTHING WAS soft and warm and fluffy. Claire had no interest in shifting, even for the smell of coffee and the warm hand reaching into her burrow. Shepherd hooked her around the waist and pulled until her messy hair cleared the blue duvet and a bleary-eyed Omega emerged.

The new bed had arrived during her dinner with Maryanne—everything in her favorite shade of blue, everything fresh. Even with the effort the Alpha had made, Claire had not felt an urge to nest for many days. But he kept putting her back in it, taking her from whatever she was doing and burying them both under the covers, caressing her belly to encourage his Omega's thoughts of the baby, until at last it just clicked and she subconsciously began to sniff at him, began to press nearer.

Rubbing sleep from her eyes, Claire sulked, unhappy Shepherd had woken her. A wise man, he gave her a cappuccino and waited for her new morning ritual, his little one peeking, trying to hide her interest in discovering what picture lay in the foam that day before she sipped and the art was spoiled.

In her cup bloomed an intricate poppy. Claire begrudgingly loved it. “Does the person who makes these have any idea who they’re for?”

Shepherd answered with a question. “You ask because of the flower shape?”

“You have to admit, it’s a little ridiculous they would give *you* a drink with flowers in it.”

“It is a courtship ritual of Dome culture for the male to offer flowers to the female. I ordered it to be prepared this way.”

Internally cringing, Claire sipped the drink and hated that she blushed at his attempted romantic gesture, that he was going to mistake her embarrassment for coyness, that he was already looking at her with an arrogant glow in his eyes.

There was more. “Our agreement has been fulfilled.”

Claire set the cup and saucer on the bedside table, bracing herself. “And the proof?”

Shepherd brought forth his COMscreen. “May only upset you, so I am asking you to trust me and not look at the photographs.”

There was no chance in hell Claire would trust such a man. “It could not be any worse than other things I have seen in this city.”

She took the COMscreen, snatching it from his hands. The first image had been taken from a distance, all three bodies shown dangling, but not near enough to be graphic. The second was from the same vantage, Shepherd’s Followers taking them down. Claire was tempted to stop there, to accept that as good enough, but to do so would be to show weakness in the face of her adversary. Her finger slid across the screen. Bodies side by side in an open grave, rotted faces on display, only pits remaining where eyes had once been. Each corpse was still gagged, shrunken lips exposing teeth, hanging ropes embedded in their necks.

Claire could not look away.

Shepherd gently pried the COMscreen from her hands. "Are you satisfied?"

What she *was* was incredibly ill. Nodding, her mouth grew sour, Claire sank deeper into her bed in hopes he'd leave so she could run to the bathroom and puke.

Shepherd knew her every tick, knew she was unwell. Claire could either walk to the bathroom and be sick with dignity, or he was going to get involved, his scowl said as much.

Slipping out of bed, she moved past him, closing the door for privacy, and threw up everything she'd just swallowed, pretty certain it would be some time before she enjoyed a cappuccino again.

He left her in peace, waited for her to wash her face and brush her teeth, and when she came back, Claire began to dress as if nothing had happened.

Brushing her tangled hair, she turned to the man still sitting at the end of the bed. "What would you like me to paint for you?"

He took a contemplative breath, voice almost jovial when he spoke. "A portrait of yourself, little one. One I will appreciate."

With the brush mid-way through a tangle, Claire mused, unsure if Shepherd comprehended how difficult self-portraits would be. “That’s out of my scope. It might not be any good.”

He flicked his fingers, beckoning her closer. Apprehensive that she would be expected to perform the other requirement of their agreement at that very moment, Claire stiffened, but went to him.

Taking the brush from her hands, he set it aside and pulled her to rest on his knee. “I want you to sing for me now.”

“I already sang for you.”

The man smirked, sly as he spoke, “Our agreement did not stipulate a number of times. You simply said you would sing for me, and I desire you to do so again.”

Claire suspected it was far more for her benefit than his, a distraction that would shift her thinking in a more settling direction. “If you set this precedent and begin bending the rules, it’s only going to backfire eventually.”

He touched a finger to her nose. Shepherd squinted, and the man cooed, “Please.”

She sang the first thing that came to mind, a relic anthem about war… a song that was poignant, sad, and far too expressive of the plight of Thólos.

“Do you still feel ill?” Shepherd asked, aware of her little musical mutiny as he gently touched her belly.

Claire did not usually feel well upon waking, especially after being dragged out of bed to see pictures of victims Shepherd had murdered, and she told him so.

“The punishment meted out to those women was earned.” The man was unmoved by her declaration. “If your death would have brought them gain, they would not have hesitated to kill you. You were kind enough to see them buried. Do not mourn them further."

"Do you not wish to be mourned when you die?" Claire asked, non-threatening, only interested in his answer.

Stroking over the baby, the tiny thing that had yet to distort her figure, Shepherd asked, "Would you not mourn me, little one? Or would you relish the death of your mate?"

Claire was not inhuman. She had natural feelings and felt a discord in the link, the sudden uneasy throb in her chest that seemed saddened by the mere thought of the bearer of the bond's death. Deeper still, she suspected his death would not equate to her freedom—too much had been done. She would languish as she had when the bond had been damaged. She would die. Unsure how to answer his question, she rubbed her hand over her face and refused to respond.

"The thought upsets you." Again it was the gentle, manipulative voice and the soft touches of a man she knew pretended to be something he was not. "You need not fear. You would always be cared for."

Sometimes it seemed as if Shepherd could read her very thoughts. Other times it seemed he was so far off base it was as if they lived on separate planets.

Claire had to get off his lap, she needed to think. Shepherd allowed it.

Smoothing back her hair, she thought to press on another subject. "I cannot make myself understand. What is it you want from Thólos? You are king with a list of ambitions, but you let your lands decay. You rule everything under the Dome, but hate your subjects."

Shepherd put his elbows on his knees, spoke with acumen as the Omega paced. "My number of loyal Followers have swelled beyond even what I imagined. Hardship distills the soul."

The things she had seen in the streets of Thólos, the depravity—it made the truth of his words sting. "Those who joined since the breach are traitors who chose your doctrine out of a misguided sense of survival."

"True, but the majority of the terrorism in Thólos was perpetrated by its own citizens. I did not get involved."

Swallowing, Claire wrung her hands, looking for something she could use. "I know. I asked for help… remember? You didn't help me."

The shine of approval lit Shepherd's eyes. "But I did."

Claire thought she might lose her cool. "I will not have this fight with you."

"Think of your assault of the Undercroft," the giant reminded her. "Think of what you accomplished for the Omegas. What occurs in Thólos defines character. You are exceptional."

That was far from true. Ashamed, Claire turned her eyes to the floor and confessed, "Did Maryanne tell you what I had to do to convince her to help me?"

"I have not discussed such things with Ms. Cauley. What was done is forgiven and your motivation understood."

"I threatened her," Claire admitted, certain he must see

how his occupation had affected even her. "I threatened her with you."

Shepherd could not help but laugh outright. "How charming you are. Do not trouble yourself. You would never have followed through on the threat. We both know that."

But she had still done wrong to her friend. "I hated doing it, Shepherd."

The man nodded, entirely self-satisfied. "But it was necessary."

He was twisting her words, using the opportunity to influence. He remained unreactive, patient, and Claire wondered why he seemed pleased at her question of, "Where will it end?"

Shepherd answered like a father educating a child. "In a cultivated Utopia."

Fighting not to grit her teeth, Claire went back to the topic at hand. "Full of damaged people? How will Shanice enjoy the world that inspired her rape?"

"Had you not interfered, she would have been safe, separated from the dangers of Thólos, and cared for by her mate —who would have provided all she needed. Charles was a good man, one deserving of the gift of an Omega's love."

She was not going to beat a dead horse. "In this utopia, where is justice for my dead boy? The children suffering and dying are innocent…"

"Children are being neglected and destroyed by their own people. My Followers do not harm them."

"But they don't help them. They perpetuate the suffering. I don't understand how you cannot see what I see," Claire, green eyes wide and beseeching, said. “Shepherd, you set convicts free. You inspired brutality. You are more dangerous an infection than the Red Consumption.”

“Less than twenty-thousand men were set free in a city of millions… a city of people who chose to embrace violence rather than stand honorably—a people who are easily corrupted. I never told them to pillage, rape, or murder. Thólos is responsible for its actions.”

“You manipulate us all with a skill that is terrible, yet could be redirected.” Stamping her foot in frustration, Claire demanded, “Why not inspire goodness, why not try to change the world through nonviolence?”

“It would be pointless in a place so immoral and corrupt. You cannot reason with these types of people, little one. You cannot explain or educate. They are absolutely aware of what they do. They don’t care about you, your goodness, or anything beyond their own insatiable desires. After all, what do you know of Senator Kantor, the champion of the people? That man would do anything for power, manipulate anyone for wealth. He knows secrets that, were he to divulge them to the resistance, they would slit his throat.”

Fighting not to lose ground or be distracted, Claire growled, “You are bitter because he is still free, because he fights.”

Crossing his great arms over his chest, Shepherd said, “What makes you think I don’t know where he is at this very moment?”

She took a deep breath, she made herself look passive. “There is no resistance.”

"There never will be." Creased skin around his eyes exaggerated Shepherd's smile. "Thólossens will never rise up at the cost of their dwindling comfort."

Knowing the question would irritate him, Claire asked bluntly, "Has my flyer had an effect?"

"Yes." Silver eyes lost their mirth, their shifty furtiveness, and narrowed in disapproval.

That was something, that inspired hope. "So you're wrong."

Shepherd developed a hooded expression, answered as if reluctant. "Your picture has led to a rash of violent murders of black-haired women who look like you. My men find more every day."

Claire's voice hitched, the sliver of hope she'd had shattered. "You're lying!" But she was already crumbling, because it was just too fucking believable.

Gently, Shepherd asked, "Now do you understand just what the citizens of this city are?"

Head in her hands, Claire began to weep, the responsibility for each unknown woman's death carved into her forever.

He had outmaneuvered her again; he had won.

Even scooped into circling arms, wracked with sobs, hating herself for what her flyer had inspired and how utterly stupid she was for not recognizing what it could lead to, Claire sagged to the floor. He was inside her in seconds, purring and petting, holding her tightly so she would not hurt herself by fighting back. She cried the entire time, tears running even as she climaxed, even as he told her sweet, soothing things. When that didn't work, Shepherd proclaimed it was not her fault, that she was good, and even he knew that she could not have suspected such an outcome—she was free of guilt, she was pure, her ideals were noble… the city did not deserve her.

He told her he loved her.

She quieted a little.

The following twenty-four hours, Claire could hardly bear to leave the nest. Shepherd left her in peace so long as she ate everything he brought her, including fried potato wedges with mayonnaise and a chocolate shake.

14

When Claire woke the following day, Shepherd bathed her, dressed her, and brought out the handcuffs so that he could take her to see the sky. Deep down, she knew self-pity would get her nowhere. She wanted to rally, to get back to forging progress, because she owed it to those murdered black-haired women, but lost faith was a slippery slope, and she had nothing to hold on to.

Shepherd tried to give her that something.

He carried her to the room with the window. He locked the door and showed her his latest gift. Her mother's piano rested against the wallpaper, his Followers having dragged it all the way from Claire's ransacked apartment.

There was no bench, only a small stool he took himself, leaving her on his lap where she might frown at the scratched keys. As they were still chained, Shepherd followed where her fingers flexed, his body surrounding her like a blanket.

One aching breath and Claire closed her eyes. In a stupor, she began to play Bach just as her mother had taught her. The pedals were tricky to reach with the male serving as her seat—a man with his hand over her womb, who moved as she moved, never once hindering. They were a single creature. Even the bulky arm chained to hers followed smoothly, Shepherd never tugging the metal links, never interfering.

Breathing in time, crying softly, Claire purged. It was all there in the melody: sorrow, shame, guilt. But as the music went on, as rumbling purrs filled the air in concert, despair changed into something that hurt a little less.

Claire was no virtuoso, her fingers hit sour notes, but performing gave her pleasure. It was pleasure she allowed, that she sucked in as if starved for it. Wet eyes opened, more tears fell. Precious sound, the feeling of keys, of warmth, drowned out the pain.

But even so beautiful a distraction could not last. "I would never have made that flyer if I'd thought others would suffer."

Shepherd embraced her tighter. "I am aware."

It was only a whisper. "Thólos needed to know. They needed to see. But they have done nothing. They are doing… nothing."

Shepherd breathed at her ear. "You cannot save Thólos, little one."

Banging the keys in a mishmash of off-putting noise, Claire ended the concert. "I shouldn't have to! You should not have done this!"

Hand on her belly, scarred lips at her ear, Shepherd murmured, "If I had not come, what kind of life would you have had, Claire?"

What she'd always pictured. "I would have found a husband, had kids, painted… I wouldn't be afraid for my friends, mourning more people than I can remember. My beautiful city would not be in ruins or my home destroyed."

Shepherd used her reasoning against her. "The people you care for are safe because of you. My men watch over them. You still paint. You have a mate who would see to any need you expressed to him, so long as it did not endanger you—one who requires your patience. Beyond that, will you not find pleasure in the child I have given you?"

Hot tears falling free, Claire looked to where a very little life would be snuffed out when she ended herself—a little life that was growing daily and becoming more real, which affected her and increased her dependence on the Alpha purring at her ear.

As if he knew she refused to embrace the thought of her son, Shepherd cooed in her ear, "You will love our baby and sing for him, paint him pictures… and he will have dark hair like yours, and maybe your eyes."

Never once had she allowed herself to picture the child. Hearing so tempting a description, Claire could not stop the image from invading her mind, hating the male who whispered so sweetly for the cruelty of what he was doing in making her son real.

Insistence invaded Shepherd's attempt at gentle speech.

"You don't have to fight it, Claire. You could forgive me, forgive yourself, and your pain would end. You could do it for your son, so that he need not suffer a disengaged mother as you did."

Her breath caught, she automatically pressed the keys to hide in her music. Gently, Shepherd took her hands, preventing her attempted distraction until his point was made.

"Have things not improved in these last weeks?" He stroked the trembling Omega; he kissed her neck. "I know it has been painful for you to accept what you have faced between us, what you experienced in Thólos. I also know that you understand my purpose to a point, and though you may not want to admit it, you see how wrong this place is."

"Please stop…"

"If you wish."

His acquiescence was unexpected. Claire uncurled, tried to move her arms, and found Shepherd no longer held her from her goal. She began to play again, the melody slow and wretched. As her fingers roamed the keys, she thought of her mother, the woman who'd sat by her side for hours, patiently teaching her child the one thing she'd taken true joy in. It was an act of love Claire had always wanted to share with her own children, part of the fantasy the Omega had envisioned in her perfect future.

Thoughts of her dead mother led to thoughts of her dead father—to the scent of orange blossoms and remembrance of warm sunshine. Her daddy's laughter had been Claire's favorite sound in the world.

Another male vaguely reminded her of the man: Corday, with his silly boyish grin, his kindness, his patience.

As if Shepherd knew, as if he could tempt her thoughts back to him, he lifted Claire's skirt and caressed her thigh. It felt good, the way Shepherd touched. It felt perfectly nice as the music stirred and her attention relaxed to alter tempo in time with the Alpha's long warm strokes. He grew more daring, and her breath caught when his large fingers explored, teasing in exactly the right spot.

The way he could play her body, the ease with which he parted her folds, how simply her legs spread of their own volition to offer access so he might please her… sometimes it seemed pure. "That's right, little one."

And that voice, the heat of masculine rasps, why could it have not belonged to someone else?

A dexterous thumb exposed her clit, circled it as she mewed and stumbled badly through a musical phrase. When thick fingers penetrated languorous and deep, Claire whined, her breath caught, and it was the Alpha's name she panted.

"Shepherd."

The bliss of his fingers slipped away, but in their place he set his member free and gently lifted his mate. He sheathed himself in a slow, deliberate entry. Cock engulfed, the Alpha remained still, set no pace—he only groaned at her ear while Claire instinctively gyrated for her own pleasure.

The heat of his hand returned, plucking at her swollen nub, drawing out whimpers and little stifled cries. Claire no longer knew what she was playing or if it made any sense musically, everything was focused on the building pressure and the comfort of a familiar body. Whatever her hips did, Shepherd's fingers followed. Though his breath was labored and he badly craved to rear up into that tight, little passage, he let her take what she needed.

It was not long before Claire's movements grew erratic. At the sound of the Alpha's desperate moan, she jerked and ground down hard, climaxing so beautifully the world went white.

Shepherd followed on command, drenching her insides in warmth and her favorite scent—something that had become far more gorgeous than the smell of orange blossoms.

Claire didn't cry. For once she did not chastise herself. She simply sat on his lap with the knot fusing their bodies, felt him still spurting in the lingering minutes of his own release, and began to play Bach again—because she had to survive herself, she had to survive to give Corday his chance no matter how badly the odds were stacked against him. And she would not survive if she could not take the comfort Shepherd offered when she was so close to breaking apart again.

The Alpha growled, contented with each exhale. Nestling closer, he held her tight, and enjoyed Claire's pseudo-serenity.

He had won. His mate was allowing their bond to soothe her.

"Gimme your foot," Maryanne barked, shaking a little bottle in her hand with quick jerks of her wrist.

Stuffed full of cake—a huge tiered thing, frosted bird's egg blue and beautifully decorated, a cake that could feed half of Shepherd's army… that even after their brutal attack on it could still feed half of Shepherd's army—the friends lounged and played at girly things.

Smiling, sitting slumped in her chair, Claire picked up one bare foot and stretched it over to set in her friend's lap. "Why am I not surprised the color you brought is vampy red?"

Maryanne brushed a careful line of paint over Claire's big toe, smirking. "Too sexy for prudish little Claire?"

"Says the girl who slept with every boy we knew…"

"After I left, did you ever cave in and date that that Seymour guy? He had such a crush on you."

Claire groaned and rolled her eyes. "Gods no. I had my dad chase him off when he started sniffing around the house."

Playful eyes glanced up, Maryanne motioning for the other foot. "What about boys in higher academy?"

Claire shook her head. "I was focused on my studies."

"After academy?"

"Geez, you make me sound so boring!"

"So only Shepherd, huh?" Maryanne pretended to focus on her work, spreading the crimson paint carefully. "That's kinda too bad. I mean, think about it. If you have only slept with Shepherd you have nothing to compare it to. He could be awful and you would never know. I bet you wish you'd experimented now…"

Laughing so hard it hurt, Claire struggled to say, "Stop antagonizing him!"

"That's what he gets for eavesdropping on girl talk. There are reasons why women congregate without men… so we can make fun of them."

Claire was still laughing, green eyes dancing while *innocent* Maryanne blew on her toes. "What other interesting things do you have in your pockets?"

"Look who wants presents?" the blonde sang, reaching into her coat for a tube of lipstick.

Unscrewing the lid, Maryanne made a face like an artist creating a masterpiece. Claire leaned forward, puckered, and let her stain her lips a rich berry red.

"Well, I'm not going to lie," Maryanne shrugged, unimpressed. "It's a little trampy on you, but Shepherd might like it."

"It's the same color you're wearing!" Claire snorted, snatching the tube from Maryanne's hands. "I had a lipstick like this once, never had a place to wear it."

"What do you mean place to wear it? You just wear it," her friend replied, settling back in her chair.

Claire's soft smile was gently reprimanding. "That's easy for you to say, Alpha. If you draw attention, being as pretty as you are, you don't have to worry about potential complications."

Yawning, Maryanne shrugged. "That is just silly, Claire—and paranoid. It's just lipstick. And I guess you don't have to worry about that anymore. Ain't no one gonna to be messing with Shepherd's old lady."

Green eyes grew sad. “That’s not what I hear is going on outside…”

“What do you mean?”

A guilt-ridden voice confessed, “Women who look like me… because of my flyer.”

“You *told* her about that?” Maryanne snarled at the hostile male watching from the corner. “What is wrong with you?”

Claire could not see his reaction to her friend’s outburst, but knew it couldn’t be good. She interjected, “I am not a child, Maryanne. I asked, and he told me the truth.”

Maryanne had her own harsh take on things. “None of that was your fault, you know. I thought the flyer was pretty ballsy, but you’ve got to get it through your thick skull, girl. Thólos is a bad place full of bad people.”

“People can change,” Claire breathed, knowing it had to be true.

Maryanne cocked a brow and made a hard point. “Do you think Shepherd can change?”

The Omega tilted her head, thinking about it before looking over her shoulder. Her eyes met Shepherd’s.

He glanced down at her stained lips, seemingly intrigued.

Standing, she walked, careless of her newly lacquered toes, and went to stand before the male. So many contradictory thoughts were running through her head. His behavior towards her had changed, was far more palatable, but all of that could easily be summed up as an insincere strategy to gain her affection. After all, she was certain there had been no change in him outside their den or in his dealings with Thólos.

When her small hand reached up and the female cupped his cheek, Shepherd allowed it, unmoving as she stood between his spread legs. His silver eyes shone, focused and pleased with her attention in front of the Alpha female.

Claire pulled in a breath as if to speak, then hesitated, pouting her red lips until he purred and the back of his warm fingers stroked over her belly.

The question was for herself. "Could Shepherd change?"

It was all there in her expression—how badly she wished he could change. How hard she had tried to affect something in him. Whispering, her voice as soft as the fingertips that touched the flesh of his cheek, Claire asked, "Could you change?"

A warm, large hand enclosed hers, gently removing her touch from his face, Shepherd admonished, "You are neglecting your guest, little one." Breathing, blinking out of her trance, Claire took a step back as the male pressed some small scissors into her hand. "I have given her permission to cut your hair, should you wish it."

Looking down at the little instrument, Claire teased Maryanne. "I don't trust her with these. Everything will come out cockeyed."

From across the room, the woman blurted, "How hard could it be?"

Claire smirked, thinking of Maryanne's godawful attempt ten years prior. "That's what you said last time, and may I remind you, those terrible bangs took over two years to grow out."

She moved back to Maryanne and let the blonde trim her hair, fairly certain it would be terrible, and honestly not caring at all if it was. The only thing about the interlude Claire cared about was the COMscreen Maryanne produced, full of photos of the Omegas, and even one of Corday, who was smiling his dimpled grin as he spoke to whoever was just outside the frame. On the smallest finger of his hand sat her gold ring, diminutive, but there.

Corday still had faith in her.

Making sure not to look at him too long, Claire set the COMscreen down and remained still as Maryanne snipped.

When the cut was over, dark hair tousled, Maryanne assured in a playfully thick accent, "Very beautiful."

Handing her a pocket mirror, she frowned when Claire pressed it back, stating, "I don't need to see."

Maryanne shoved it back. "It's not bad, Claire. Take a look."

"I'm sure you did fine."

Maryanne knew what was going on, could see through the cracks in her old friend's mask.

Holding the mirror up, making a point, she snarled once the Omega turned her head away. "What is wrong with you?"

Moving the mirror to Claire's new line of sight produced the same outcome. Claire looked away. Enough was enough. Maryanne grabbed a fistful of hair and held Claire's head still, forcing the mirror before the Omega's face. "Open your eyes and look in the mirror, Claire!"

She did. Claire looked at a hated face, one with full lips that had been painted to be pretty and black hair that had been cut to frame her face. A face with green eyes and pale skin; a face she had been unable to look at for the last week without seeing dead women who looked like her. Women she had killed.

With a voice that could no long bear inflection, Claire said, "You're right. The lipstick is trampy."

"You don't need to do this to yourself, you idiot." Maryanne gave Claire's hair a little yank. "There is nothing wrong with that woman in the mirror. Their deaths are not your fault."

"Step away from her, Ms. Cauley. Go stand near the door and do not move." There was nothing but the threat of murder in Shepherd's voice, every word enunciated with chilling precision.

Maryanne darted back, the behemoth stalking forward. Watching with awe, the Alpha female saw the mountain kneel to his mate. His purr was aggressive, his hands already petting an Omega who seemed composed and patient, but was anything but.

"She didn't do anything wrong," Claire explained. "Everything is fine."

Shepherd spoke in that other language, loud enough that the Followers on the other side began to unlock the door. In a flash, Maryanne was gone. Once the door was bolted, Shepherd pulled Claire to stand and drew her to the room's luxurious bathroom.

A large mirror hung over the fine sink, and with a flick of

the lights there they were, standing side by side, framed in filigreed gold.

"Your skills at deception are abysmal," Shepherd explained, gesturing at her reflection. "So let's not waste time, shall we? Why are you only looking at me in the mirror and not at yourself?"

Humiliated that she had allowed this situation, that she had not performed better, Claire looked straight at her reflection. "My stomach was upset."

"You are lying," the male roared, hating the strange feeling that was coming through the cord. "What is wrong?"

There were no tears, only a blank stare. "I just can't look at them."

A great hand lifted as if to grip her skull. Instead Shepherd clawed through her hair, the nearest thing to a pet an angry Alpha could manage. "Continue."

In the mirror Claire was dwarfed next to the massive man, small and useless. "I am angry that I cannot do anything for anyone, that everything I tried only made things worse. I feel powerless, ashamed of myself for my failure and the horrible effect I had on women who look like me." Beseeching eyes darted to his reflection. "And I'm frustrated that no matter what I say to you, to a man I am pair-bonded to, that it would change nothing—even if I had the power to redeem you—because Thólos did horrible things when the people could have rallied and brought you down."

"The price you are exacting from yourself is not yours to pay. It is Thólos'."

She was getting angry. "I *am* Thólos, Shepherd. Born and raised here. I grew up here. My parents are buried here."

"Look at yourself in the mirror, Claire O'Donnell." The male reared up as he spoke. "You are an Omega, physically small and weak, yet incredibly intelligent. That said, however shrewd you may be, you are also foolish enough to think you must bear the burden of others' sins… That is your true flaw. The psychological trauma you are causing yourself is both immature and pointless. It does nothing to change the scenario. And though I am honored you would consider the thought of my redemption as worthy, it is your own peace you need to focus on now. Self-pity and playing the martyr help no one."

The woman gave a caustic snort. "Well, I failed at playing the hero."

In a voice that was hard and assertive, Shepherd snarled, "But you didn't, and you know it. Forty-three people are alive because you had the nerve to stand up to me. You won, Claire. No single adversary has ever beaten me before. Ever. Take your victory."

It was not that simple, not when the world and her mind were in a constant state of turmoil. Not when she was only breathing to buy time.

In the midst of chaos, there is also opportunity. - Sun Tzu

Rubbing her lips together, she felt the unfamiliar slide of lipstick and met Shepherd's eyes again. "The lipstick *is* trampy."

"And your hair?"

"Looks nice."

"And the dress?"

"Is something I would never have chosen for myself in a thousand years. I look like the poster girl for a pre-plague Omega housewife—which I suppose is fitting, as I am barefoot and pregnant."

"Are you attempting comedy?" For once the man actually sounded unsure.

Claire smirked and shook her head in the negative.

FOR DAYS she wasted paper while the Alpha stared, watching her paint her promised portrait for him. Claire was beginning to suspect that Shepherd was trying to drive her crazy with the constant appraisal of her work. But there was a method to his madness, even Claire understood that. He was forcing her to look at herself over and over, until it was no longer quite so nausea inspiring, until it was her face on the paper and not some unknown woman Claire had conjured up.

A deep breath, the type that preceded some grand speech the bastard was going to make, passed Shepherd's lips. Claire's eyes shot up, blazing warning as she snarled, "I swear to the Gods, Shepherd, if you say one thing about this painting, I am going to scream."

Undaunted, he cocked an eyebrow and stated, "I want you to paint yourself smiling more."

Pounding her fist on the table, biting back the rising noise in her throat, Claire let out a stream of obscenities so vulgar the man began to laugh. Paint-stained hands balled up the picture, Claire throwing it right in his face. Then it was her turn to laugh at the absolute look of murder in his eyes.

Popping her lips, grinning impishly, she reached for another piece of paper and ignored the swelling, angry male. Innocently, she dipped the brush and began the outline again, painting the same smug grin she was wearing at that moment. When the basic form was drawn, she arrogantly held it up, and watched him narrow his eyes and appraise.

Before he could speak, a knock came to the door and a man whose voice Claire didn't recognize spouted off something in their language. Shepherd's attention focused on what he was hearing, the Alpha already standing as he replied in kind.

Shepherd immediately began pulling on his armor.

A strange anxiety twisted in her stomach, this situation not having arisen before. Watching him dress for battle at a summons and not simply because he was leaving for the day, meant something was going on—something that could be dangerous to him, to Thólos, to anyone.

"You do not need to be concerned, little one." There was a smile in his voice.

When Claire's eyes darted up to meet his, she found him collected and calm. But *she* felt incredibly uneasy, all humor from only a few moments ago evaporating. "What's going on?"

The purr began. Shepherd pulled on his coat and came to where she sat, alarmed and stiff. Stroking the line of her jaw, he explained, "There is nothing. I simply lost the hour playing your game with the paints."

He was lying. The man always knew what time it was without the presence of a clock. “I don’t believe you.”

Ignoring her accusation, he cracked his neck and looked down at his worried mate. “I will be back shortly, and when I return, I expect to receive the remaining portion of our agreement.”

She fought to maintain an impassive expression while Shepherd traced her lips with his thumb and leveled upon her a liquid gaze brimming with lust and ravenous expectation. He dipped his thumb between her lips, growled richly as if he was about to fuck her, and left her sitting in a little pool of slick.

Dazed, Claire stared at the closing door. She knew what he was calling due, what he had left sitting between them for weeks—in order to fulfill their bargain, Claire was expected to initiate sex.

Unsure whether he had chosen that moment as a means to distract her from her worry, or if it was some sort of victory celebration for whatever he was doing, she shifted uncomfortably at being left in such a state.

It was not as if she’d forgotten what she’d offered for Lilian and the others to be laid to rest, but she’d had other far more pressing things to center her thoughts upon. Besides, physical intimacy with Shepherd had taken place countless times. She knew what he liked, where to touch him to draw out a reaction… so how hard could it be to initiate it?

Hard.

Looking for a distraction, Claire showered and cleaned up the paints, expecting him back at any second. But hours passed and she began to grow anxious, worried about what might or might not be going on in Thólos.

Was it an insurrection? Corday—had he found a way to end this?

Claire was on the edge of full-blown panic when the lock finally shifted. Gritty metal whined and the door swung inwards. She stopped her customary pacing, turning with tangled relief to face the largeness of her mate.

15

The severed head of Senator Kantor still lay on the table, wrecked and unmoved from the place it had been dropped once Jules had pulled it from the pike outside the Citadel and brought the repugnant thing to Shepherd. There was no clean cut where neck had been severed from shoulders, just a torn stump of muscle and tendon. Around it lay a splatter of blood, leaking fluids, and the fingers of a man gripping the table so tightly his knuckles had gone white.

Before Shepherd had left, they'd argued, the Alpha's bulging arms crossed over his chest while he'd stared down his second-in-command. "You went against my orders and killed him while he was still useful to us?"

"No…"

Svana.

She had done this. She had murdered her uncle. Who else

could move with the stealth to slip right under the noses of trained Followers? Who else would stick the head on a pike outside the Citadel as if to taunt not only Shepherd but the city she sought to destroy? Who else would gain by this?

It was a delicate thing, tormenting a population just enough to keep them miserable, Shepherd having exercised caution not to press millions past the point of desperation. Hanging a traitor as part of a public trial and execution spread the blame on all who watched. It made the population impotent and held Thólos responsible. This… the Champion of the People and leader of the resistance's head had been mutilated for show, loudly broadcasting the wrong sentiment.

That was what had earned Shepherd's anger, not Jules' accusations that Svana had done this to undermine them all.

Riots had already begun to bloom, Followers acting in mercenary fashion.

Even faced with this kind of proof of Svana's treachery, Shepherd did not see an imprudent mistake—yes, Svana could be difficult, but she would not break rank, not when she stood to gain the most from their great plan's success. If she had done this, it had been for good reason.

Jules had lost his temper. He'd smashed his fist against the table and roared.

Shepherd had only put a hand on his friend's shoulder, both as comfort and as warning. "Do not allow this complication to cloud your thinking. Patrols must be immediately increased to counter potential uprising, rioters dealt with quietly. We cannot continue shooting citizens in broad daylight, to do so would only encourage more unrest. I need you in the field."

Jules swallowed, lips tight. "She seeks to control the rebellion."

Squeezing the smaller man's shoulder, Shepherd growled, "Brother, if what you believe is true, it would only benefit our cause to have Svana at the helm of our enemy's forces."

There was some stinging truth in his leader's words. Had the woman in question been anyone but Svana, Jules may have even agreed. The Beta would not allow her to stir up animosity, having seen years of her manipulations and spite. He would not give her the pleasure. The best course was to follow orders. "Understood."

Shepherd had left him to oversee the sedation of potential riots, to be seen in the Citadel.

Alone, for an hour, Jules crouched, eye level with the severed head of Senator Kantor.

Up close, Kantor's eyes displayed the hazy film of developing cataracts. Between lids half drooping, retinas mismatched in the direction they pointed, and the gaping mouth, the Alpha finally looked as monstrous on the outside as Jules knew he'd been on the inside.

The Champion of the People… had been the vilest of men.

Jules' lips parted and from his mouth flowed malice. "You murdered my children. You took my Rebecca from me."

He spat fully across the corpse's bloodied face.

"And I have watched you be lauded and adored for a

decade. I have watched you lie and pollute, and I have bided my time so that you might know true suffering." Raw fury twisted through Jules' hiss. "Your death was *mine*, and I will make her pay for stealing my vengeance. Svana will bleed for this."

Thank you for reading Born to be Broken! Shepherd and Claire's story is far from over.

Now, please enjoy an extended excerpt of REBORN…

REBORN

Alpha's Claim, Book Three

Collar of his coat flipped up to protect his neck from the growing cold of the halls, Shepherd returned at last from being called away by his soldiers. He found his mate nervous, the acrid scent of Omega fear spoiling the air. But, mostly she was expectant and blissfully unaware of just what was going on above ground.

And he would never tell her.

Shepherd made no move to approach the panicky woman, he simply stood as Claire looked him over from boots to skull. The Omega searched out any hint of what had called him from her, looking for blood splatter, or the swelling of his knuckles, relieved when she found nothing out of the ordinary.

His Claire was angry, but far more reassured that he'd returned seemingly *normal*.

When the Omega stepped forward to touch him, to initiate what had to be done to seal their bargain, Shepherd spoke. "You are hungry, little one. We will eat first."

We will eat first?

Shepherd did not go to the door to fetch food. Instead, he went to where he stored his clothing and began pulling off his coat, armor, and boots. Bunched muscles flexing, he pulled his shirt over his head, handing it to her. Unthinkingly, Claire took it and put it, as he expected, in her nest.

Distracted by the task, the Omega chewed her lip, taking time to arrange the scented fabric and remove something old to be washed.

A knock sounded, Shepherd barking for the visitor to enter.

Jules came in with their food, set it down and left in seconds—the trivial familiarity he shared with Claire completely concealed by his indifference. She found it minorly amusing, especially the way Shepherd shifted to put his body between her and the Beta.

When the door closed, Claire found it very difficult to suppress a snort.

"What is funny?" the male growled, narrowing his eyes.

"*You* are funny, Shepherd." Claire arranged herself at the table. "That man has brought me meals dozens of times when you are not here—so you must trust him. Yet there you are, glaring at him as if he were not your friend. You have serious issues..."

Shepherd only grunted in answer. Dressed only in trousers, he came to the table. "It is a natural reaction for an Alpha to guard his Omega from dangerous men."

But not dangerous women...

Glancing at the food, Claire felt wholly disillusioned. She began to comprehend what was going on, what he had arranged for himself. This, the meal, was a show—a show where she was not spectator, but entertainer. She was expected to perform for the man lowering himself into the seat across from her. Reminding herself their agreement only required she initiate sex, nothing more, she picked up her fork and chose not to argue. Instead, Claire focused on the beautiful dinner, the male mirroring her movements and tasting the food.

It seemed awkward, the silence, and out of habit and good manners, Claire found herself wanting to make small talk, knowing it would be both pointless and something Shepherd would not respond to.

Except, he began it. "I have been told this is one of your chef's most famous dishes."

Cocking a brow, Claire looked up from the steamed fish and nodded, momentarily confused. "My chef? You do not eat his cooking?"

"Her cooking, and no."

That seemed strange. "What do you normally eat?"

"What my men eat. Communal food amongst those who've endured the Undercroft bears an importance I do not expect you to understand or submit to."

There were a great many things about the man she didn't understand.

Seeing that the woman was puzzled and still tense, Shepherd offered a modicum of explanation. "After years subsisting off mold, our digestive tracts have altered. *Followers'* diets must be bland, and the required nutritional additives have an unpleasant taste and smell. The bulk of my meal was consumed before I returned to you. This is… supplementary."

Was that why he never ate in her presence? She looked at

the beautifully arranged plate. “Well, considering all your other physical attributes, I think it’s only fair you have one restriction.”

The male smirked, gratified. “Physical attributes?”

“You are very tall,” Claire quipped flatly, taking another bite, not at all interested in padding the Alpha’s ego.

His foot bumped hers under the table. “List another attribute.”

Dodging Alpha pride was something Claire had years of experience with. “You are bald. It must save time not combing your hair.”

Narrowed eyes matched his agitated reply. “I shave my head.”

Claire sneered, pleased her slight had pricked him, and took another bite of dinner.

“You are playing with me, little one,” he added, intrigued, once he saw her mischievous expression.

Gesturing with her fork, Claire explained. “You’re arrogant enough. I am not going to feed that beast.”

Shepherd countered, his own evil smirk appearing. “You will later. When I move inside you tonight, you will hum about my prowess and strength… You will want to say all those things and more.”

The self-satisfied expression, the fact she knew what was coming—worse still, the fact he could inspire such a declaration—made Claire’s cheeks flame. She would cry out for him, admire him physically with her hands and tongue, but she would keep her words to herself. “We shall see.”

The grin that spread his scarred lips, the absolute hunger

in his expression, only added to the Alpha's excitement. "A challenge from the coy, little Omega..."

For a second, Claire believed he might reach across the table and devour her. Even the way Shepherd breathed as he watched her eat implied his exercise of control warred with his impulse to mount her.

"You seem like you are in an awfully good mood." Claire thought back to how he had left her earlier, lingering anxiety matching the disapproval in her voice. "What did you do today?"

"Nothing of importance, aside from wondering what would be waiting for me in this room when I returned," Shepherd purred, charmed by her attempted interrogation. "I think of you often when we are parted."

Gods, even his scent was dripping sex.

The whole secret lies in confusing the enemy, so that he cannot fathom our real intent. -Sun Tzu

Sucking her lower lip into her mouth, Claire tried to figure out if he was trying to distract her, or mislead her. Looking at him, at the exposed musculature of his chest and arms, she found Shepherd sat with arrogance and authority, as if her regard were his due. Claire cocked her head, testing. "If you were so eager for the remainder of our bargain, then why are we eating together?"

"Out of respect for my mate. I had fine food prepared and we are engaging in conversation, as you stated you desired... and as Dome culture dictates."

Claire understood at once, this was not just a shared meal. It was Shepherd's attempt at another courtship custom—like the foam flowers in her coffee. Pushing her hair behind her ear, her nervous blush deepened.

He exercised the softer expression he saved for the kill. Claire saw it, and knew at once her assessment was correct. Shepherd was, in his way, trying to woo her.

Unsure, Claire murmured, "This is to relax me."

"Yes."

"So I perform better for you?"

He gave her a long look that said yes, no, and a thousand other things. Unsmiling, his head just a tick to the side, Shepherd grunted. "You do not appreciate the effort?"

There was definitely a wrong answer, and that was the only one she wanted to blurt out. Biting her tongue, she looked at the shirtless man and said, "You are courting me."

"According to your customs, yes."

She was not sure what made her curious, but Claire had to ask, "Wouldn't they also be your courtship customs?"

The man seemed momentarily at a loss for an easy answer. "There was no concept of courtship in the Undercroft. Men just took what they wanted. Violently."

All too familiar anger bubbled under her skin, Claire aware that was exactly what he had done to her. "So that is the culture you choose to identify with?"

It seemed like such a simple question, but Shepherd took his time measuring his reply, as if tailoring it in his head first. "I choose to identify with military culture."

The corner of her lips curled, Claire took another bite, wondering how on earth the crazy man across the table existed.

Shepherd disliked her reaction. "You find my answer unsatisfactory."

Waving her fork, she stated blandly, "I find it unique. Very Shepherd-like."

"Explain."

Claire leaned forward and met his eyes with a harsh look in her own. "You have strong opinions on *my* culture, have made several claims of our failings and vices... but you do not have a culture of your own. Considering the aspersions you cast, it seems your personal experience with real society is negligible."

The male straightened in his chair. "I have extensively studied Dome life for many years. I lived above ground and below. I watched, learned, followed, and remembered."

The man was completely missing her point, or he was redirecting her on purpose. "Have you participated in *my* society before you tried to ruin it? Only watching doesn't count. Your military culture, the ethos you created for your Followers, is just Undercroft society tailored to conveniently meet your manifesto."

Shepherd warned, "We have our own traditions and an honorable philosophy, little one."

"That's right, a whole army of honorable monsters who probably roast humans on a spit for fun."

The man answered with a very droll, "We only do that on high holidays."

Claire almost choked when Shepherd actually made a joke. Coughing into her hand, chuckling despite herself, she found the male very pleased with himself for rousing her amusement.

She could feel the wheels in his mind turning, understood he had tried to banter in the same manner he'd witnessed between her and Maryanne. It was very strange to witness the way Shepherd's mind processed and adapted. He was like a sponge that absorbed interaction but didn't quite know how to apply it. So he practiced, usually falling short. Except that time... that time had been perfect.

Taking another bite so she could hide her smirk, Claire asked, "Enlighten me, Shepherd. Where do Omegas fit into military culture?"

Shepherd began to consider. It seemed like such a human gesture, the way he sucked his plump lower lip into his mouth, so totally normal, Claire could not look away. A moment later, Shepherd offered, "Napoleon was an Omega."

Claire blinked, cocked her head, and argued. "No he wasn't."

Shepherd grinned, leaning closer. "It is a well-documented fact, little one. A fact pointedly removed from the Dome's retained version of history. Unlike you, I am not afraid to read forbidden books."

If such a thing were true, then why was it considered dangerous to know?

Claire did not believe him. "Are you telling me an Omega pillaged through Europe's monarchies and created an empire?"

Self-righteous to the core, Shepherd nodded. "That is exactly what I am telling you."

The idea he might be right, made Claire doubt herself. "Why would that knowledge be forbidden?"

"Because it did not fall into line with the Callas family's crafted society all those living under the Dome are slave to."

"Or maybe it was because that man was a megalomaniac and a monster. Napoleon was insane and not the best role model for Omegas." Even as Claire disagreed, she didn't support her own bad argument. It was obvious in her uncertain tone and disappointed expression.

"Napoleon's rule, even his ultimate defeat, led to enlightenment, art, and the emancipation of the slaves in Britain. Napoleon changed the world through his violent actions and commitment. He was a very clever tactician devoted to his cause." Shepherd offered what he perceived as a compliment. "Would such an outcome not please you, *little Napoleon*?"

Her soft breath conveyed trepidation. "Is this where you try to convince me he was a good man despite all the terrible things he did? That you are a good man?"

"No."

Claire ran a hand through her hair, a nervous habit, and offered, "You could be a good man, Shepherd."

He leaned towards her, expression soft and voice natural. "We are not so different in the absoluteness of our dedication to change the world for the better. You gave up your very sense of self to the mob, reprimanding the city with your flyer—exposing who you were, trying to inspire. I do what must be done, because I am strong enough to do it, and I understand truly evil men in a way I pray you will never know. So you must grasp that I cannot be, in my duty, what *you* define as good—just as you could never safely live amongst Thólos society as Claire O'Donnell ever again. We both sacrificed our lives for the greater good."

She didn't know why she felt compelled to ask, but the question came before she could stop herself. "What was your reaction to my flyer?"

His entire expression darkened. "I was afraid for you, little one."

A cold chill, a creeping icy thing, scratched down Claire's spine. She was wise enough to grasp that for the Alpha, fear was something long ago conquered and not at all welcome. To know she'd inspired it was unnerving.

His grim honesty continued. "I desired very intensely to alleviate the pain displayed in your photograph. I was even impressed with how unfailingly brave you were to do such a thing, though I abhorred it."

Claire's attention went to her plate; she felt like weeping and didn't know why.

Her lack of words did not alter the undeniable tone in the thread. The connection was normalizing, vibrating, and creeping deeper. Before there might be anymore *courtship rituals*, before there might be a greater consequence, Claire stacked their cleared plates, ready to get her duty over with.

"Did you enjoy our meal?"

She nodded, even thanked him politely, hearing his instant purr when Shepherd's eyes flashed at her praise. The feel of his hand on her arm, the long stroke of light fingers, stopped her movement. She watched, stunned, as the man lifted her hand to his lips and tenderly kissed it.

Slightly hoarse, Claire admitted, "I am not entirely sure where I should begin."

He held her gaze, lightly flicked his tongue against her sensitive palm. "You could touch me."

The worst calamities that befall an army arise from hesitation. -Sun Tzu

Her entire strategy centered on action, on pushing boundaries between them, on growing stronger as she sought out his weaknesses. There could be no room for hesitation if she wanted to gain ground.

Resting a hip on the table, Claire did as he suggested. He wanted to be touched, so that's what she did. She traced his jaw and nose, ran her fingertips over his lips as he had done so often to her. Next, she stroked down the back of his neck, kneading the flesh he'd once claimed caused him pain.

Shepherd turned his head up to her, his mercurial eyes watching with such intensity Claire found her gaze rested far more comfortably on the Alpha's broad shoulders.

Keeping her mind separate from how familiar his body had become, Claire tried to approach it clinically, unsure if she was doing well. When a large hand came to rest on her hip, she took his touch as encouragement to continue. Her palms flowed over his arms from shoulder to wrist and back again, forming to the contours of honed muscle and absolute strength. She reached around his back to lightly scratch her nails over the broad expanse of flesh.

He liked that. His breath hitched, and Shepherd made little grunts and groans as she traced his spine.

When his purr grew husky, she rose from her perch and

took his hand so he could stand from the chair and she could continue. With his great height, there was a shift in power, Shepherd suddenly so much taller.

Her uncertainty returned.

Timid, Claire's hands went to his belt.

Shepherd took her lowered chin, brought her face up so she might see the contented expression on his. "You are doing well."

His voice was gently encouraging, those expressive silver eyes liquid. Claire assumed he wanted her to continue, and licked her lips, trying to seek out the fastening of his pants. Fumbling, she pulled down his zipper and eased the fabric from his hips. Shepherd stepped out of his remaining clothes and stood naked under her touch.

When the Alpha made no move, Claire understood she was expected to continue.

Her hands found a path from his thighs, near his groin, and across the hard planes of his stomach. She nosed his chest, and pulled in his scent exactly as she once imagined she would do with the husband she'd hoped for all her life. Holding on to the comfort of that fantasy, she put the conjured image in Shepherd's place, and pressed closer, breathing in the smell of his excitement.

The fabricated man in her mind loved her, he honored her; he believed she was more than just an Omega.

It was so much easier to stroke and hum as her imagination unraveled, Claire didn't even hesitate to tease. Pretending he was hers, the mate she had dreamed of, she let it all go. Biting his chest, she playfully scratched near enough his groin that his cock twitched in expectation of attention—attention she denied, to instead reach around and caress his buttocks, relishing his groan of pleasured frustration.

By the time she closed her fist around his cock, touching it for the first time only to please him, Shepherd was already dripping, pulsing in her hand, and arching into her grip.

He wanted more. Hands settling on her shoulders, he began to press her to her knees.

Claire knew he wanted her to take him in her mouth, a thing she'd only ever done in the heat of estrous. At first she resisted, a hiccup in her uncertain seduction. Eyes closed tight, hesitant, Claire counted to five before she could make herself obey.

Drawing in a deep breath, she acquiesced, kneeling to suck Shepherd's swollen crown between her lips.

The Alpha answered with a deep, rumbling groan.

Claire's hooded eyes dilated further at one taste, a dreamy hum expressing pleasure when more moisture dripped onto her tongue. Tangling his hands in her hair, gathering it from her face so he might watch, Shepherd relished her hollowed cheeks and the beauty of her pursed lips stretched beautifully around his cock.

Directing her movements, guiding her skull, with each bob of Claire's head, the male knew bliss.

She seemed so absolutely willing that he grew exceedingly excited, thrusting deeper between her lips, pulling her hair when that wicked little tongue swirled. Almost as soon as it began, he was on the brink of spilling into her pretty mouth.

His thrusts growing forceful, Claire gagged when he pressed too far, but did not fight back... she let him use her. When the Alpha reached down to cup his tightening sack, when he roared, Claire obediently swallowed around his girth and sucked harder for her prize.

Watching her little hands wrap around the forming knot to squeeze so it might feel like he was inside her, Shepherd spurt the first gush of semen down her throat, the male careful not to choke her on the copious fluid.

Claire gulped as much as she could, one stunned Alpha watching her effort, mesmerized by a stream of his seed oozing from the corners of her mouth.

Lost in the mating high, in her fantasy, Claire licked him clean, nuzzling into the broad palm settled on her cheek.

Shepherd's great thumb wiped up the spilled trickle running down her chin and pressed it back between her lips, the man groaning in approval when she eagerly lapped every last drop. "Look at me."

Claire, eyes black, hardly a trace of green surrounding the pupils, obeyed. She was so far gone, never had he seen her give in so completely. Seizing the opportunity, he pulled her to a stand, Shepherd taking her lips, kissing her and tasting himself in her mouth.

Even consumed as she was, Claire did not return the pressure.

Growling in frustration, he kissed her harder... but was penalized by the loss of her touch on his body.

Panting, aroused by the challenge and annoyed she continued to deny him her kiss, Shepherd changed tactics.

The straps of her dress were flicked from her shoulders and the fabric tugged down. Breathing in her sweetness, biting and licking the valley between her breasts, Shepherd growled and offered in a voice rich with need, "Will you spread your legs for my mouth?"

Lost on another plane, Claire breathed, "Yes."

The Alpha reared and stalked forward, backing the little Omega towards the bed. "Do you desire my tongue?"

"I do."

He lightly shoved her down and fell upon his prey, his mouth everywhere but where she was wet and eager. Claire arched and writhed, exasperated to receive, but no touch came to ease the growing throb between her legs. Shepherd made her wait until he had marked her in featherlike bites, tasted every inch, until she was dripping slick from her enjoyment of his lips—the Alpha never having growled to call forth such a sweet scent.

Lifting her flushed body in the exact position to perfectly display her cunt, he pinned her. Her pussy was pink and throbbing, her hips wriggling against his hold, all the while her little hole twitching like a tiny sucking mouth.

Slick trickled out to tempt him, Shepherd flicking his tongue in the river of fluid, lost at only one taste. While he lapped up every drop, Claire moaned like a whore, rolling her hips to each flick of his tongue, grinding against his face when he burrowed that writhing muscle deep in her pussy.

With her mind still in that place she'd always imagined for herself, with her body in the hands of an expert Alpha she pretended might be the husband she once longed for, the feeling of a powerful climax swelled—something mindlessly perfect almost in her grasp.

Then Shepherd stopped, he stopped at the pivotal moment, and held her spread to watch her pink little pussy flutter as she tried to buck up to the mouth hovering warm above her. When she whined, his tongue stretched out and gave the lightest of licks, taunting her.

Fighting to move, to find relief from the coil of need he engorged with each darted swipe of his tongue, Claire's agitation turned to anger.

She had given him pleasure, and now her mate was contorting the vision, denying her the perfection of the dream by toying with her. Looking down between her spread thighs to glare at her tormentor, Claire aggressively growled.

The mass of muscle, the thing that was supposed to be fucking her with his tongue, prowled possessively over her body, negating her hips' movement each time Claire tried to rub against him for relief.

Brushing his wet lips over hers, Shepherd purred deeply. "Kiss me, little one, and I will give you great pleasure in any and every way you wish."

Wound up tight, instant wrath drove away all reason. Eager to punish for his attempt to claim something that was not his, to discipline for destroying the perfection of her dream, Claire pulled her lips back from her teeth. Nails scraped the hardness of sinew, her mouth attacking the bulging muscles between his shoulder and neck. In a rush, she pressed her teeth to his flesh and bit down with all the strength of her jaw, heard him catch his breath in surprise, and sunk her bite even deeper.

She wounded Shepherd with all the power of her indignation, all of the rage building up since she'd first looked at the behemoth, and the unfulfilled lust he had taught her body to crave and thought to use against her.

She didn't even want to fuck anymore; she just wanted him to bleed.

When the head of his cock skimmed between her folds, she dug in her claws and refused to let go. Shepherd penetrated her anyway, his warm lips at her ear where she could hear every gasped groan as he invaded her sopping cunt in erratic, desperate thrusts of his hips.

Shepherd began to speak. She refused to listen. He moaned out his name for her. She only growled like a rabid animal. He hit the place where her nerves were raw and need was everything, and that horribly powerful internal itch grew again, blossomed and divided her—blasting her into a sideways place where she had no name or purpose but to fuck and be fucked by her mate.

It was all there inside her, the raging storm that took away reason, it crashed and tore, and finally blissful expansion arrived.

Her teeth left the flesh she had deeply punctured. She swallowed the pooling blood in her mouth, and came as wildly as she'd grown feral. One more hard thrust, and the size of Shepherd's building knot grew impressive. It elongated her climax and tied the twitching thing to him where he could keep her still while his cock pumped her full of spurting streams, bathing her womb with soothing liquid heat.

The taste of blood was thick in her mouth, the red stuff under her fingernails, all ignored as her mind flew away in the intensity of her orgasm. Time seemed irrelevant, an endless field of grey... until a face distorted her vision. The beast whose heartbeat hammered against her red stained breasts asserted himself. Iron shaded eyes full of history and greatness, the silver of deceit and lust... those gunmetal disks looked at her with the devil's version of tenderness.

Full lips panted words, a rich musical voice undistorted by the rasp his scarred lips imposed, distracting her between kisses over her cheeks. "Little one, that was very pleasing. I am very, very pleased."

His mouth brushed her blood smeared lips, Shepherd looked deeply into hers, as if waiting for some act the female was supposed to offer. Claire lay there with his blood pooling on her chest and vague realization began to dawn. In horror, she grasped the consequences of her self-indulgent lack of control.

The depth of the bite... the placement...

In her fervor, she had ripped claiming marks deeply into Shepherd's flesh, almost as savagely as he'd marked her.

The purring brute's forefinger traced over the blood on her lips, the trail that had leaked from the corner of her mouth, sniffing and panting and still deeply knotted. The warm heat of his tongue began to lick her clean of the red, bathing her mouth and neck, tending to a thing half in shock. The second his knot began to abate, the smooth plunge of his cock began again, Shepherd knowing to fuck her immediately before her pupils contracted and his unexpected victory became her sorrow.

Making love to her until the Omega's exhaustion pulled her past consciousness, Shepherd did not allow her a moment of regret—not when everything was so perfect. Not when she was finally responding as the Gods intended.

CORDAY'S HEAD was in his hands, every last testament of violence he'd found stirring up a more horrible thirst than his worn out, simple desire for revenge. What he longed for in that moment, what he craved, were the whims of a violent psychopath.

He wanted to see Shepherd suffer. He wanted to watch him bleed.

Corday wanted to torment his rival himself until the sounds of the monster's screams might drown out the noise of the madness knocking about in his skull.

It was hard to swallow, even harder to admit there was no way to balance what he was with what a darker corner of his mind tempted him to become.

It was the room. It was the broken furniture. It was the blood.

The safe house where the Omegas recovered from the drug pushers' brothel, the place they had been promised, protection was ransacked. The two Beta enforcers set to watch the women lay dead on the ground, wracked with bullet wounds.

Nailed to the wall, his hand raised in a wave, drooped a headless body hung like a sick banner. The clothes Corday recognized, the stature, the smell not quite ruined by the stink of carnage.

Senator Kantor.

The leader of the resistance had been taken, tortured, and murdered, and it had been done right under their noses.

Shepherd was toying with all of them–laughing at them.

There was no sign of the few Omegas who'd called this place home. Though before they had been stolen, based on the stink of terror in the air, Corday imagined they had been forced to watch whatever had been done to a man he looked up to like a father.

"Are you going to say nothing?" Leslie stood at his side, staring forward, her lips bloodless, her expression dazed.

The safe house had failed the women it was set up to protect. The few remaining Enforcers, the stunted resistance, were failing the city they'd sworn to save. The one man unifying the flagging population had been butchered.

What was there to say?

Corday was crumbling no matter the stern look he kept locked on his face. There was nothing left.

Staring at the stump of mutilated neck, at the blood, and the open cavity of the man's torso, stepping over the entrails piled and stinking on the floor, Corday could find no worthy words for the corpse's niece. "We should take him down."

Leslie shook her head as if she couldn't bring herself to

touch the abomination. “What do you suppose they’ve done with his head?”

He had no intention of answering a question they both, deep down, must know the answer to. Instead, he turned his attention to prying the body as gently as he could from the wall.

When it was done, what could be gathered was collected into the only receptacle they might find–garbage bags. Corday stood covered in his mentor’s blood. “I am very sorry, Leslie, for agreeing to bring you here. He told me to keep you hidden. Had I listened, I might have spared you this.”

“You needed help carrying supplies. *I* needed to do something useful, for once. The months of my seclusion have shown us one truth, over and over. My uncle was wrong... I was wrong. My access to Shepherd’s communications did nothing to further the resistance’s cause.” Leslie let the Beta see her need for vengeance. “The proof is on the wall before you.”

Corday’s response was automatic. “You have interpreted messages that have saved the lives of many of our brothers and sisters.”

“How did they find him? How did no one know he was missing until this morning?” Face pinched, she whispered, “What if Shepherd... what if he only let us think we operated out of his influence?”

An ironic, painful chuckle escaped the Beta.

Rubbing her skull as if it ached, Leslie sighed. “Your visitor, that Maryanne woman, may have been right. If they found Senator Kantor, they know where the resistance gathers. Shepherd knows where you live. He knows about me and my access to this commutations network."

Exactly Corday's unspoken point; the resistance was in ruins.

Leslie had more to say. "What if your Omega Claire had made a deal with her mate? He may have been watching us this whole time." A question wracked with doubt trailed off, "How else could this..."

He didn't want to hear it. Corday didn't even want to think it. "We must get back to headquarters. Brigadier Dane needs to be told what was done here."

Leslie Kantor grew vehement. "This has to end."

The word left him in a breath, he was at a loss. "How?"

"I have been to your meetings. I've spoken with my uncle! Brigadier Dane, Senator Kantor, refused to engage Shepherd's army. All they did, *all she will do*, is police the population and bribe potential recruits with food and false hope, while our enemy grows more powerful."

Everything Leslie was saying was true. Corday agreed with her, but the resistance was too undermanned. Weaponry was scarce, bullet stores diminishing by the day. Had they attacked months ago as Claire had suggested, a rebellion might have stood a chance. Now... the only prayer they had was to find the contagion and wait for the city to implode.

Senator Kantor had been trying to prevent such an outcome. He'd been trying to save as many lives as possible. He had tried to outthink a man far smarter than him.

Corday repeated himself, robotic and unable to even hint

at what was going through his mind. “We need to take this body to headquarters.”

Leslie softened her eyes and offered a sad smile. “No, darling Corday. There is no more time to hide away. I will not hand our city over to the inept hands of Brigadier Dane’s failing leadership. There is another place we can go, a place my uncle refused to consider. Inside there might be food, supplies, guns, ammunition... everything we need to take a stand and end this.”

Eyes bone dry in their sockets, feeling as if all life had been sucked from him, Corday made himself engage. He knew the very place she suggested and understood why it was off-limits. “During the breach, while my fellow Enforcers were trapped in the Judicial Sector, dying from plague, Callas’ home went into lockdown. For all we know, the contagion was let loose behind that steel barricade. To force the gate could expose the population and kill us all.”

She turned her back on the blood in the room, moving to the dwelling’s small window and its slice of sunlight marking the ground. “There is another way inside, Corday, a small, secret entrance. Like my uncle, I know where it is.”

The information did not surprise him. In fact, he, others in the resistance, had suspected there must be secondary access—an escape hatch in case of emergency. It had been Senator Kantor who fervently refused to risk the lives of millions to find out what might lie within the Premier’s home.

Leslie answered his silence, turning her head to see him motionless, the corpse of her uncle wrapped in plastic and cradled in his arms. "If nothing is done, we are going to die. The proof is in this room. Salvation might wait beyond Callas' door, and Shepherd would never suspect the resistance would gather there. Let him think he's won, that we've disbanded while we rally behind walls he cannot penetrate. This is our only chance, Corday."

There was another roadblock, the woman the resistance would look to for leadership. "Brigadier Dane will stand against you on this."

"That's why we are going to open it, you and I, before we go to her. When we come to the resistance, we come bearing hope, or we die as we should for our ineptness." She sounded so much like her uncle in that moment: imperious, confident. "Now, put him down. Leave my uncle here. He would not want us to waste time or endanger ourselves simply to cart his body to be gawked at by the people he loved."

He put the remains down on the room's only table, took a step back. Spinning the golden ring on his finger, twisting it around and around, Corday turned his furious attention to Leslie Kantor. "If you are wrong, we will unleash the virus."

"That was my uncle's argument as well. Well, here is mine: consider where Shepherd is from, how he thinks. The man created an army, still recruits to swell his numbers. He wants to rule. He has total control." Leslie's passionate words put a stop to Corday's endless spinning of the ring. "An animal like him would rather die fighting than submit to death by infection. Do you really think he would leave the virus lying around where it might be set loose to ruin all he has built? Even Judicial Sector, once exposed, was purified by incineration protocol. What virus infected those charred halls was destroyed the instant Shepherd's point was made. The people of Thólos saw the suffering, they saw the flames. But, we have not seen what happened in the Premier's Sector. Why? Why keep the population in the dark?"

She was as good an orator as her surname implied. Even shaken as he was, Corday could feel a small spark of lost hope threaten to chase away his despair. He wanted to believe she might be right.

"We can end this, Corday." The Alpha female edged closer, offering her hand. "Come with me. Help me."

Possibility warred with the chance that obliteration might lie down the road Leslie would lead him. Something felt wrong, but life was wrong, the resistance had been wrong, and it was time to put his faith in something new.

The Beta took her offered palm and sealed the fate of the Dome.

Read REBORN now!

ADDISON CAIN

USA TODAY bestselling author and Amazon Top 25 bestselling author, Addison Cain's dark romance and smoldering paranormal suspense will leave you breathless. Obsessed antiheroes, heroines who stand fierce, heart-wrenching forbidden love, and a hint of violence in a kiss awaits.

For the most current list of exciting titles by Addison Cain, please visit her website: addisoncain.com

facebook.com/AddisonlCain
bookbub.com/authors/addison-cain
goodreads.com/AddisonCain
amazon.com/Addison-Cain/e/B01E1LKWMY

ALSO BY ADDISON CAIN

Don't miss these exciting titles by Addison Cain!

Smoldering Standalones:

Swallow it Down

Strangeways

The Golden Line

Thirst

A Night by my Fire

The Alpha's Claim Series:

Born to be Bound

Born To Be Broken

Reborn

Stolen

Corrupted

Wren's Song Series:

Branded

Silenced

The Irdesi Empire Series:

Sigil

Sovereign

Cradle of Darkness Series:

Catacombs

Cathedral

The Relic

A Trick of the Light Duet:

A Taste of Shine

A Shot in the Dark

Historical Romance:

Dark Side of the Sun

Twisted Tales:

The White Queen

Immaculate

Omnibuses:

Shepherd (Alpha's Claim, Books 1-3)

A Court of Poison